If we wo to gether can 'Beat' anything

Butterflies

D E McCluskey

Stay Safe

D E McCluskey

Copyright © 2020 by D E McCluskey

The moral right of the author has been asserted.
*All characters and events in this publication,
other than those clearly in the public domain,
are fictitious, and any resemblance to real persons,
living or dead, is purely coincidental*

All rights are reserved

No part of this publication may be reproduced,
stored in a retrieval system, or transmitted in any form
by any means without the prior permission, in writing, of
the publisher, nor be otherwise circulated in any form of binding or
cover other than that of which it was
published and without a similar condition including this
condition being imposed on the subsequent purchaser.

ISBN 978-0993449062

Dammaged Production
www.dammaged.com

Butterflies

For Ashley, Joanne, and Emily

Family...

D E McCluskey

1.

TODAY WAS THE day! The day that Olivia Britt would officially become Olivia Martelle. It was the day that she had been looking forward to for more than a year, although it had felt like a lifetime.

She was alone in the hotel room that was to act as her and her husband's—she just couldn't get used to calling him that—bridal suite. The room was beautiful; it was large, bright, and airy; living up to every penny of the extortionate price they had paid for it.

A huge window served the main bedroom of the suite, and Olivia was standing, bathing in the morning light as it streamed over her via the breath-taking view.

The view was Lake Geneva in early August; a true sight to behold. The mixture of summer and autumn colours collaborating with the blue and green of the lake and sky caught her in its ambiance of calm; an oasis that she sorely needed this morning.

Olivia was thirty-two years old. Her shoulder length, wavy hair, which usually hung loose around her shoulders, had been sculpted almost into a work of art. Her makeup was on point, accentuating her large brown eyes and blending with her beautiful olive skin. Her svelte figure had been eased and teased into a lace corset, and she was all set to slip into the most exciting dress she would ever wear.

Today was to be the happiest day of her life.

Or at least it was *supposed* to be…

Just this morning she'd had to sort out three bridesmaids' hair, prevent two of them from killing each other over a brush, arrange for a replacement makeup artist as the first one had come down with some sort of pox, and finally, she'd have to find her mother, who had gone out with them last night for a last-minute hen night drink, and, up to now, had not made it back.

Today was supposed to be all about her!

Finally, she'd managed to snatch a modicum of peace, just a moment or two to breathe and take in what was happening to her. This moment was to be all about her and the best friend she had in the whole world: her great aunt, Penny.

Penny really was her great aunt, in every sense of the word. Olivia's grandmother had died suddenly, shortly after giving birth to her fifth child, and Penny had taken all the children under her impressive wings and brought them up. Secretly, Olivia knew that she had always been Aunt Penny's favourite. Olivia's mother had been very young when she fell pregnant, and as she'd always had a wild streak in her, she had not taken to motherhood very well. So, Aunt Penny took another little wayward chick under her massive wing.

'Well, just look at you,' Aunt Penny remarked as she entered the room, ready to tie the laces of the corset. 'I always knew you'd find yourself a good man, and here we are. I was right.'

She *was* right too. Paul Martelle was indeed a catch. He was the most generous person Oliva had ever known, and the funniest. He was a fantastic cook, funny in public, and extremely attentive in the bedroom. He understood her every longing, every desire, and every need, sometimes even before she did. She could honestly say that she had never been quite so fulfilled until the day she met Paul.

And now, here she was marrying him.

The first twinge of nerves, like a small kaleidoscope of butterflies, began to flutter around her stomach. Was it the pending nuptials? The lavish honeymoon? Or was it the thought of living the rest of her life with Paul, her knight in shining armour? Olivia thought that it was a little of all the above.

She was more than a little flustered as Penny tied the last of the straps on her underwear. Along with the corset, she was wearing white stockings and a garter belt, the perfect timelessly fashionable accessories for her gorgeous dress. She had the added benefit of knowing Paul would go crazy for them, and the French lace panties too. They were the textbook finishing touch.

He aunt stood back to admire her, shaking her head, attempting to stifle tears that were threatening to fall. 'Seeing you here with that lake as your backdrop, it's taking my breath away. Paul truly is the luckiest man alive.'

'Oh, Aunt Penny, you always say the right things.' She turned and wrapped her arms around her aunt in a big, heartfelt hug. 'Now...' she continued, dabbing a tear from her eye with a white handkerchief. '...let's get this dress on and bag me a man.'

Penny retrieved the dress from the wardrobe. It was a long, Victorian style, made from white satin with a cream brocade. It was a family heirloom. Olivia had always loved it, ever since she was a child when Aunt Penny would allow her to try it on during boring, rainy weekends. A few alterations had been made to make it relevant for today's tastes, but they had been few and far between. She'd seen photos of Aunt Penny back when she was a younger woman, and she'd had the same figure then as Olivia did now.

Butterflies

'Right, come on Ollie, step in,' Aunt Penny ordered, and Olivia raised her stockinged leg to step into the offered dress. 'Strap that over your shoulders... there, now hook this at the back, and... slip this on... and we're done.'

Penny stepped back one more time to regard her niece. This time there was no stopping the threatened tears; they came in floods.

Olivia wrapped her arms around her elderly relative again, giving her another tight, loving squeeze.

'Oh no, Ollie, don't,' she said pushing her away. 'I'll get stains all over the dress.'

'Don't worry about that, Pen. I love you with all my heart and soul. A few stains are not going to stop that.'

Both women shared their tears before the door opened and one of the bridesmaids bustled in.

'Hey, you two, quit the love in, the car's here.' She paused for a moment to take in the vision that was Olivia, surrounded by the lake in the background. 'Oh, my God!' she gasped. 'You look fucking gorgeous!'

She turned and saw Aunt Penny; her face went bright red, and she put her hand to her mouth. 'Oh, Aunt Penny! I'm so sorry.'

'Don't worry yourself, Jan. I think she looks fucking gorgeous too,' she replied with a twinkle in her eye.

2.

THE SPARKLING ROLLS Royce pulled up to the church amidst much whispering and cooing. As Olivia stepped out, everyone in the congregation gasped. They were all in agreement that she was one of the most stunning brides they had ever seen.

The most obvious alteration Olivia had made to the wedding dress was a cut at the front. She'd had it tastefully cut at the front, allowing her to showcase her shapely legs, and the waist had been brought in to accentuate her curves.

She exited the car to a flurry of photographs. It was all she could do to smile and wave as her feelings overwhelmed her. She felt like a celebrity dealing with the onrush of paparazzi, as she made her way towards the nave of the church. The butterflies in her stomach were fluttering again.

Aunt Penny, who was to give her away, flashed her a smile.

'Can I really do this, Aunt Pen?' she asked.

The smile turned into one of Penny's warmest. 'Yes,' she replied, nodding her head. 'You really can!'

Feeling buoyed by the reassuring arm of her best friend and biggest idol, she began to make her way up the aisle, intimately aware of all the heads turning to look at her. Everyone was happy, smiling, and waving.

She spotted Angela, Paul's older sister, sitting in the congregation. She was the only one in the whole church not smiling. *Will nothing ever cheer that miserable cow up?* she thought as she tipped the woman a curt nod.

Angela's husband—Kevin? She could never remember his name—was sat next to her. She had always felt a little sorry for him; she had witnessed him being henpecked by Angela on more than one occasion, but he had always been quick with a smile. In a million years, she would never have put those two together, they were just so different. Angela was thin and flat, her shoulder length black hair was straight, and that was really all she could say about her. Kevin, or Brian, Olivia had no idea, was a large man with rugged good looks and the colouring of someone who worked outdoors. *Opposites attract,* she thought as she walked past them. He flashed her a big, genuine smile and gave her a brief wave. She felt instantly guilty about not remembering his name as she waved back.

Then she saw Paul, the man who would be her husband very soon.

Her heart felt like it skipped a beat.

He had always had the ability to do that to her, even without trying. He was stood at the altar in his perfectly tailored wedding suit, with his freshly cut hair and his shaven face. Her hungry eyes greedily looked him up and down as Anthony, his best man, turned him around to look at her.

Her vision tunnelled. All she could focus on was him. The handsome best man standing beside him may well have not even existed. For her, it was all about him. His six-foot-two frame had been squeezed into his expensive suit, and the results were spectacular.

As he turned towards her, his face glowed. Olivia thought that his look was the very definition of beaming. His white teeth dazzled her, and she fell deeply, madly, in love with him all over again.

Aunt Penny released her arm and passed her over to him with a stern, but playful, look. He accepted her. He took her face in both his hands and lifted her veil. He looked deep into her eyes and whispered, 'I love you.'

Butterflies

3.

OLIVIA THOUGHT THE service was excellent. Ten minutes in and all her pre-wedding jitters had passed. She had to keep reminding herself that she was *really* here, standing in a church on the banks of Lake Geneva, marrying the man of her dreams, not only once, but twice.

'I do...' he said as his deep blue eyes pierced her dark hazel ones.

He's looking towards our future, she thought. *To the rest of our lives together.*

She swallowed a sob.

'Miss Olivia Penelope Britt, do you take this man, Paul Edward Martelle, to be your lawful wedded husband? To have and to hold, in sickness and in health, for richer or poorer, 'til death do you part?'

'I... do,' she replied. *Oh, my God, I nearly said 'fucking' in the church*, she giggled to herself.

Paul gave her a wry grin. 'What's so funny?' he mouthed.

She just shrugged and smiled.

'I now pronounce you husband and wife,' the priest announced. 'You may now kiss the bride.'

They were the words she'd been waiting for, for the whole of the service. As Paul turned towards her, she turned to face the congregation. She felt his warm and strong hands on her, gently pulling her back towards him. He kissed her on the lips, and she responded in kind. For a moment, she was only peripherally aware there were other people in the room with them, people who seemed to be whistling and cheering.

After a few more blessings and the signing of the legal register, they walked back down the aisle as husband and wife. Mr and Mrs Martelle.

They appeared outside into a massive shower of confetti and rice. There was so much being thrown that they could hardly see their way to the car waiting to whisk them the full two hundred metres to where the photographs were to be taken.

The bride's family were taken first, then the groom's family, then both families. Photographs with the bridesmaids, with the best man, with the ushers, then, finally, everyone joined in.

'OK, people,' the photographer shouted in his best English. 'I have just the Bride and Groom, please? Everyone else, if you could go into the hotel over the road, they will make you all comfortable.'

As everyone shuffled towards the hotel, the photographer walked with the new couple over to the shores of the lake.

'Can you, erm, kiss your bride?' the photographer asked, again trying his best English.

Without warning, Paul grabbed her by the hand and, placing his other hand around her back, tipped her over like a dancer.

'You don't need to ask me twice,' he said loud enough so the photographer could hear him while not breaking eye contact with Olivia. He then kissed her deeply. She relished the taste of his lips and the feel of his tongue as it lightly probed and played with hers.

Butterflies

'I think we might need to stop, or this guy might get a few shots he never bargained for,' he whispered into her ear, giving her tingles all over her skin.

'Ahem...' the photographer coughed to get their attention. 'Can we please get a few more shots before... eh...' He gestured with his hands, a not entirely rude gesture, but one they got the gist of.

They both laughed, and Olivia blushed slightly; the kiss *had* gone a little too far.

Blushing himself now, the photographer asked for the garter shot. 'Right, Mr Paul, I want you to be on one knee in front of Mrs Paul... Please, can you put one hand on her thigh and the other on the garter?'

Paul sidled down onto one knee in front of her. She delighted as his hand slid along the inside of her thigh. Cheekily, she opened her legs a little, allowing him to probe a little further than he should have. He brushed the material of her French knickers, and the butterflies in her stomach stirred into life.

'Yes... yes... that's right, just please both a look at me...' The photographer was clicking away, but Olivia could honestly testify that at that point, she had forgotten he was still there.

'OK, Mr and Mrs Paul, I think we're all done here. Let's go into the hall and take a few party shots, eh?' He sped off in front of them towards his car, removing his camera strap as he went.

'You're a cheeky bastard,' she said, jokingly poking Paul in the ribs. 'I was well onto you there, you dirty old man.'

He looked at her as if to feign his innocence. 'What?' he asked, shrugging.

She walked on ahead of him and then stopped and turned abruptly. He was smiling that big cheeky grin of his, the one she could never resist. She looked back around to see if there was anyone looking, and when she was confident no one was, she slowly parted the long cut at the front of her skirt, just enough for Paul to see the sheer white lace of her French knickers.

He stopped and shook his head. 'You are fucking gorgeous!' he said, his mouth hanging wide.

She closed her skirt and turned back around, cocking her head to one side as she walked off towards the hotel. 'You're the third person to say that to me today,' she tutted.

Butterflies

4.

WITHIN A FEW hours, the party was swinging. The band was killing it on the stage, and the guests were loving it. The food and the drink were flowing, and everyone was having a good time.

Even Angela!

Olivia laughed as she watched Paul's sister spin around on the dance floor with her husband. *Is it Kevin? Keith?* She'd have to find out before the night was over. He seemed like such a nice man, maybe too nice to be married to her.

All her friends had flown over from England on Paul's insistence. He'd paid for flights and accommodations in their hotel on the lake. It had cost him a small fortune, but he'd said if it made her happy then it was totally worth it.

Where is he? she wondered as she scanned the faces of the revellers within the function room. It wasn't long before she spotted him propping up the bar with a few of his friends. She eyed him up and down from afar, admiring everything about him. It seemed that every time she looked at him today, a sprinkle of sexual desire coursed through her. *I could get used to that,* she thought.

A small but devious plan hatched in her mind.

Her oldest friend and chief bridesmaid, Katie, was strutting out of the toilets looking, and obviously feeling, like she was a million dollars. Olivia had to stifle a laugh as she noticed a small trail of toilet paper stuck to the high heel of her black shoe.

'Katie,' she shouted over the thumping bass from the dance floor. Her friend turned and waved. 'Check your shoe,' Olivia mouthed, pointing towards her own feet. Katie gave her a confused look. 'Your shoe,' she mouthed again, wildly exaggerating and pointing to her own shoes.

Katie must have thought Olivia was doing a strange dance routine, as she began to dance in time to the music but pointing down towards her own shoes.

Olivia shook her head. 'NO,' she mouthed, then she pointed to her eyes and then down at her shoe.

Katie did this move too, wiggling her backside in her tight-fitting bridesmaid dress.

Shaking her head, but laughing, Olivia made her way over to where Katie was dancing.

'Your shoe,' she whispered into her ear.

Katie saw the toilet paper and laughed. Embarrassed, she leaned down and pulled it off.

'You're such a lucky bitch, Ollie,' Katie shouted over the music. 'Just look at that man you've married.'

Olivia did, and once again, she felt that fantastic sprinkle. 'Your fella's no slouch either,' Olivia said, pointing to Katie's current boyfriend. A rather handsome, café-crème complexioned Adonis was standing alone at the bar with two drinks.

Katie grimaced a little. 'Yeah, I know, but unfortunately, so does he.' They both laughed as they caught him looking at his reflexion in the mirror behind the bar, running his fingers through his hair. 'When we're having sex and he wants to do it in front of the mirror, I just know it's not me he's looking at.'

Olivia laughed again and grabbed her best friend's arm, pulling her closer in a conspiratorial manoeuvre. 'Katie,' she began, looking around the room as she addressed her friend. 'Was there anyone in the bathroom when you were just in there?'

'In the ladies? No. It's only got three cubicles, but the marble sink and mirror in there are to die for. Why?'

'Oh, no reason,' Olivia said with a crooked smile. 'Will you tell Paul that I need some assistance in the ladies' in... shall we say, two minutes?' Olivia's face twisted into an even more mischievous one. 'Tell him he'll need to knock five times.'

Katie smiled, and her eyes came alive. 'Oh, you dirty bitch, I love it. I'll go and tell him right now.'

With an exchange of knowing smiles, the two girls set off in different directions, Olivia towards the ladies' toilet, Katie towards Paul at the bar.

As she got into the toilets, the first thing she did was check if there was a lock on the door. There was. *Excellent,* she thought.

A large couch ran along one wall, and there were three cubicles along the other side. She checked they were empty; they were. At the opposite end of the room was a mirror with a marble double sink beneath it. As she checked it out, she realised it was a little bit too high for her needs, but then she saw the marble bench, and that was just the right height. She allowed herself a small, nervous smile.

The door handle rattled, and her stomach flipped, her heart was racing so fast. 'Is there anyone in here?' a female voice shouted through the locked door.

'I'm... err... cleaning, ma'am, I'll be done in ten minutes. There are other facilities on the other side of the room,' Olivia shouted back in her best/worst foreign accent.

'Shit!' came the reply from outside. 'Come on, baby,' the disembodied voice said. 'We'll have to use the gents.'

Olivia stifled a laugh; there was another couple with the same idea as her. *It must be the effects of the lake,* she thought.

Another knock on the door brought her back to her current mission. This was the one she was waiting for. One knock, then two, then three… Adrenalin began to course through her body. Four knocks, then five… Then no more.

It was Paul.

She unlocked the door and looked at him.

There was a light sheen of sweat across his forehead from his exertions on the dancefloor, his tie was loosened, and he'd unbuttoned the top two buttons of his shirt. To Olivia, he'd never looked as sexy in all the time she'd known him.

'Get in here, and lock that door behind you,' she hissed.

Flashing her a dazzling smile, the dimples on either side of his face making her blood pressure soar, he did exactly as he was told. She'd never wanted anyone as much as she wanted him right then.

'Stay there until I tell you it's OK to enter,' she whispered once she saw the lock turn on the door. Then she backed away towards the small bench next to the sinks.

He shook his head. 'Whatever you say. You're the boss.'

She continued backwards towards the marble bench and leaned on it. Without taking her eyes off his, she lifted her dress.

His eyes were drawn to her, just as she'd intended them to be. Her hand slid down between her legs, and her fingers began to caress the delicate fabric between them.

She watched as his eyes widened and his beaming smile was replaced with a lustful pout. These changes emphasised the subtle bulging in the front of his tailored suit. She liked how her little idea was shaping up very much.

Butterflies

Her hand made its way down inside her French knickers, and her fingers wandered even further. A tingle of sexual electricity buzzed throughout her body, rousing the sleeping butterflies in her belly.

The bulge in the front of Paul's trousers told her everything she needed to know; he was enjoying her little show.

With her other hand, she beckoned him closer.

As his strong hand caressed the back of her head, she noticed that he was careful not to ruin her hair. *God this man is fucking perfect,* she thought.

Then he kissed her.

She had braced herself for a strong passionate kiss full of tongue and saliva, as men are usually wanting to do in these situations, especially after a few drinks, but he surprised her with a light peck on her cheek, and finally one on her lips.

Shaking, no, quivering because this man was driving her wild, she thought she could quite happily live with this treatment for at least another fifty or sixty years.

His hands wandered down her body, reaching their intended destination in a short time, and she gasped as she felt the heel of his hand press in-between her legs. It sent a flow of the same electricity as before pulsing through her body. Her breath was lost in the moment. She couldn't believe he hadn't even touched her yet, skin on skin, and she was already soaking wet.

Expertly, he slid her expensive French undergarments down her legs and over her suspender belt and stockings. The cool fresh air teasing the wet warmth between her thighs was refreshing and stimulating in equal measures. Without taking his eyes off hers, he unbuckled his belt and lowered his trousers. She could feel the effect of her, and the moment, pressing against her.

His hand traced the contours of her face, and he cupped her cheek as he edged her onto the marble bench. She flinched as the cold stone bit at her naked buttocks beneath the fabric of her uplifted dress.

But this was all part of the experience.

With ease, as she was so wet, she felt the delight as he entered her. The feel of his tongue inside her mouth, and the hardness inside her down below, was almost too much for her to bear.

Everything flashed by her, the whole day; the dress, her underwear, the little flash earlier, the lake, the surprise kiss, the fact they were doing this in the toilet of their own wedding, the danger of it all. All of this was all the foreplay she needed. Before long, she had that exquisite feeling, the one that began in her toes before moving to her stomach, eventually spreading to every nerve in her body.

He rocked her back and forth on the marble ledge. She could feel she was about to go; she couldn't hold on for much longer.

Then it dawned on her that his breathing had become faster too.

Her body let go of all control, and it released the millions of caged up butterflies into her stomach. She tried her best to suppress her moan but couldn't. As their wings flapped and tickled inside her, she no longer cared.

Paul came at the same time as her, the pleasure she felt as his love surged inside her was all consuming.

'I fucking love you, Mrs Martelle,' he whispered lightly in her ear once he had his breath back. He pulled his head back to look at her, and she flashed him her best girlie smile, the one she hoped that he had fallen in love with.

She raised her eyebrows and returned his love. 'I fucking love you too, Mr Martelle!'

Butterflies

5.

IT WAS APPROACHING midnight, and the party was raging. The band was still playing, belting out all the crowd-pleasers. The newlyweds were doing the rounds of the guests, a seemingly never-ending regurgitation of the same sentences. 'Thanks for coming and making our night special, thanks for your lovely gifts, thanks for coming, it's been too long since we saw each other last…'

While performing these duties, it was becoming obvious to everyone present that neither of them could keep their eyes, or their hands, off each other.

'Jan, I think we need to put them out of their misery, don't you?' Katie shouted, leaning over their table, trying to be as quiet as her drunken state would allow.

'Ah, yeah, let's have a word with the band and get their dance on.' The two girls staggered off towards the dance floor.

'OK, ladies and gentlemen,' the lead singer of the band announced. 'It's that time in the night when we bring together the lovely people who are the reason we're all here tonight.' The ravers on the dance floor began to clap, shout, and whistle; all of them looking around the room. 'Can we have Paul and Olivia to the dance floor, please? Paul and Olivia. Are they here? Or have they done a runner to have a quick sha—Oh, here they are.' He pointed as they both made their way towards the stage. Cheers and laughs in response to the joke accompanied them.

Paul was enjoying the moment, taking the time to have a little dance with everyone who clapped them on, but Olivia was a little embarrassed. She pulled an 'I'm going to kill you two' face towards her bridesmaids as Paul guided her onto the dance floor. He took her in his hands and looked deeply into her eyes. She felt a shift somewhere deep inside her; it was a nice feeling. *Hmm, not for the first time tonight,* she thought, *and hopefully not the last.*

'What are you smiling at?' he asked as they stood face to face in front of the baying crowd.

'Oh, nothing,' she whispered in reply. 'You'll find out later.'

Paul's grin stretched from ear to ear.

The band began their romanticised version of 'Something' by The Beatles; a particular favourite of the new Mr and Mrs Martelle.

Olivia was acutely aware of all their family and friends watching them dance. She looked at Paul for a little help as she had never really liked being the centre of attention, but he was singing along at the top of his voice with his eyes closed. She pulled him closer trying to hide a little from everyone's scrutiny, and got a little, or maybe not so little, unexpected, surprise.

Paul was rock hard.

She pulled away, and he opened one eye. A sly grin spread across his face as he raised his eyebrows and winked at her.

At that point, all the guests began to pile onto the dance floor, giving them a little privacy even though they were in company. Feeling naughty, she rubbed herself on him, enjoying the feeling of his excitement through his trousers. *Fuck, I need to get upstairs with him,* she thought. 'Let's go, right now,' she whispered into his ear.

'I thought you'd never ask,' he answered.

Butterflies

A minute or two later and the song had finished, everyone was clapping and cheering. Paul, after fixing himself discreetly, walked onto the stage and took the microphone.

'Ladies and Gentlemen, I have to thank you all for being here tonight. For making our day so special. I know most of you have travelled a very long way to get here today, and for that, I thank you.'

Someone from the back of the hall shouted, 'You paid for it, son, so, thank *YOU*!'

Everyone laughed.

'Well, I'd like to let you know that the band is going to play on until two am, isn't that right, fellas?' He turned towards the band, and they give him the thumbs up. Everyone in the hall applauded. 'The bar staff will be serving until three am, isn't that right, people?' He offered his hands out towards the bar, and everyone cheered louder than they had for the band. 'But...' He held up his hands to the crowd below him. 'Unfortunately, it's proven to be a long day for the missus here, and she's informed me that...' he paused for dramatic effect,'...she's tired and needs to go to bed!' He gave a theatrical bow and the crowd responded with wolf whistles and shouts.

Olivia flushed bright red.

'So, on that note, on behalf of my better half and myself, I'll thank you all again, and say goodnight.'

As Paul led her towards the door, Anthony, his best man, grabbed the microphone and shouted, 'Everyone, let's hear it one more time for Paul and Olivia Martelle. THE BRIDE AND GROOM!' The band broke into a rocked-up version of the wedding march, and everyone held up their glasses and cheered as the happy couple headed towards the exit.

It took a while, but eventually they made it, and Olivia collapsed into his arms. The band had started a rather popular rock song, and everyone inside seemed to be enjoying themselves.

The lobby was empty, except for a bored looking bellboy and one young girl manning reception.

'The lift's this way,' Paul said, almost dragging her in the direction.

The lift came, and they got in. 'Floor six,' he said as he pushed the button. He leant back against the wall, looked at his wife, and smiled.

She could see her reflection in the full-length mirror that he was leaning against, and she took a little while to study herself. *I do look fucking gorgeous*, she thought with a grin.

Paul leant forward as the fourth-floor light turned off; he pressed the HALT LIFT IN EMERGENCY button, and the carriage shuddered to a stop.

'What are you doing?' she whispered, her voice shaking.

'This,' he said as he moved her closer to him, slipping his hand behind her neck, pulling her in close. His normally strong hands were shaking, this small detail melted her heart. It pleased her to know that he was as nervous as she was.

He kissed her, and it was the kiss she was expecting earlier in the toilets, filled with passion and love. A warmth began to creep into her belly, and she sighed as it began to slowly spread down between her legs. *This is how newlyweds are supposed to kiss*, she thought. Her hands ran down the front of his tailored suit, and she could feel the smoothness of his flat stomach through his shirt and waistcoat. As they probed further, they stopped at the front of his trousers. The bulge there was even harder than it had been on the dance floor. Without stopping, she unbuckled his belt and made short work of unzipping his fly. Sliding her hands around his waist, she pulled at his trousers until they came down, bundling at his knees.

There was a comical moment when his underpants got stuck over his erection, and she couldn't help but giggle as she pulled them down all the way. He didn't even notice. She slipped her hands around to cup his buttocks, skin to skin.

She eased down and knelt before him. The result of his sexual attraction almost hit in her face, and she squeezed it a little. She smiled as he inhaled sharply.

She looked up and noticed that the smile had left his face to be replaced with a breathless abandon and a ruffled brow. Her eyes found his, and she grinned saucily up at him. With their eyes locked, he began to shake his head ever so slowly.

She caught her reflection in the mirrored wall opposite her and realised that she had never witnessed herself in this sexual position before. 'I look fucking gorgeous,' she said with a laugh before continuing what she had started.

She noticed he was looking upwards to the ceiling of the carriage, and for the first time, she saw that it, too, was mirrored. He was watching her doing what she was doing from a different angle.

This excited her even more.

After a few moments, his breathing began to deepen, and she felt his hands grip her hair. She took this as a cue to speed up. The knowledge and anticipation of what was about to happen made her heart beat faster, and her movement kept pace with the throb.

His breathing sped up, getting faster and faster, and his hand grasped tighter at her hair. She loved everything about this, and waited in a blissful anticipation for the inevitable to happen…

The alarm on the lift rang out, and a concerned voice shouted up the elevator shaft. 'Hello up there. Are you stuck? I'm going to call the repairmen, don't worry, we'll have you out in no time!'

Olivia fell back against the mirror laughing, as did Paul. He covered his modesty and pulled her up from the floor. Then he wrapped his arms around her and hugged her close, burying his face into her hair. Goose-bumps rose on her neck as he took in a deep breath. 'I love you so much,' he whispered into her ear.

Olivia giggled like a love-struck schoolgirl. 'I love you too,' she whispered back.

Butterflies

6.

BACK IN THEIR suite, they were still laughing about the elevator incident. Paul kicked the door closed behind them, and suddenly they were shrouded in twilight. The only illumination was from the glow of the full moon reflecting off Lake Geneva and shining in through their window.

They fell into a kiss. She held his face in both of her hands, caressing him gently on the mouth. 'I've got a surprise for you,' she whispered, pulling away from him.

He smiled back at her. 'I've got one for you too,' he replied with a wink.

She made her way into their en-suite bathroom, closing the door behind her. She wanted privacy for this. Looking at herself in the mirror, she noticed that her hair was looking a little dishevelled, mostly due to Paul pulling it in the elevator, but apart from that, the day hadn't taken much of a toll of her at all. Most of her was still pretty much intact.

Her makeup was still good, her dress was still cleanish, and best of all, her new shoes hadn't hurt her feet all day—which was excellent as they were a big part of Paul's surprise. She began to undo her hair, pulling out the million-and-one clips that had kept it in place all day, when there was a light knock on the door.

'Can I come in?' Paul whispered through the door.

'Yeah, I'm just taking my hair down.'

He opened the door and peeped in at her. 'Thank God you haven't undone your dress yet,' he said.

'Why?'

'Because I've been dying to do that all night.'

He stepped up behind, brushing hair away from her neck. The feel of his breath on her exposed nape sent her skin back into goose-bumps. She dropped her arms and watched his reflection in the mirror. His hand traced along her shoulders, and her skin tingled at his velvet-like touch, making her squirm in his embrace. His lips brushed her sensitive skin and the goose-bumps intensified ten-fold. His hands continued their journey down her back and only stopped when they reached the bow of her corset, midway down the garment.

She held her breath as he fingered the bow before giving it a small tug. As he un-looped the ribbon from each eyehole, he kissed her neck. The shivers travelled up and down her body, and she closed her eyes, relishing every one, as she allowed him to undress her.

Eventually, the garment eased its restrictive hold, and she felt an instant relief as it fell. She caught and held it over her breasts. Taking a trembling breath, she looked at his refection. 'Right, Mr Martell. It's about time you left this bathroom and let a girl do what's needed to be done.'

'Tease,' he said, feigning grumpiness.

'Out!' she demanded, pointing towards the door.

Pulling a sad face in the mirror, Paul left the bathroom.

As he left, Olivia smiled and let her corset go. She reached for her travel bag underneath the mirror and removed a few bottles and a small black plastic bag with a large white dot in the middle. She wriggled out of her wedding dress skirt and slowly unclipped her suspender belt, then rolled her stockings down her legs. Finally, she removed her silk knickers. 'You did a good job, girls,' she giggled.

She gazed into the mirror at her naked body. It was the first time, in a long time, she could say that she was pleased with the way she looked. She fingered her long chestnut hair as it cascaded in ringlets past her shoulders before leaning in and studying her hazel eyes. They were complemented by the expert makeup job. *Thank you, Jan,* she thought.

Her slender shoulders were covered in an even tan; the five days at the spa in Marbella with the girls had done her the world of good.

She had always loved her breasts; they were full, perky, and rounded with small brown nipples. They had never let her down in the past. She had been disappointed that she hadn't been able to lose the small pouch of her stomach, but it was the best that it had been for a long time, her personal trainer had seen to that. She had inherited her mother's hips, a little too curvy for her liking, but all the boys she'd known never had any reason to complain about them.

All in all, even though there were parts of her that she would change if she could, she couldn't really complain about her body too much.

'Right, girlie, this is a dirty job, but someone's got to do it,' she told herself, picking up one of the bottles and giving it a vigorous shake. She poured the oil onto her hands and rubbed them together to warm it up. She then began to apply it onto her skin, starting with her shoulders, making her way down to her breasts. As she covered them in the oil, the slight breeze from the air conditioner caught them, hardening her nipples instantly into tight, oiled buds. It sent a pleasing tingle throughout her body; she loved having sensitive nipples.

She finished off oiling the rest of her body and gave her skin a little sniff. The orange and coconut flavours were gorgeous. She opened the black bag and removed the lacy, two-piece underwear set.

She eased herself into the black bra and the small, lacy thong, feeling a rush of anticipation, wondering what her surprise could be.

Slipping her high-heeled wedding shoes back on, she climbed into one of the hotel's thick towel robes and opened the door into their room.

Paul was lying on the king-size bed. He was also wearing one of the hotel robes. In front of him on the bed was a large silver bucket filled with ice, with a dark green bottle-top sticking out of it.

'Is it nearly time for my surprise?' he asked, sounding like a kid in a candy store.

'Almost,' she replied, cocking her head to indicate the bucket on the bed. 'Is that my surprise there?' she inquired.

He gave her a small wink and a naughty smile. 'It's part of it, but I think it's only fair if you go first.'

'Why me? Maybe we should both go together. On three…'

He got up off the bed to face her, and they both began to untie the belts on the robes.

'One… two,' she counted slowly.

'Three,' he said faster, then whipped off his robe.

He was naked underneath, except for his own small black thong. The word GROOM was written on the front in white writing. At the crotch, there was a red light that was flashing on and off. He stood with his hands on his hips, thrusting his pelvis towards her in time with the red pulses.

It was too much for her, and she creased over with laughter. 'Hang on a moment,' she laughed between her hands. 'Don't go anywhere.' She backed away towards the dressing table, not able to take her eyes off her pulsing groom. She fished about for her mobile phone. 'This is definitely going into the wedding album,' she laughed as her camera clicked away.

Satisfied with the shots, she put her phone away. 'Come here, you,' she commanded him, her face suddenly serious.

Paul made his way over to her and took her in his arms.

She slowly undid her robe and let it fall open.

'This is your surprise,' she whispered. 'It's yours to do what you want with, forever.'

She pushed him away playfully, and he fell onto the bed. As he lay there, the pulsating red light filled the darkened room. *Is that thing flashing faster?* she thought as her robe fell to the floor.

He leant up on the bed, and his eyes widened as they lapped up the vison before him. It always amazed her that no matter how many times he saw her naked, each and every time was like the first.

'Do you like this?' she asked, edging herself closer to the side of the bed. Because of the funny angle the red light was now flashing on his underwear, she surmised that he did indeed like it. It made her feel special when that happened; she loved the feeling of control it gave her.

She bent over him and eased the novelty thong off before flinging it onto the bedroom floor next to her robe, where it continued to strobe. 'Do you want me to continue where we left off in the lift?'

'Fuck, yes,' he replied with a breathy voice.

~~~~

Wave after wave of butterflies beat and flapped at her stomach as she made love to her husband. With each thrust of his passion, more of them awoke and joined the throng inside her. *How many of those things do I have?* she thought with a secret smile as, yet another bolt of ecstasy tore through her.

Twice, she felt herself on the brink of orgasm, and twice, she let herself float along with it, suspended on the immense, blue gossamer wings of her beasts of ecstasy.

There didn't seem to be any stopping Paul, he was like a machine tonight, and Olivia could feel herself gearing up to her third orgasm. *Three?* she thought with abandon.

Paul's rhythmic breathing began to deepen, and her butterflies began to fly in anticipation of what was about to occur.

They were in almost perfect sync with each other as Paul began to push deeper and deeper inside her, his moans getting louder with each thrust. She knew that she was only moments away from a personal best for her, if only her man could contain himself a moment longer.

She hugged him closer, raking her manicured fingernails across his moist back. *Nearly there,* she coaxed herself, *nearly there...*

Then Paul was away. He screamed as his love released into her, taking her away with him.

Her butterflies soared and swirled around their cavern, the wings brushing every sensitive part of her body, making her back arch and blood rush to her face.

She was aching now, but a deep sense of loss encompassed her as Paul slowly pulled out of her and collapsed onto the bed, drained, spent.

She was throbbing. Her eyes were closed, but there were light-flowers blooming and spots forming behind her eyelids. 'Oh... my... word...' she sighed. 'I'll be feeling that tomorrow,' she laughed. *Or at least I hope I will be.*

She turned to look at him, and, like a true romantic, he'd fallen asleep next to her, his once proud erection now wilting. She couldn't resist the urge to flick it, and he mumbled as she did, turning and

Butterflies

wrapping his arm around her. He nuzzled his wet face into her shoulder and fell back asleep.

Everyone would still be partying away downstairs for at least another hour. *What do I care?* she asked herself. *I'm happy up here with my sleeping Paul.* A smile spread across her face.

'Yeah. More than happy!'

7.

THE NEXT MORNING, Olivia was wide awake at seven and was feeling fresh. Paul was still sleeping the sleep of the just. As she swung her legs out of the bed, she felt a delicious ache between them. Every movement she made was a reminder of what they had done together the night before. Making her way to the bathroom, she turned on the shower and then looked in the mirror. *Did I ever come so hard before in my life?* she questioned herself; she knew the answer was no.

The warm, powerful gush of the shower against her skin invigorated and refreshed her as she allowed it to cascade over her body. Reaching for the soap, an excited chill coursed through her. *I have the rest of my life to feel like this.* Grinning, she lathered the soap over her skin, washing the sleep away.

As she washed her hair, she became engrossed in their itinerary for the day: breakfast, pick up their hire car, drive out into the countryside of Switzerland, discover some castles or something, back here for dinner and who knew what else.

She was so caught up in these thoughts that she didn't hear her husband enter the bathroom. With shampoo in her hair and over her body, she had her eyes closed and gave a little start when a hand reached around the shower door and grabbed her bottom.

'Hmmm, now that's what a man should wake up to every morning,' he said as he slipped into the steamy shower cubicle behind her.

She moved over, allowing him access to the warm spray, and he began to kiss her neck. The feel of the hot water coupled with his lips was unbelievable, and she felt herself go moist in parts of her body she hadn't even gotten around to washing yet.

'Paul, we can't this morning. I'm still sore from last night,' she protested breathlessly, and rather weakly. She knew it was a hopeless fight as he had already stiffened up, and she wanted it as much as he did. He continued to caress her neck and shoulders. His hands sliding up her sudsy skin, from her thighs to her belly, before continuing to her soapy breasts. He cupped them in his strong hands, and she felt the intense sensation of her nipples becoming harder than they already were. The feel of Paul's erection becoming even harder made her lose any inhibitions she may have held.

Closing her eyes, she lifted her head and enjoyed the feel of the warm water streaming over her face.

The feel of Paul behind her, enjoying her as much as she was enjoying him, heightened her feelings towards him, and she knew she wanted him—no, that didn't give her feelings any justice, she needed him—deep inside her.

This was how she wanted every morning to start for the rest of her life. She wanted her butterflies, their little light wings, to flutter her awake every morning. Paul certainly knew how to get them going.

When he entered her, she could feel her body braced for another explosion.

As was his.

Her knees began to buckle as the slow orgasm began to build through her body. She grabbed hold of the shower door to stop herself from falling as her body gave in to the pulsating wings of the butterflies. She felt his body tense and then shout as he reached his own climax.

Once their bodies began to relax from their exertions, she turned to him and smiled.

He flashed his gorgeous, wide smile, his wet hair and blue eyes making him look like a young boy.

'Is it possible to fall in love with you again?' she asked. 'That must have been about the sixth time since yesterday.'

He laughed, and she leaned into him on her tiptoes, brushing her hard nipples against his wet chest, giving herself another little chill. She kissed him.

The shower water continued to stream over them as her lips searched for his.

'I love you, Mrs Martelle,' he said, allowing the water to fill his mouth.

'I love you too, Mr Martelle,' she replied.

He then squirted the water from his mouth over her face. She jumped back, laughing in surprise, and swatted him on his muscular rump. She pushed him out of the shower. 'Don't you think you've splashed me enough this morning? Now get out, you've made me dirtier than I was before I got in.'

'I never had you down as the dirty type,' he laughed, shaking his head. 'To think, I have a dirty wife.' He grabbed a large towel from the heated rail and left the bathroom with a swagger.

She stood under the warm water and continued to wash her body. There was a smile spread across her whole face.

Butterflies

8.

ONE HOUR LATER, they were both dressed and en-route downstairs to breakfast. They caught the elevator and shared the ride with an elderly couple.

'Ollie, do you think we should carry on where we left off last night in this elevator?' Paul asked, loud enough for the couple to hear, and the devil languishing in his smile. She gave him a poke in his ribs as she blushed a deep crimson.

The elderly couple looked at them. 'Are you the couple who were married here yesterday?' the lady asked, her face a picture of pinched lips and a ruffled brow.

'Erm, yes,' Olivia rushed, and held out her hand, flashing her rings for her to inspect. 'Mr and Mrs Martelle.'

The lady took her hand and closely inspected the diamond in the thick platinum band. 'Oh, that ring is to die for,' she remarked. She looked at her husband and linked his arm before looking back at Olivia and Paul. 'We got married here a little over fifty years ago.'

'Did you? That's wonderful,' Olivia gushed. 'I bet this place has changed a bit since then.'

'Oh yes, for one thing, they didn't have elevators then,' she said with a twinkle in her eye.

Paul laughed as Olivia blushed redder still.

'Son, you have a good one here. Make sure you look after her. You know it only gets better with age,' the old man said, shaking Paul's hand. 'May I?' he asked as he moved to give Olivia a kiss.

Paul nodded. 'Of course, sir.'

'I was talking to her,' he said, laughing as he pointed at his wife.

'Oh, you,' the wife laughed, and swiped at him with her hand.

Olivia took him by the hand and planted a big kiss on the older man's lips. 'Of course, you can, sir,' she said.

The couple got out on the floor above the dining room. 'I think we might be going to the naked sauna on level two,' the old man said with a smile and a raise of his eyebrows as they shuffled out of the elevator.

'Oh, get out, you dirty old man. The last thing they need is to think of you in your towel. Goodbye, and I hope you have a long and healthy life together,' the woman said, addressing them both as the doors began to close.

'Naked sauna, eh? Might check that one out later!' Paul shouted to them as the doors closed.

'No, you won't,' Olivia replied. 'You'll be too busy checking ME out.'

Butterflies

9.

MOST OF THEIR friends were already in the restaurant for breakfast, and a huge cheer erupted as the newlyweds entered. Everyone seemed ready for party number two.

They sat and ate and laughed and drank tea with everyone for over an hour before they announced they had to go, as today was a busy day for Mr and Mrs Martelle. Again, another huge cheer erupted from their guests, complemented with more than a few wolf whistles.

'Remember that surprise I had for you last night?' he asked as they were leaving the restaurant, hand in hand.

'Yeah, the one I've got on my mobile phone?' she laughed.

He shook his head. 'Nope, the one I never got around to giving you.'

'The Champagne? It's still in the fridge.'

'Wrong again,' he said, smiling. 'It's this one.' He held out a set of car keys.

Her face lit up as she looked at the outstretched gift. 'Paul!' she said, the shock evident in her high-pitched voice. 'What are those?'

His face revelled in her delight, 'These my dear, are the keys to… that.' He gestured towards the outside of the main hotel doors where, sitting in the driveway with the lake and the glorious sunrise as a backdrop, there stood a brand-new Aston Martin DB9 Convertible.

'I thought we might just go for a little spin into the countryside in your new car. We could stop off, have a little picnic, maybe make a little love in the summer breeze with the top down,' he said, flashing his trademark wink.

She looked the car over, revelling in its beauty. It was metallic green with a beige, full leather finish dashboard and matching seats. She was breathless as she turned towards him. 'Oh, I don't think we'll be making love in this.'

Paul's face dropped a little at the statement.

'Oh no…' she continued, '…in this car, we fuck!'

His smile reappeared and stretched so wide she began to worry the top of his head may just fall of. Tossing her the keys, he shouted, 'Right then, let's get going.'

10.

THEY DROVE OUT into the glorious sunshine for about an hour, taking the back lanes around the countryside, circumventing the great lake, and enjoying the breath-taking scenery. From one spot where they parked, Olivia had a clear and unobstructed view of the whole lake.

'Paul,' she said dragging her gaze away from the vista before them. 'I don't think I've ever been so happy in my entire life. I know it sounds cheesy, but it's the way I feel right now.' She smiled and held his hand tight.

'Baby,' he said in a mocking American accent with a deep booming voice, 'You know I just about feel the same. I think today has been… AWESOME!'

They drove on for miles and miles, enjoying the fresh air in their faces, their hair blowing in the wind, the sun on their skin, and the fresh new wedding rings on their fingers. *And not forgetting the butterflies in my stomach either,* she kept a special thought aside for them.

'I'm starving. Let's pull over and tuck into that picnic.'

'Great idea. I'm so hungry I could eat—'

'A tramp's sock?' she finished for him.

'Ewww, no,' he replied, pulling a mock-disgusted face. 'I was going to say I could eat that whole picnic to myself.'

They were still laughing as they pulled into a secluded spot with another great view of the lake. Olivia could make out one other car in their whole vicinity. It, too, was parked up, and it looked like the owners had the same ideas as they did.

Picnicking.

From the back seat, Paul pulled a huge wicker basket laden with picnic style goodies. There were sandwiches, sausage rolls, roast chicken, and cake. There was also some non-alcoholic fizzy wine and two crystal flutes.

'Well, mister, it seems you've thought of everything.' She planted a kiss on his forehead as they sat down to eat.

Once they'd eaten their fill, they lay back to look up at the sky. Olivia was trying to make out shapes in the clouds, and by the sound of his rhythmic breathing, she guessed Paul had dozed off.

She was right.

She reached her hand over and stroked it down his arm. 'We should think about getting back,' she said, getting up and collecting their things together. 'Some of the guests are leaving this afternoon, and I wouldn't mind saying goodbye to them.'

Reluctantly, he agreed with her and helped gather everything together and put it into the boot of the car. When they were ready to go, she threw the keys over to him. 'Your turn to drive, I think.'

She knew he'd been dying for a go.

Grinning, he caught the keys and ran around to the driver's side door. 'Yes,' he shouted as he got in and began to make himself comfortable. 'Get ready for the ride of your life.'

'I'm already on it,' she laughed.

Butterflies

He did a small wheel spin start and whipped the car off onto the winding road 'Sorry,' he shouted over the roar of the engine. 'I couldn't help myself. I've always wanted to do that.'

'Just you slow down,' she shouted.

He grinned at her and proceeded to accelerate.

'Paul,' she shouted again. 'Slow down.'

He complied, smiling, and she sat back in her seat, relieved.

On their journey outward, Olivia had noticed a small nook of a path, maybe just big enough, and private enough, for them to park up for a few moments, or maybe an hour. As they returned, she kept a keen eye on the road, trying to recall any of the landmarks around where it was.

Then she remembered, when they'd passed an old lighthouse, there had been a long fence for about a mile and a half. The path had been at the end of that fence.

It would suit her needs perfectly.

The lighthouse made its appearance in the distance, and she knew it was time to put her saucy plan into action.

As Paul concentrated on the road, she expertly slipped her bra off while turning away from him. The breeze coming off the lake, coupled with the naughty thoughts running through her head, made her nipples begin to stand out underneath her thin, white t-shirt.

He was lost in his driving of the beautiful car and hadn't noticed what she was doing, but as he stole a glance her way, the car swerved a little. He oversteered and careened the car over into the oncoming lane. Luckily for them both, there was nothing coming the other way.

She winked at him. 'Keep your eyes on the road, Buster.'

He veered back into his own lane, shaking his head. As he corrected the car, she crept her hand into his crotch and began to unbutton his fly.

He looked at her, his smile confused but excited.

'Do you want me to stop?' she asked.

'No!' He almost spat the word out in his elation.

'Good, then drive. I want you to look out for a small road off the end of the fence by the lighthouse. When you find it, use it,' she commanded.

Paul smiled a cheeky grin. 'OK, ma'am, right away,' he replied, saluting comically with one hand.

I really can't believe I'm about to do this, she thought as her fingers slipped into his trousers. She was not the least bit surprised to find that Paul was very nearly hard.

He raised his backside, arching his legs, and she managed to pull his trousers down around his thighs.

Her head travelled down, and she began to kiss his stomach. As her lips caressed his skin, she felt him stiffen in her hand. She didn't think she would ever get bored of that reaction. The thought sent naughty feelings right through her stomach.

Fly, my pretties… She thought about the butterflies waking up in her stomach and giggled.

'What are you laughing at down there?' he asked, taking his eyes off the road again.

'The Wizard of Oz,' she replied.

'What?'

Her head moved down lower, and the car swerved once again.

She looked up at him. 'If you can't drive this thing, I'll have to stop,' she warned.

'I can drive, I can drive,' he replied with a gasp.

She noticed, with more than a little humour, that every time her tongue hit a certain spot, his foot automatically hit the accelerator and they went a little faster. She toyed with this for a while, enjoying the feel of control.

Butterflies

It was a wonderful sensation, feeling the thrum of the road beneath her as he ran his hand through her hair and down her neck towards her nape.

Suddenly, the car slowed, and she felt it pull off the road. She looked up to see where they were and was happy to see that it was the dirt road she'd noticed earlier. *Excellent,* she thought.

The car pulled into a small wooded area and stopped. Paul engaged the handbrake and turned towards her in one fluid motion. He grabbed her lightly, but forcefully, by the hair, pulling her towards him. He kissed her, his hands grasping at the buttons on her shorts.

'Oh, yes,' she gasped as her breath was almost sucked from her mouth. 'Yes, yes, fuck yes...'

His probing hands found their way into her white cotton panties and pulled them roughly to one side.

'I want you inside me, and I want it now,' she panted.

He distanced himself from her and removed the hindrance that was his trousers. She fell back into her seat and removed her shorts and cotton panties. The fresh breeze on the wet warmth between her legs sent tingles up and down her body, spurring her butterflies back to life.

She leaned over towards the driver's side and supported her hand on the window frame, pulling herself over towards him, straddling him. She hovered above, just for the slightest of moments, enjoying the delicious anticipation of him entering her. She looked down and saw that he, too, was savouring the moment, and the view.

Not able to wait any longer, she lowered herself onto him. He slipped effortlessly inside her, releasing her captive butterflies from their anticipation.

Completely ignoring that they were outside, on a public road, she let herself go in wild abandon. Her feet begin to tingle, and it raced up the inside of her thighs. *I'm sitting in my new car, making love to the man of my dreams, and I'm about to...* this thought was never finished.

Wild sensations surged through her. She had never felt anything like this before. There was pain, pleasure, cold, heat, wetness, warmth, tightness, all hitting her at the same time.

She was lost in a whirl of pleasure and butterflies. She squeezed every drip of orgasm, every dot of feeling out of her. Holding her breath helped, closing her eyes helped, digging her fingers into his arms helped.

Eventually, the orgasm released its hold, then she felt the second rush of his release deep inside her.

Then they both relaxed, spent, at the same time.

~~~~

Her hair was hanging over his face, sweaty and tangled, her hands were leaning on the seat, either side of his head. She felt he might need to pick her fingernails out of his skin. He was still inside her, and she loved the feeling of him wilting away.

Lifting her head, she looked at him. Her eyes were filled with love and satisfaction. His eyes were still closed, and his face had the glow of someone who had been deeply sexually satisfied.

One eye opened, and he gave her a lopsided grin. 'Mrs Martelle,' he whispered. 'I'm going to do that with you for the rest of our lives.'

'You best had,' she whispered in reply.

11.

TEN MINUTES LATER, they were both dressed, decent, and ready to commence driving. 'To look at you right now,' he stated. 'You wouldn't know that ten minutes ago you were a writhing mad woman, hungry for the seed of passing virile young men.'

'Men?' she laughed in reply. 'Can you just drive, you lunatic? I'm starving again.'

He tipped her a wink and pulled out of the dirt road into the main road.

The roar of the oncoming vehicle was the loudest, most horrific noise she had heard in her entire life.

Then the world went black.

12.

SHE WOKE TO pain.

Pain in her arms, pain in her chest and back, pain in her face.

She also woke to whiteness.

White on the walls, white on the bed, white on the curtains around her.

Everything was a blur as she opened her eyes. Her vision was hazy at best, but there was a figure within the haze, one that stood out in clarity from everything else around her. When her vision finally focused, she recognised the figure as Aunt Penny.

'Where am I?' Olivia croaked through an extremely sore and dry throat.

Aunt Penny leaned over the bed to stroke her hair. 'You're in the hospital, darling; you were in an accident. You're OK now, so just rest, everything's OK.'

She did as she was told; Aunt Penny could always sooth away any pain with a few comforting words.

Slowly, the older woman got up and walked out of the room. Olivia heard her calling for someone. A young nurse blustered in, along with an older man wearing a white coat. She began to fuss around the bed, lifting Olivia's head slightly to adjust the pillows while the doctor leant in and shone a light into her eyes. They both spoke with broken English as they busied themselves around their patient.

'Tell me, young lady, can you see how many fingers I am holding up?' the doctor asked.

Olivia attempted to focus on his hand. It looked like he was holding up more than one, as her eyesight was still so fuzzy. 'Three?' she croaked in a guess.

The doctor's face dropped in disappointment, but he managed to smile anyway. 'Can you tell me your name, young lady, and your age?'

'My name is Olivia Martelle, nee Britt, and a gentleman shouldn't ask a lady her age…'

In her head, she'd made this joke very eloquently, but in reality, she sounded like an old hag who had smoked sixty cigarettes every day of her life.

The doctor smiled and patted her arm at the joke. There was a little concern in his face, but the smile put her at ease. He left the room muttering to the nurse, who was running behind him taking rapid notes, leaving Olivia with only the comforting presence of Aunt Penny for company.

'The doctors say that you need plenty of rest, but that you'll be OK. Thank heavens,' her favourite person in the whole world reassured her, while making herself comfortable on the chair next to the bed.

Olivia promptly fell back into a deep sleep.

13.

OLIVIA AWOKE AGAIN in the same room. The light streaming in through the window told her it must have been sometime past midday. She raised her head and gave the room a scan. Her head throbbed and swirled from the effort, making her vision blur again. But one thing was clear: she wasn't alone. Aunt Penny had left, but had been replaced by Kevin? Keith? Brian? *Oh, why can't I ever remember his name?*

Angela's husband was sat at the bottom of the bed, looking nervously towards her. 'Hi,' he whispered. 'I hope you don't mind me being here. Penny needed to get back to her hotel room, and she didn't want you left alone.'

'No, no, it's great that you're here to see me looking my very worst.' She sounded like she was speaking through sandpaper. 'You couldn't pass me some water, could you please?'

It was then that Olivia noticed Angela outside her room talking to—or was it at—a doctor. She didn't look happy, but then, she never really did.

'I'm so sorry, but I think this accident has played with my head somewhat. I know you are Angela's husband, but your name has gone completely out of my head. I'm so embarrassed.'

Butterflies

He laughed a little and gave her a nice smile, 'Don't worry about it. I'm Richard, and I'm pleased to meet you.'

'Richard, what's going on out there? Why is Angela looking so angry?' Olivia could feel herself becoming upset. 'Richard, where's Paul? Why isn't Paul in here to see me?'

His face dropped, and Olivia's emotions went into turmoil.

'Richard,' she sobbed, 'Where's Paul? Where's my husband? WHERE IS HE?'

The doctor outside the room turned away from the woman shouting at him to see what was happening. He walked away from Angela with evident relief and into Olivia's room.

Richard was stood at the foot of the bed, looking both scared and useless. As the doctor and Angela walked in, he turned to look at them. 'I'm sorry, so sorry, I didn't know what to say…'

'It's OK, sir, I'll take it from here,' he said, putting a hand on her forehead. Olivia marvelled absently on how warm his hands were. 'Mrs Martelle! Please, you must calm down. My name is Doctor Hausen.'

'Doctor, I need to know what's happened to me. Why am I in here? And where is my husband?' Olivia was pleading between her sobs.

'Mrs Martelle, please, you and Mr Martelle were involved in a road accident. You need to be aware that your husband is quite alive…'

The weight of the world suddenly lifted from her shoulders, she closed her eyes and relaxed back into the deep pillows behind her. 'Oh, thank God, thank the lord, thank whoever I need to thank. Paul's alive!' She rejoiced as the good news sank in.

Dr Hausen saw her delight and gripped her hand tighter. His face took on a more solemn look; this look troubled her. 'Mrs Martelle, he *is* very much alive, but there is something you need to know.'

Her stomach dropped, and her heart skipped a beat. She could feel the murmur of butterflies somewhere deep. These were not the bright blue ones she had gotten used to with Paul. These were black and ominous.

She closed her eyes, not wanting to hear what was coming next, but at the same time, it was *all* she wanted to hear.

'Mr Martelle received trauma to the side of his head. It has caused an intracranial hematoma. He has a massive blood clot, what we call a subdural hematoma. Basically, Paul is in a coma. Physically he seems otherwise fine, there are no breaks in his bones, but for the moment, he's comatose.'

Olivia's world caved in. She fell back onto her pillow with her eyes closed. The black butterflies swarmed all around her, beating at her with their vile, leathery wings. She closed her eyes and fell into a deep, and blissfully dreamless, sleep.

14.

SHE SLEPT FOR sixteen hours straight. When she eventually awoke, it was mid-morning, and there was no one at the end of her bed. She was bursting to go to the toilet. She flicked the blankets off and attempted to manoeuvre herself off the bed. Although she did have feeling in her legs, they just steadfastly refused to work correctly. *You'd better start to work, stupid legs. There's no way I'm wearing an adult nappy.* She smiled at that thought, but then instantly thought of Paul. Her Paul, the man she had planned and dreamed of being with forever. *What if he comes out of this coma and can't walk? What if he has brain damage? What if he never comes out at all?* Her mood shifted between light bemusement and black depression.

A nurse saw her trying to get out of bed and fussed into the room. 'Mrs Martelle,' she scolded in broken English. 'You can't get out of bed on your own yet. Even though you haven't broken anything, your body is recovering from the trauma. Let me get you a bed pan.'

Olivia was shocked. *I can't pee into a bedpan,* she thought through the pain. *The indignity!*

She came back with the most peculiar object Olivia had ever seen and instructed her how to use it. She thought there was no way she could do it like that, it was so… unnatural. But, when she got down to it, nature took its course, and the relief was instantaneous.

'You'll be up and about within a couple of days,' the nurse said absently as she removed the strange metal pan. 'You have had a severe concussion, Mrs Martell. Plus, there was a deep cut to your thigh, and your ankle was badly sprained. You will need to relax and take it easy until your body had healed from its trauma.'

'Is there any news on my husband?' she asked hopefully.

'Not yet. As soon as we know anything, you'll know it too.'

'Will I be able to see him today? Please.'

'That's not for me to decide,' the nurse replied, grabbing hold of her hand—obviously for comfort, but she found precious little within it. 'The doctor will be around momentarily; he'll let you know what is happening.' She flashed a small, well-meaning smile, but Olivia found it the hardest thing in the world to look at.

As the nurse left the room, Olivia felt her heart might just break in two, but at that very moment, Aunt Penny blustered in with two huge bouquets of the most gorgeous flowers she had ever seen.

As soon as she saw her, she burst into tears.

Penny hurriedly put the flowers down at the side of the bed and fussed her way over to her. She flung her arms around her with the deftest touch, enough to give the comfort required but not enough to hurt her fragile body.

Olivia marvelled at this wonderful woman.

'Pen, I still haven't seen Paul. Have you seen him? What does he look like? Is he very badly injured? Will he make it Pen, will he?'

'Oh, Ollie,' Aunt Penny chided. 'He's in the best care. The safest hands in the business are looking out for him. You need to concentrate on building up your own strength so you can be there for him when he wakes up.'

She had the knack of saying the right things at the right times.

Butterflies

'Anyway, I've got some news about your mother.' Penny always had a disdainful look when she talked about Olivia's mother. 'It seems the man she met on your hen night is taking her to live in Las Vegas. She said she'll be in a bit later to tell you all about it. I have to be somewhere else this afternoon, so I'll leave it to you to give her my best wishes.'

Aunt Penny had always been wary of Olivia's mother She was a wayward, carefree woman with no maternal instincts, and she treated Olivia as if she were a friend, at best. It had never bothered Olivia; she knew that Aunt Penny was her rock. Let her mother do what she wanted to do; as long as she was happy, Olivia didn't really care.

'So, about Paul…'

Penny grasped Olivia's hands and gave them a squeeze. *This is so different from the nurse's grasp,* she thought. *I suppose you can just tell when there is true feeling.*

'There's still no change. The doctor is on his way shortly. He said it might be good for both of you if they took you round to see him this afternoon. He looks good, though, Ollie, and they said because he's so strong, there may well be a chance of him waking up soon.'

Olivia knew Aunt Penny. She was not a good poker player.

'Anyway, Angela is in there with him right now. Oh, she's a bossy one, that girl. Her poor husband has run around getting coffee and tea for everyone while she's stood yelling at all and sundry, telling them what their jobs are. I got out before she had me fluffing the pillows.'

Olivia smiled her first and what would be her only smile of that whole day.

15.

THE DOCTOR MADE his way around to Olivia's room by eleven a.m. Aunt Penny had left half an hour earlier because of a pressing appointment that she apparently just couldn't shake off.

They had embraced before she left, taking all the joy of the day with her.

When the doctor found her, she was sitting up in bed, blankly staring at the small TV screen in the corner of the room. A Swiss soap opera was on with the sound muted. It looked rubbish, but then she wasn't in any mood to be entertained.

'Mrs Martelle?' A strong, deep Germanic accent boomed from the doorway. 'I'm here to update you regarding your progress, and to take you to see your husband.'

'Oh, thank you, Doctor.'

'The good news is…' he began, still booming in his authoritative, masculine voice. '…your sprained ankle will heal, as will the laceration on your upper thigh, and we are confident there will be no permanent damage other than a small scarring. When the bruises heal, you will be fit as a fiddle. There is nothing wrong with your bones or your internal organs. You seem to be recovering well from your concussion, although it was a bad one. I would recommend at least another three full days of rest, and then you can go home.' He smiled at her, but she didn't have it in her to smile back.

Some home, she thought fighting back tears.

Two male porters entered her room on the gesture of the doctor, one of them was pushing a wheelchair.

'Right, I think it is time for you to see your husband. I'll explain his situation to you on the way.'

The two porters helped her out of the bed and lifted her into the chair. She grimaced as a bolt of pain ripped through her. They removed all her electronic monitoring patches and uncoupled the drip from the apparatus so they could take it with them on their journey.

'So, this is what you need to know about Mr Martelle. He has suffered a severe blow to the head. The extent of any damage, we will not know until his brain has stopped swelling. We are stemming the swelling from any dangerous levels with complex drugs, but unfortunately, the drugs render him completely still. I'm telling you this as you may feel distressed when you see him. The drug's effects leave the patient in a comatose state, one that resembles death. The machines around him are doing the breathing and blood regulation for him.' He stopped their small entourage for a moment and looked at her, his face devoid of any humour. 'I assure you, Mrs Martelle, your husband is still very much alive.' He took hold of her hand and gave it a reassuring squeeze. 'You just have to be strong for him.'

Is this what people do these days to give comfort? she thought. *He's the third person today to squeeze my hand.*

She returned his gesture with her own little squeeze, but steadfastly refused to smile.

16.

THE ROOM WAS dark inside, a little too dark for her eyes, and they took a moment to adjust. The bed was in the centre, with ample access space on either side. These spaces were filled with technology. Olivia had never seen so many machines. It reminded her of the time her uncle had taken her into the cockpit of a Boeing 747 during a flight to Spain when she was a child. The lights and dials had dazzled her then as these lights dazzled her now. The constant suck and hiss of the ventilator, somewhere in the room, was almost deafening in its whispered, laboured breathing.

Olivia signalled for the porter who was pushing her to stop. 'Dr Hausen, I want to go in alone, if I may?'

The doctor replied with a whisper. 'Yes, Mrs Martelle, of course you can.'

She wheeled the chair into the room and manoeuvred herself over to the bed.

Lying within it was a man.

His face was covered with tubes entering his mouth and nose. His eyes were closed, and there was a bandage wrapped tightly around his head. His arms were free of the blankets but covered by more tubes of red and white and yellow.

Butterflies

Olivia looked at this poor man with pity before raising her gaze up towards the nameplate above the bed. It read:

Mr Paul Martelle, NOK Mrs Olivia Martelle.

This brought home to her why she was here, in this room. The lifeless man, the husk lying on this bed, was her husband. It was Paul, the same man she made love to in the toilets during her wedding, the same man who wore the silly underpants with the flashing lights. Her Paul, her husband, her life… her future.

A small tear welled in her eye. It burst its barrier and travelled down her cheek. She felt the warmth and tasted the salt as her lips parted ever so slightly, allowing it to disappear into her mouth.

The tear was quickly followed by another, and then another.

The floodgates had opened, and a river of tears coursed down her face. She tried to catch her breath, but every time her mouth opened, another deep sob gripped her, taking the precious breath with it.

A strange thought came to her: every tear was another dead butterfly!

Dr Hausen entered. He gripped her wheelchair. It was shuddering with each of her sobs, so much so that it took him a few moments to control it. Once he did, he leaned in and whispered into her ear. 'Come now, Mrs Martelle, I think it's time to get you back to your room.'

Olivia had no recollection of the journey back, or of being helped into her bed, or of screaming Paul's name over and over and over. There was no recollection either of the medication administered to her to calm her down, or of falling asleep crying, her face and blankets soaking wet from the tears of raw emotion and pain streaming down her face.

17.

TWO DAYS LATER, Olivia awoke from her sleep. She had been encased inside a heavy, black cloud of depression since seeing Paul, and nothing anyone could do or say could remove it. Aunt Penny had been an almost constant companion throughout her ordeal, and a blessed one too. Her mother had made a welcome, albeit brief appearance. Apparently, she had to catch a flight out to Las Vegas to begin her 'new chapter' now that she knew her 'little baby' was going to be fine.

Last night the nurses had reduced Olivia's drugs, and she felt a little better for the good night's rest. She stretched, mindful that her body was still sore, and searched around the room for Aunt Penny. Her brow ruffled, and she cocked her head when she saw Richard once again at the foot of her bed. He was asleep in the big chair by the door.

He looked like he'd been there all night.

She stretched again, and as she did, she felt a little movement in her bowels. It was only a little movement, but it was definitely there. She needed to go to the toilet, but there was no way on God's green Earth she was going to ask Richard to take her. She removed her bed covers and shifted to the edge of the bed. She grimaced at the swollen ankle and the bandage that was covering the cut on her upper thigh. She could see the deep bruising spreading out from under the dressing; it looked like a bad makeup job from some cheesy horror film.

She was determined to get to the toilet herself right now. The dizzy feeling that she had been experiencing was not quite gone, but it was almost minimal.

This was her mission, and she chose to accept it.

There was a jolt of pain as her foot made contact with the floor, and the aches in her body made her feel like she had been doing an intense workout, but she was determined to do this.

With Herculean effort, she limped across the floor, making the whole fifteen metres or so to the bathroom completely unaided.

It was a triumph.

As she sat on the toilet, she thought about her situation. She had come to terms with knowing that Paul was in the best possible hands. Moping around being sad and miserable was not going to bring him back any sooner. It was almost as if her early morning exercise had brought with it a wave of positivity.

As she exited the small room, Richard was stood outside, waiting for her. There was a huge grin across his face.

'Wow, Ollie, this is great news. I'll ring Aunt Penny and let her know that your back up on your feet. She had to go home last night. I told her that I'd stay and watch over you. She looked tired.'

'Oh, thank you, Richard, that was so thoughtful,' she replied, covering the shock in her voice at seeing him outside the toilet. She was glad that she had closed the door behind her.

'Ah, it was nothing. Angela had spent most of the night on the phone to the British Consulate trying to organise getting Paul back to the UK, so I—'

'What?' Olivia asked, interrupting his flow. She was not one hundred percent she'd heard him correctly.

'She wants to take Paul back to the UK so he can recover in familiar surroundings,' Richard replied, looking a little sheepish, as if he'd said something he shouldn't. 'She's fighting with them as they've told her he'll have to pay for the transfer and any special requirements he may have for the journey out of his own money. Sorry, I, erm, I meant, your money.'

'Over my dead body.' Olivia instantly regretted using that particular phrase, but she carried on regardless. 'Paul's in no fit state to travel to the UK. The doctor told me the drugs he's on to stem the swell of his brain are the only thing keeping him alive. If they move him now, it'll kill him.'

She sat back on the bed, the anger in her was swelling, she could feel it tingling in her sprained ankle.

'I need to find Angela,' she said, panting. All the energy in her body was sapping from her, and she would have fallen if Richard hadn't been there to steady her.

'Whoa, little lady,' he said as he caught her. 'I think you should slow down a bit.'

'I need to see Angela. She has to stop whatever she's doing.'

Richard helped her into her wheelchair. 'Well, wherever you're going, it doesn't look like you're walking there. I know where she is, but do me a huge favour—'

Olivia was in too much of a rage; so much so she wasn't even really listening to him. 'What?' she snapped.

'Please, for my sake, don't tell her it was me who told you this.'

Remembering her recent promise to herself regarding smiling, she laughed a little and reached up to squeeze his hand. 'OK, your secret's safe with me.'

18.

RICHARD WHEELED OLIVIA to the hospital administrator's office. Inside, a fierce argument was raging. The female voice sounded commanding while the male voice sounded like it was tiring.

'It's my bet they've been going at this all night,' Richard said in a non-so-happy voice. A voice that sounded like he was speaking from experience. 'She'll get her way, you just watch. She'll grind him down until she wins by submission.' He shook his head. 'She's like that with everything she does.'

Olivia knocked, and both voices stopped jabbering and bickering at once. The door opened, and a man in his late fifties stood inside. Although handsome, tanned, and quite athletic looking, Olivia could see he was tired.

His face lit up as he saw Olivia, and he made a rather theatrical greeting to her at his door. 'Ah, Mrs Martelle, how very nice to see you. Please come in.'

Richard leaned down to Olivia. 'Right, I'm off. Tell her a nurse pushed you here.' Without any further ado, he turned on his heels and sped off in the opposite direction.

Mr Gunnet, the hospital administrator, wheeled Olivia into his spacious office. Angela was sat on a large, expensive looking chair facing Mr Gunnet's desk. She didn't turn to greet Olivia as she entered the room.

'Angela,' Olivia greeted her sister-in-law. 'It's nice to see you. I haven't seen much of you around lately.'

'Olivia,' Angela took her offered hand. 'I'm so sorry, but I've been attending to the needs of my brother,' she replied curtly.

'Oh, yes, well thank you for all your efforts, they've been very much appreciated, but I'll be taking over from here, being his wife and legal heir and all.'

Angela smiled, and Olivia could have sworn she felt the temperature in the room dip, quite extensively. 'I'm sorry, Olivia, but I think not. I have a legal document stating that I have rights of attorney in the event of you not being of sound mind and…' She looked at Olivia's wheelchair, '…body.' As she said this, she indicated towards a file of legal documents on Mr Gunnet's desk.

Olivia smiled back, suddenly feeling tired and drained. 'I think you'll find me of both sound mind *and* body, Angela.'

The thin, angry woman looked her up and down. 'Really, Olivia. Can you walk to the bathroom unaided? Did you sleep last night without the use of drugs? Can you make it through the day without huge doses of pain killers? I'm awfully sorry, but this is my decision, and I've decided Paul is to be moved to a private facility in London, with hand-picked doctors. He has been here for the best part of two weeks now, with no progress and no diagnostic information to hand. This is not acceptable. My brother has financial and business interests that need to be addressed, they cannot be—'

'Angela, shut up!' Olivia shouted at her, suddenly angry and tired at the same time.

She looked at Olivia as if she'd been slapped. 'What?' Her face was filled with exasperation.

Olivia guessed that she had never been spoken to like that before. 'I said shut up. The doctors here at this facility are doing their very best. This *is* a private facility, after all, paid for by Paul's money, not yours. I'm about to make an appointment with a clinical psychologist who I'm sure will give me the signed approval of sound mind and body.'

'Hmmm…' was Angela's only reply.

Mr Gunnet sat at his desk, his eyes wide and looking impressed at the way she had cut through Angela's shell.

'I'll contest any decision that is made in your favour. Paul is my brother, and I'll do what's best for him.' Angela stood, and promptly left the room.

After the door had slammed, Olivia turned to the hospital administrator. 'Mr Gunnet, is moving Paul a feasible option?'

'Not right now, Mrs Martelle. As I told your sister-in-law, the brain has not stopped trying to protect itself. This is a most dangerous time. The brain, like any organ, will do what it needs to protect the damaged areas, but it does not have the capacity to swell due to the restrictions of the skull. We have to stem it, but also protect the damaged areas at the same time.'

'OK, leave it with me. I'll guarantee Paul will not be moved from this facility.'

'Thank you, Mrs Martelle. Can you also guarantee me no more visits from Mrs Grantham too?' he asked, smiling, although Olivia could see he wasn't joking.

19.

MR GUNNET PUSHED Olivia back to her room himself. She was far too angry to have any sort of real conversation. That was until she saw Aunt Penny in her room waiting for her.

She stood up and smiled as Olivia was wheeled in.

'Oh, Pen, please sit down,' she said. 'I'm fuming. That bitch Angela is trying to take control of my husband. *My* husband! I told her where she can get off, there's no way that she's taking Paul back to Britain for any treatment. She's totally mad. Mad, I'm telling you.'

'Ollie, I have cancer!'

'Just moving him from one room to anoth—WHAT?'

Penny dropped her head. 'I have cancer. It was confirmed today. Secondary cancer of the liver.'

'Secondary?'

'Yes, Ollie, secondary. That means that it's spread from somewhere else. I've been getting tests. I didn't want to tell you; you had your own problems.'

Olivia suddenly felt constrained by the wheelchair. She cursed her stupid ankle for not allowing her to stand up, to rush towards her aunt and wrap her arms around her, hold her.

'Oh Pen...' All she could do was hold out her arms out to her. As she did, she did something that she that she had promised herself she wouldn't do today.

She cried.

Penny bent down to her chair and accepted the embrace. She, too, was crying. They stayed like that for almost five minutes, both sniffing and blubbering in each other's arms.

When the sniffling had stopped, Penny helped Olivia onto the bed. 'I have to go back to England, Ollie. My medical insurance won't cover me while I'm abroad. That, and all my medical records are over there too,' she said as she sat down in the chair next to the bed.

'I've got the money to help you, you know that. Besides...' Olivia said between sobs, '...we need to look after each other now.' As she broke down, she turned her head and buried it into her pillow. *My stupid fucking ankle,* she screamed in her head, *I can't even stand up and give her the hug she so desperately needs.*

As if reading her thoughts, Penny leaned over the bed and gave her a hug. 'Everything will be fine, you'll see. I love you, Ollie.' She kissed her on the top of her head and then left, leaving Olivia alone in her room. Alone with all the time in the world to think.

20.

A FEW DAYS later, Olivia woke early. She was getting plenty of movement back into her legs and was more than eager to make headway on her walking. As she woke, she gave her toes a little wiggle and then moved her legs. There was a little pain but a lot of movement. *I must be on the up,* she thought with absolutely no joy whatsoever.

She cast her mind back to the last few days. There hadn't been any improvement in Paul, and now Aunt Penny had been diagnosed with cancer. Things couldn't possibly look any bleaker. At least Angela had been silent in her battle to control Paul and his estate.

Truth be known, Olivia didn't care much for the estate or for the money. All she wanted was to be happy, as happy as she *had* been for a few brief moments before all these black clouds had swarmed in. *Since my butterflies turned black,* she thought.

Over the last two days, she'd been having physiotherapy as an attempt to get her ankle and her leg working again. Dr Hausen had been extremely pleased with her progress. She'd gone from not being able to put any weight on it at all, to getting around pretty well on crutches within a few sessions.

Butterflies

Secretly, she was enjoying the physiotherapy. It gave her something to concentrate on, something to centre her thoughts on other than Paul and Penny.

Today, she thought, *I'll shower myself. I'm a confident, positive person.* She smiled at this thought, grabbed her shower bag, both crutches, and made her way determinedly to her shower.

The bathroom in her private room was spacious. It had a disabled toilet, a large bath, and a wet-room style shower. Each visit, there had been a nurse in with her to help in and out of the bath or off and onto the toilet. *But not today, s*he thought.

One hour later and one huge triumph for team Martelle, Olivia emerged from the bathroom, clean, refreshed, and ready for whatever this day could throw at her.

Right, the three Cs, concussion, coma, and cancer, I'm ready for you all, she thought with a strong smile. *Oh, and, legs, if you think I've forgot about you, then you have another thing coming.*

It was a day of positives for her.

Firstly, she had absolutely no contact from Angela; this was always a blessing. Richard did turn up to see her, though, just to see how she was doing, and she thought that was very nice of him.

Penny had her first consultation regarding her therapy. The oncologist seemed to be rather optimistic.

She had also received emails from Jan and Katie, asking how she was and what Paul's condition was. They obviously didn't know about Aunt Penny, otherwise they would have asked about her too. *Nosey cows,* she laughed to herself.

She was also feeling stronger than she had over the last few days; the doctor thought she may well be able to go home soon, as her concussion had healed, and their worry about post-concussion syndrome had proved unwarranted. The movement in her ankle was getting so much better, and her mobility was building.

She had the strength to go and see Paul for a few hours too. There were a couple of tears and a wobbly moment when she first walked into the hushed room and saw him lying on the bed; but her strength held, and it enabled her to sit with him and hold his hand.

Later that evening, she had booked her very first psych evaluation. She was nervous as hell, but it was something that just had to be done. The temporary reprieve from Angela's attempts to take Paul back to England relied on the outcome of her mental health.

She knew that she was of sound mind, but she just needed to prove it.

21.

SHE KNOCKED ON the door of the office of Dr Michaelsson. She straightened her shirt and tidied herself up a little before entering on cue. Dr Michaelsson was a woman, and a gorgeous woman at that. She had long mousey-blonde hair tied back in a loose ponytail; she wore black-rimmed glasses and very little makeup.

She intimidated Olivia straight away.

For starters, Olivia was wearing jogging bottoms with a pair of worn out carpet slippers. Dr Michaelsson was wearing a black pencil skirt with a long cut, emphasising her toned legs. The t-shirt Olivia was wearing used to be white but was now a comfortable worn-in grey. The doctor's blouse was a pearl colour, and very expensive looking. *At least I'm clean, thank God*, she thought, but was hyper aware of the rushed, tight ponytail and her ears that were sticking out. *I think I should nip back to my room and grab that photo of me in my wedding dress, just to show her how good I can look,* she thought.

'Hello, Olivia. May I start our session by saying how sorry I am for you to find yourself in this situation. This can't be the best honeymoon scenario.'

'Thank you, Doctor,' Olivia replied, touched by the emotion in the woman's voice.

'Oh, please call me Lauren. I'm a doctor, but that mantle makes me sound so old,' she smiled.

'Hello, Lauren. I'm please to meet you.' Olivia extended her hand and they shook.

'So, psych evaluations, eh? You must have something to prove? Could you tell me what that is?'

Instantly, Olivia was on her guard. This woman was sharp as a tack, and twice as pointy. 'Because of the concussion after the accident, I need to prove my mental health to contest a stupid decision that's being made without my consent. It's a decision that could ultimately kill my husband.'

'And, may I ask, what is that decision?'

'My sister-in-law has been given power of attorney while I'm, erm, incapacitated. I need to prove that I'm quite capable.'

'And how do you intend to do this?'

'By convincing you that I am.'

'Do you think you *need* to convince me? Trying to convince me tells me that you are maybe acting, and you're not OK, but in fact far from it. If you were OK, then you would need to show me you are, not convince me you are.'

Lauren Michaelsson has just wrapped me around her little finger without me even noticing, Olivia thought in disgust. This was going to be harder than she thought.

An hour of cat and mouse ensued, thrust and parry, thrust and parry.

Ultimately, the battle ended when Dr Michaelsson wrapped up the session. 'OK, Mrs Martelle, there's not much more we can do here today, but we have made some progress. Shall we resume this tomorrow at the same time?'

Butterflies

Oh, do we have to? Olivia thought, flashing a brilliant smile. 'Why not?' she said, struggling to her feet. She offered her hand out to Dr Michaelsson once again. 'Until tomorrow.'

Dr Michaelsson shook her hand.

'Until tomorrow, Mrs Martelle.'

This whole episode had drained her more than she'd realised. She made a brief, tearful stop at Paul's room for ten minutes before finally making her weary way back to her room. She planned on reading some of those legal documents pertaining to the power of attorney, but as soon as her head hit the pillow, she was asleep.

22.

THE NEXT DAY started well. She was up early, with another toilet and shower session on her own. Small victories.

Dressed and ready, she made her way to Paul's room. The doctors had asked her to spend some time each day sitting with him and reading to him. 'You never know, the stimulation might do him the world of good,' they told her.

As she got there, she bumped into Angela, who was leaving as she entered. *Oh well, there goes the end of a perfect morning*, she thought, while swapping pleasantries.

'Angela, good morning,' Olivia offered.

'Ah, good morning, Olivia. How are you today?'

'I'm fine. Getting stronger by the day,' she replied, raising her eyebrows at Paul's sister. 'How long have you been here?' she asked, aware of the early hour—it was not far off eight-thirty.

'Oh, just a few hours, you know, we need to keep him stimulated.'

The doctors had obviously given her the same talk.

'Listen, Angela, we need to talk about this move to England…'

Angela was instantly interested. 'What about it?'

Butterflies

'I think it's a good idea. I just think it's impossible right now. These drugs to stop him from moving, he's taking them for a reason you know…'

'So the doctors tell me, although I'm not convinced he needs them. It's been nearly three weeks since the accident with no change in his condition. Sometimes I feel like I'm the only person *really* looking out for him.'

Olivia's face clouded over as the rage inside her burst. 'What did you say? The only one looking out for him. I'm here every single day, Angela, in between my physiotherapy, my psychotherapy, thanks to you, and every-fucking-thing else I have to do while I mend. What are you doing? Scheming behind my back to steal my husband away in his hour of need.'

'He was my brother a lot longer than he's been your husband,' she snapped, and with that, she walked away.

BITCH! Olivia yelled in her head. She wanted to scream it down the corridor after her, but she didn't want to alert anyone—well, anyone who could report the incident back to Dr Michaelsson at least.

As she entered Paul's room, Richard, who was looking a little flustered, accosted her.

'Olivia, have you seen Angela?' he panted.

'Yes, she left about a minute ago. She was headed for the restaurant, I think. Is everything OK?'

'I don't know, I got a message to meet her here ASAP,' he replied. 'I'll catch up with you later, goodbye.' With that, he ran off down the same corridor Angela had disappeared down.

She shook her head as she watched him disappear. *Poor man,* she thought, *she calls, and he comes running. How come Paul is so normal?*

23.

OVER THE NEXT week, Olivia recovered well. Her body was getting serious workouts, as was her head. Her latest session with Dr Michaelsson had gone well; Olivia was getting the sense that she had only pushed her at first to see how far she would go.

Paul, however, was showing no signs of returning to normal. The doctors had successfully stemmed the swelling in his brain. They said it was returning to its normal size, but at present, there was still nothing to indicate when he would wake up; he was still unresponsive to all stimulus. The worst thing about this situation, was now he was looking physically better, there was less of a reason to keep him in Switzerland. She knew it was pathetic, and petty, but she hated the idea of Angela knowing he could now be moved. In truth, she really needed to be back in the UK herself, with everything that was happening with Aunt Penny, but the thought of bowing down to Angela made her baulk.

Now that she was on the mend, she needed to consider Penny. The thought of her undergoing chemo with no one there for her pained her. But first, there was her last 'treatment' to contend with.

24.

OLIVIA LOOKED INTO her mirror. 'You look much better than you did on our first meeting,' she told herself. This brought back a pang of sadness as she thought about her wedding day, which felt like it had happened about three hundred years ago. 'No, I won't dwell on the past, not today. Today I'm going to get signed off as psychologically fit enough to act with the power of attorney for my own husband. I am a confident woman.' She gave herself a little smile and dusted her clothes down in the mirror. 'Let's do this,' she said aloud.

Knocking on the door of Dr Michaelsson's office, she had never felt so confident about anything else in her entire life. *Today I take back my life.*

'Come in, please, it's open,' came the sexy Swedish voice from inside. Olivia strode in. Dr Michaelsson was sitting at her desk; she had arranged a couch and chair set up in the corner of the room.

'Mrs Martelle, thank you for coming. I thought that, due to the nature of our last meeting, we could investigate a little of your subconscious today. Just a little light hypnotism, a little regression to find out your real feelings regarding Paul and your accident. Do you mind?'

'Err, no, not at all. It's just a little bit unexpected, that's all.'

Dr Michaelsson cocked her head. 'If you are not comfortable…'

You tricky bitch! Olivia thought. 'Oh, no, it's not that, it's just I've never been hypnotised before.'

Dr Michaelsson smiled warmly, and her eyes softened. 'Don't worry, I'll be very gentle with you. You won't be running around like a chicken, I promise you.'

Olivia kicked off her shoes and got onto the couch. She lay rigid and uncomfortable, and closed her eyes.

'Mrs Martelle, I need you to please relax,' the doctor said in a smooth silky voice.

Olivia let out a deep breath and relaxed, then gave a little jump as she felt the doctor's hands reach out and undo the top button on her blouse.

'There, I need you nice and comfortable. I need you to listen to the rhythm of my voice, the slow constant rhythm and the intonation of my voice.'

Olivia had always been sceptical about hypnotism and could not believe she was feeling sleepy right now.

'You are relaxed and sleepy; my voice is carrying you away on a cloud. You need to trust me. Take my hand as I lead you back inside your own head. Deeper and deeper into relaxation. You're safe and warm, you're relaxing on a cloud, rocking back and forth, back and forth, back and forth…'

> Olivia is on a beach. She is stood on the most beautiful beach she has ever seen in her life. The sand is almost white, and it's warm between her toes; the sea is the deepest blue, then green, then blue again.

Butterflies

She can hear the song of the gulls circling up high. There isn't anyone else on the beach; she is alone.

Realising that she's dressed in her best white blouse and long black skirt, she begins to undo her buttons. The feel of the sea breeze and the heat of the sun on her skin is delicious.

She removes her top and slides herself out of her tight skirt. Underneath her clothes, she is wearing an orange, two-piece bikini. The elation she feels from being free of the confines of her stuffy clothes is almost overwhelming. She drops them into a pile, slips off her shoes, and runs.

She runs across the warm white sand, towards the sea. The water is inviting; it's refreshing to be so free.

She stops at the water's edge; the white froth of the wave laps at her toes sending chills up her legs and through her body. Her nipples harden at the electric buzz that's coursing through her.

She takes another step into the water, then another, and one more. Before long, she is wading through water that is waist deep. All she wants to do is to dip her head under the water and float away in the warm eddies.

A splash from beside her startles her. She thought she was alone. She covers herself up, not wanting any strangers to catch her out and ruin this feeling.

She turns towards the sound of the splash, and her heart almost misses a beat. Paul, her husband, is emerging from the water. He is smiling at her as he takes her hand in his. 'Ollie… it's been too long.'

Butterflies dance around his head, butterflies that are changing from black to an array of vibrant blues. She hasn't felt so much joy in what feels like a long, long time. He leads her out of the water and back onto the beach, where there's a towel already waiting, along with a blanket and a full picnic laid out.

As she reaches for the towel, she realises she is already completely dry, as is Paul. He reaches a hand towards her and fixes her free-flowing hair behind her ear. He brushes his warm, strong hand against her cheek and brings her face close to his.

He kisses her. She can feel her skin responding to his embrace. It has broken out in goose-bumps, and her nipples have hardened once again.

She places her hand on top of his; but then pulls back to look at him. His deep blue eyes are changing with the rhythm of the sea; green, blue, green, blue…

Butterflies

His smile fills her heart with love and desire. She can feel herself moisten intimately. She wants him, she needs him, she is lusting for him. Everything feels perfect; making love here on this beach would be the piece de resistance.

Looking at his slim, athletic build, she can see that he wants her also. His nipples are hard, and she notices with a sly smile that they are not the only things that are.

As the butterflies dance around them, he places his hand around the back of her head and pulls her close. He whispers something into her ear.

She can't quite make out what he's saying, but she knows it's something she doesn't want to hear.

Suddenly, the butterflies around them double in number, then treble, then quadruple. They cover him, obscuring him from her view.

Then he's gone; she's back at the pile of her clothes on the beach. Slowly, she climbs back into her skirt, then her blouse.

That's when she sees the couch.

A couch, standing alone on the sand. As she approaches it, she undoes her top button again and lies down. She closes her eyes and listens to the rhythm of the waves hitting the beach.

'And, you're back in the room, Mrs Martelle...'

Olivia opened her eyes to the familiar scene of the doctor's office. Dr Michaelsson was sitting opposite her with her legs crossed and an A4 pad of paper on her lap. She was smiling. 'OK, I think we have concluded our meeting here. I would say there is no need for any further therapy.'

Olivia was confused. 'Did you make notes on my dream?'

Michaelsson tapped her pad with her pencil and smiled. Olivia felt reassured by the gesture. 'Yes, I did. You relayed everything to me. It was very enlightening. Your descriptions were, shall we say... descriptive?'

Olivia blushed, remembering the fading dream.

'Basically, you wanted to free yourself of any constraints and run free. You wanted to shun your responsibilities, but the rock of your responsibility towards Paul, and life in general, brought you round to sensible thinking. If you had dipped your head into the water, or if you had indeed made love with Paul, then we would have needed more sessions. As it is, I'm satisfied with your progress.'

After a few more exchanges, mainly the one giving her a clean bill of mental health, Olivia got up off the couch, slipped on her shoes, and left the office with a satisfied grin.

OK, she thought, *time to find Angela...*

25.

EVENTUALLY, OLIVIA MADE it back to her room. She was tired after having spent the last hour and half with Paul, offering stimulation and support and telling him about her good news. She was upbeat regarding her diagnosis, but also down regarding his condition... and her dream. It had been so vivid. *Would it have been wrong of me to embrace the freedom and have made love to him, just one more time, even it was only in my head?*

This daydream was brightening her mood, right up to the moment she opened the door to her room, and there stood Angela.

Olivia's heart sank into her chest. She was expecting a clap of thunder, a streak of lightning, and a sudden downpour of torrential rain to announce her appearance, but none of that happened. She turned around to look down the corridor just in time to see Richard running towards her. He saw her looking at him, stopped, and mouthed the word 'sorry' towards her. He then turned and ran off in the opposite direction.

How does Paul not hate this woman as much as I do, and quite obviously as much as Richard does too? she thought. It caused her to smile a little as she entered the dragon's lair.

'Angela, your hair looks lovely today,' she lied. It didn't; it looked the same as it did every day; flat and tied back. 'I'm so pleased to see you.' She wasn't. She'd have rather bumped into a horny bull than to have seen her right now. 'What can I do for you?'

'You know why I'm here. I want Paul moved back to the UK, and I want it done within the week. We've procrastinated on this far too long. He'll get the—' Angela started.

'I agree,' Olivia said, interrupting her, while making her way over to the desk in the room. 'Let's get the planning done and move out on Friday, shall we?'

'—best treatment, he'll be in his familiar… What did you say?'

'I said, I agree. It *would* be in Paul's best interests to be home.'

Angela's mouth hung open. She had obviously been building herself up for a huge argument, and now she had nothing to say. Olivia just stood there looking at her, smiling with raised eyebrows.

'Well, I… well, I'm, err, glad you've finally seen sense,' she stuttered. Her shocked look was begging to dissipate, and she puffed her chest out. 'I've been treating my brother around the clock and overseeing his business interests. Until you're declared sound of mind, I will continue to do so…'

'I've been declared sound of mind.'

For the second time in as many minutes, Angela looked like she had been slapped in the face. 'What? When?'

'Today. Dr Michaelsson is in the process of drawing up the papers that declare me sound in mind and body.' She spoke the last part in her poshest voice. 'So, we really do need to talk, don't we?'

Angela threw her a look.

If looks could kill, Olivia thought with a sly smile.

Butterflies

26.

WITHIN THE WEEK, they were all back in the UK. Olivia had invited Angela and Richard to stay at hers and Paul's house, as the flat in which they currently lived was quite far away. This was against her better instincts, but as she was still prone to fatigue, it would be reassuring to have Angela and Richard looking into Paul's affairs while Olivia concluded her convalescence.

They installed themselves in the spacious granny flat at the bottom of the garden. It wasn't really a granny flat, it was more of a compact, self-contained house, with two bedrooms, kitchen, and utilities, and it fitted their needs perfectly.

Since they had been back, Angela had become a constant pain in Olivia's backside.

One time during a row regarding Paul's hospital room, Olivia had a vision of grabbing a lamp off the table, pulling the bulb out, and poking Angela in the eye with it. Fortunately, all she did was smile nicely and promise to look into it for her.

Another time Angela was bitching on about something or other. Olivia was recovering from a bad day both physically and emotionally; she turned around to her sister-in-law and shoved her out of the kitchen door, into the garden, back towards her little house.

'You can't do this to me. You can't,' Angela screamed.

'Yes, I can, and yes, I just did. Now leave me alone.' She slammed the door behind her and leant back on it. She exhaled a long slow lingering breath. 'One... two... three... four... five.'

Once she had calmed down, she turned and opened the door. Angela was still stood there, looking angry. Olivia screamed and slammed the door again. 'SIX... SEVEN... EIGHT... NINE... TEN!' she shouted aloud, took another breath, and then cautiously opened the door again.

'FUCKING HELL... I can't believe you're still here.'

'All I want to say is—'

Olivia slammed the door once again. As she did, she shouted, 'Angela, go away now. I will not be opening this door again.'

She walked out of the kitchen holding her head and lay on the couch. She cried herself to sleep.

27.

OLIVIA AND HER Great Aunt Penny were sat in their favourite restaurant. Penny was not eating, just kind of pushing the food around her plate.

'...and then I opened the door about an hour later, Pen, I swear I'd have hit her with something if she'd still been there.'

Aunt Penny laughed. As she covered her mouth as the laugh turned into a cough.

Olivia looked at her with a frown. 'Pen, how are you? Really? I need you to start letting me come with you for your chemo sessions.'

Penny flapped her hands at her while catching her breath. 'No, no. I'm serious, I don't want you to come. It's nothing nefarious, but I've developed some good friends there. Believe it or not, we have a right laugh. It feels good to be able to laugh with nice people, especially in the face of something so nasty.'

Olivia grabbed her hand and looked deep into her favourite person's eyes. 'You know I'm here for you, don't you? I love you and will be here, stood next to you every step of the way.'

Penny smiled and patted her hands. 'I know, child, I know.' They sat for a few moments, just holding hands, and looking at each other.

'What you need, young lady, is a good girl's night out,' Penny said, finally breaking the silence between them.

Olivia's face brightened. 'You know what? I think maybe you're right. Are you up for it?'

'Oh, you don't need a sickly old lady dragging you young ones down. I couldn't make it out anyway.'

'Yeah, but you could be there at the house when we're all getting ready and having a little drink.'

Penny smiled wistfully. 'It would be fantastic to see all your friends again.' Her face a lit up, more than a little theatrically. 'You know, you might have to invite Angela.'

'Penny, I love you, but you can be such a bitch sometimes,' Olivia replied, laughing.

'Plenty of life in the old girl yet.'

The waiter came to take their dishes away. 'Excuse me, madam, is this finished?' he asked, indicating towards Aunt Penny's dish.

'Yes, young man, tell the cook it was delicious. I just didn't have the appetite I thought I did.' She flashed him a grateful smile, which he returned as he removed the remains.

'Can I get you two ladies anything from the dessert trolley, or some coffees?'

'No thank you, just the bill, please. It's been a long day.' It was Olivia's turn to flash a smile.

When they'd paid, they began to make their way towards the car park, about five hundred yards away. Penny had to stop and rest halfway. She had lost all her colour and looked tired. 'Ollie, would you mind bringing the car around to me? I'm feeling a little bit…'

Her heart sank as she watched Aunt Penny flop down onto a nearby bench. 'Pen, Penny, are you OK? Do you want me to get you anything?' she asked. *Or maybe take you to the hospital?* she thought.

Butterflies

'No, no, no. I'm fine. The doctors told me this would happen, side effects of the chemotherapy and all of that. No, you go and get the car. This'll have passed by the time you get back.'

'Well, OK, if you say so.' Olivia kissed her on the top of her head, and Penny brushed her hand against hers. As she walked off in the direction of the car, she looked back to check on her frail aunt. 'Oh, my God, please don't let her be dying,' she prayed as she walked. 'I can't lose Paul *and* Penny at the same time.' *NOW STOP IT*, she scolded herself, silently. *You're not losing either of them. Be positive, Ollie, we'll all get through this.*

She pulled the car around to where Penny was sitting and noticed that she was looking a little better. Her funny turn had passed. Penny almost jumped into the car, buckled herself in and said, 'Right, what about this night out then?'

Olivia laughed and shook her head at the tenacity of the old bird next to her and drove off towards Aunt Penny's apartment.

'Hey, Pen, here's a thought, why don't you move in with me? I have the room, and while Paul is still in the hospital, I'm just rattling around in that big old house.'

'Ollie, Ollie, Ollie, you don't need me hanging around while you work out all the things in your head that need working out. Paul is going to need a lot of time and effort on your behalf. When he comes home, he's going to need around the clock care, his journey back to health will be long and arduous. The last thing you'll need is me taking up some of that precious time you'll have together.'

'Nonsense, after all you've done for me in the past, what would make you think I'd abandon you now? It's decided, I won't take no for an answer. Anyway, Paul will be in the hospital for quite a while; you'll be all better by the time he gets out. When that happens, then I'll kick you out on your bony ass.' She threw a look across to Penny, who reacted in the same way.

'I'll get some men to move your stuff, starting tomorrow. Tonight, you stay with me. Girlie night in. Agreed?'

'What about Angela and Richard?'

Olivia shook her head and pulled her aunt a theatrical glance. 'Oh, Pen, you really know how to kill the mood, don't you?' she laughed.

28.

OLIVIA WAS JUST coming home from the hospital after a gruelling stimulation session with Paul. There was a requirement to keep his limbs as active as possible while he was still in his coma. This was to arrest muscle and tendon atrophy and reduce the risk of bedsores. The activity had taken it out of Olivia emotionally rather than physically. She had wanted to be the one who performed the exercises, as she felt she owed it to him somehow. But the feel of Paul's dead-weighted limbs in her hands dampened her spirits every time. It made her realise that his recovery was no closer than it had been while they were still in Switzerland.

The last thing she needed was for Angela to be waiting for her when she got back to the house, but fate was very cruel.

'Angela, I'm so sorry but can this wait? I've just got back from seeing Paul and I'm drained…'

'I'm sorry, Olivia, but it can't. It's to do with some of Paul's contracts. His business interests are suffering while he's in this limbo. I know we both have more important things to think about, but if you want to keep this house, then you need to start picking up on his business accounts.'

Olivia did not have a head for business. She'd been studying for a business degree in university, but she'd swapped over for a fine art degree, as she craved a little more creative freedom. She'd received a first-class honours degree in her adoptive subject, but business was just not for her.

'Angela, you've got a head for business, haven't you? Didn't you run your own publishing franchise?'

Angela was looking a little excited in anticipation of what Olivia was about to say.

'If I get the papers drawn up…'

'Yes?' Angela's eyes were wide open now, and she was almost salivating.

'Would you take control over the financial and business interests of Paul's estate?' As soon as this had escaped her mouth, Olivia felt a huge weight lift from her shoulders. Not only had she got away from any business dealings, but it would also keep Angela busy most days, and therefore out from under her feet.

Angela closed her eyes as if in thanks, or as if to say, *at last*. She was in serious risk of nearly cracking a smile, but then the real Angela returned, and the smile disappeared almost as fast as it appeared.

'So how is Paul?' she asked, almost business-like.

Olivia sighed, a resigned breath escaping her mouth and nose. 'He's doing as well as can be expected. There's still no change in his condition, but I've been helping with his physical exercises. That was a little uplifting, but also a little disheartening too.'

Angela's face fell as Olivia answered the question, her head giving little shakes as if it could not possibly be true. 'You, you were helping with Paul's exercises?'

'Yes.' Olivia wished she hadn't said anything now. 'It was…' she found herself trying to think up excuses for being with her own husband, '…just because I was there at the time.'

Angela began to fuss about, fidgeting as if something was irritating her. 'Oh, right, well, very good. I'm glad he's getting all the stimulation he needs. So, if you can get the papers written up, then I'll manage the business interests. I'll give you accurate and frequent reports. You have nothing to worry about on that score. I must rush now; Richard is taking me out shopping this afternoon, and I have to get ready. Bye.'

As she rushed off, Olivia watched her go. *How can two people so closely bonded be so completely different?* she thought, shaking her head.

The mobile phone in her pocket rang. She picked it up, and her heart leapt. It was Katie. 'Oh, thank the lord for small mercies,' she said to the god of mobile phone conversations. 'A little light relief.'

She pressed the button to answer the call. 'Katie, thank God you rang at that precise moment. I've just had another 'conversation' with our favourite in-law of all times.'

'Angela? Ollie, I don't know how you put up with that—that cow!'

Olivia laughed. 'Neither do I. I must have a proper glittering crown in Heaven.'

Katie laughed down the phone. 'So, tell me, how is that handsome husband of yours coming along?'

Olivia dropped her cheerful tone, only for a moment, but long enough for her best friend on the other end of the line to notice. 'Oh, he's…' she started.

'He's still the same, isn't he?' Katie finished for her.

'Yeah, it's killing me each time I see him.'

'Well, that's what I'm ringing for. You, me, Jan, and a few of the others are going out on the razz. You're going to forget all about your woes and about that wicked Angela-stein for one whole night at least. What say you?'

'I say, let's do it, and—' Olivia held her hand up in a Girl Guide salute. 'I promise not to be maudlin all night.'

'You're on,' Katie shouted. 'I'll let Jan and the others know, and we'll be round tomorrow, if that's OK? Oh, and please don't invite Angela. I may not be able to hold my tongue. Gotta go, byeeeeee!'

Katie hung up, and Olivia managed a smile for the first time that day. As she walked to the front room of the house, she could see Angela and Richard outside by their car. He was struggling to carry some boxes. She was stood next to him shouting, pointing, and tutting at everything he did.

Oh, my God! She thought, *that woman, what does he see in her?*

She watched as a box dropped onto the floor. He struggled to pick it up when another one dropped, and then another. Soon all the boxes were on the floor, and poor Richard was sweating, on all fours, trying to gather them up.

Olivia stifled her laugh with her mobile phone to her mouth. She felt a little guilty enjoying the comedy unfolding outside.

She received a text message; it made her jump as it vibrated against her mouth.

> OK Jan Karen Helen + Anna r up 4
> 2morrow... 630 @ urs OK??? K8 xxx

'I hate text speak...' she said aloud, before re-reading the message again, slower this time. She got the gist of it the second time around.

Butterflies

I hope Penny will be up to making an appearance. With this pleasing thought in her head, she strode off towards her aunt's bedroom.

She knocked lightly on the door. 'Pen? Pen?' she whispered. 'Is it OK if I come in?'

Penny's croaky voice filtered through the door. 'Of course, dear, you know my door's always open.'

Olivia entered the room and was instantly hit by the gloom inside. Aunt Penny's room had never, ever been like this. Olivia didn't like it. 'Aunt Pen, are you sure you're OK?'

'Yes,' the voice from somewhere deep within the darkness croaked. It sounded like an old man's voice. 'I'm just having a bit of a bad day, that's all. It happens.'

Olivia's eyes adjusted to the darkness, and she watched as Penny sat up in bed and patted the mattress next to her, 'Come and sit here, child, and tell me everything. You have a look about you that says, *up and down.*'

'You never cease to amaze me, you know,' Olivia replied, shaking her head and smiling. She went on to tell Penny all about her morning with Paul and about the exercises she was involved in. Penny seemed to take this as good news. 'But, Pen, it was like moving a lifeless corpse. He was warm and flexible, but that was it. It's like he's a husk of a man.'

Sensing Olivia's tears were close, Penny reached out and put her arm around her.

As she was pulled close by the woman she loved more than anything in the world, Olivia felt how thin her aunt's hands and arms had become. *Oh, no, Pen,* she thought, *you're just skin and bone.*

'Tell me about Angela.' Penny managed a smile. 'Your favourite subject.'

Olivia wiped away a few of the rogue tears that had broken free of their confines and snuggled into Aunt Penny's embrace. 'Oh, well, that's why I'm a little bit happy. I think I've managed to kill two birds with one stone.'

'How so?' Pen asked with interest.

'Well, I've decided to give her full access and full control over all the business concerns relating to Paul's estate.'

Pen nodded. 'Good decision, clever girl.'

'Yeah well, I wasn't going to do it. But now I've got rid of her, out of my life and Paul's, at least through the week. But that's not what I've come up here to tell you.' Oliva sat up and looked at her Aunt. 'I've spoken to all the girls, and they're all coming around tomorrow night for a bit of a shindig. Do you think you would be up for making an appearance?'

Penny's face beamed. 'Well, I'll certainly try my best. You know I love a good girl's night. Right now, though, if you don't mind, I wouldn't mind going back to sleep. I'm feeling a little light-headed. I'll catch up with you a bit later.' She tapped Olivia's hand as if to dismiss her.

'Oh yes, of course. You have a sleep, and I'll make us some dinner for later.'

'Oh, you are a special girl, Ollie,' Penny said shaking her head.

Olivia bent over and kissed her on the head, then she tucked her into bed. Walking out of the room, she noticed Aunt Penny was already lightly snoring. She stood there with her back against the door, listening to the soft, regular breathing from inside.

It wasn't that long ago that you were tucking me up into bed, she thought. Her heart began to beat out of control, and her palms began to sweat. She banged the back of her head lightly against the door and wondered just *HOW* she was going to get through all of this. Paul,

Butterflies

Penny, Angela—her life had become more complicated than she could comprehend, and in such a small amount of time.

After another few moments and a couple of teardrops, she inhaled and walked away from the door, towards whatever craziness life was about to throw at her next.

29.

THE NEXT MORNING was completely Angela free. As she was getting ready to go to the hospital to spend some time with Paul, Olivia bumped into Richard. He was looking a little more cheerful than of late, a big smile beaming on his face.

'Hey,' she shouted to him. 'Look at you. I don't think I've seen you looking this happy for a long time.'

Richard blushed a little at the attention. 'If I told you why, I'd probably have to kill you,' he laughed.

'Go on, you can always try.'

Richard blushed deeper again, *I think he fancies me,* she thought, blushing a little herself.

'It's Angela. I've just got to thank you for putting her in charge of the business dealings. It was all she could talk about last night. I haven't seen her this happy for years.'

'Oh, and that makes you happy then?'

He smiled a wise smile. *He is quite attractive*, she thought, and her face bloomed again.

'No, it's just that it keeps her out of my way.' He tipped her a wink and walked off towards the garden, whistling.

Butterflies

Penny was still not up, so Olivia left her a note to let her know where she was going. Then she left the house.

As she got into her car, she found herself thinking about Richard. Thinking about the way he blushed when he talked to her. She used to find him a little creepy, but now, out from under the wing of the dreaded Angela, he seemed rather sweet. *Don't forget a little dashing too,* she thought, and completed a hat trick of blushes for the morning.

30.

THERE WAS NO change with Paul. His breathing was regulated, his heart and pulse monitored, and his temperature controlled. The only difference was that the swelling in his brain had been confirmed as arrested, which was good news.

Good, but not brilliant.

Once again, Olivia came away from the hospital with a heavy heart. *Is it so wrong to hate coming in here to see him?* she pondered as she got back into the car. It had been a few months since the accident, and she'd expected some change in his condition by now. She sat in the car for a moment, collecting her thoughts.

After a short spell of wallowing in self-pity and worry about her husband, she collected herself. She looked in the vanity mirror and marvelled at how a few small tears could mess up her mascara so badly—she thought she looked like a singer in a goth rock band.

'Right, missy, tart yourself up and go and have a good time with the girlies,' she said to her reflection in the mirror. She smiled a sad smile. *It may be sad,* she thought, *but at least it is a smile.*

She started the engine and then instantly heard her mobile phone buzz as a text message came in. It was from Jan.

Butterflies

Cnt w8 4 2nite... c u l8r

'Why, oh why can't they just send messages like normal people?' she tutted. This, however, was just what she needed, a night with her friends. She drove off with a slightly lighter heart.

When she got home, she was in for a very pleasant surprise. Aunt Penny was up and dressed and had made her lunch. 'What's all this?' she asked. 'Are you feeling OK? Do you want me to call you an ambulance?'

Penny's face brightened.

My God, how her face changes when she smiles like that. How have I only noticed it now? Olivia thought, wiping a rogue tear from her eye.

'My dear, you're crying. What's wrong? Was it something at the hospital?'

'Well, yes and no,' Olivia replied sniffling. 'Seeing Paul lying there like a vegetable, and then seeing you all full of life, it makes me think that my life is just so full of ups and downs. It's making me really appreciate what I have.'

Aunt Penny did what she always did: she made Olivia feel better. She walked over and wrapped her thin arms around her shoulders. She could feel the chemo-ravished body underneath her clothes, but she could also feel the enormous warmth of love radiating from her, and the fierce beat of a strong, and loving, heart. A heart that just wouldn't stop giving.

Feeling very loved, Olivia burst into a flood of tears.

'Come now, Ollie, carpe diem, darling, carpe diem. Shush them tears and let's enjoy while the enjoying's there. I've made us lunch because I'm starving.'

'I'm sorry for crying, Pen. It's just, I don't know... everything!' Olivia wiped the tears from her eyes.

'I'm not surprised you're crying; look at what your life has become. You've gone from the happiest woman on the planet to what amounts to a widow and a cancer nurse. You are a fantastic, strong, independent woman, Ollie. If anyone needs to let some tears out now and then, it's you. I'll be here as long as I can to mop them up for you. You're my rock.'

These words from Aunt Penny cheered her up, and a small smile escaped from the misery that was plastered over her face.

'There she is,' Penny said, wiping the tears from her cheeks, much like she had done right through her childhood. 'There's the gorgeous girl that I know and love.'

Olivia laughed and kissed her on the forehead. 'Have I ever told you that I love you?' she asked the elderly lady.

Penny grinned. 'Not nearly enough,' she replied.

31.

LUNCH WAS LOVELY, mainly due to the fact Penny was eating for once, but also because Olivia felt like she had something to look forward to for the first time in a long time.

When it was over, Penny announced she was going for a lie down. Olivia decided that, as it was a nice day, she was going to do some work in the garden. She slipped into a pair of shorts and a t-shirt before making her way outside.

As she entered the garden, she could hear shouting coming from the granny flat at the bottom, where Angela and Richard were living.

'I'm telling you, Angela, this is no marriage. Every time I even lay a finger on you, you wince. Am I that fucking unattractive to you?' It was Richard shouting. It seemed strange as she had never heard him shout before.

'Oh, don't be stupid. Don't you think we have more important things going on in our lives at this moment? If you haven't forgotten, my brother is lying in a hospital bed in a coma. I've been given all the responsibilities for his estate, and I'm working my fingers to the bone so we can afford to get our own house and some grounds… And all you're interested in is a grubby little jump in the afternoon.'

'Angela, it's been nearly a year since we even looked at each other naked. This is going to sound pathetic, but I'm a man, and I have needs.'

'Aww, poor you and your manly needs. Richard, I can't bear to look at you right now. Please leave, I've got work to do.'

'What? Well, you just go fuck yourself, Angela. I suppose that's what you must do or get someone else to do it for you.'

Stifling a nervous laugh, Olivia heard the slamming of a door and the rattle of the frame. 'Oh shit,' she muttered when she realised that she was just about to get caught eavesdropping on their argument. She sloped off and hid behind a large rose bush. She watched as Richard stormed out of the cottage and made his way through the garden towards the gate.

'Hi, Olivia,' he shouted to her as he opened the gate.

'Oh, hi, Richard. How are you?' she replied in embarrassment, as it was only too obvious, she was trying, unsuccessfully, to hide.

'You know, another day in paradise.' He flashed her a rather forced smile and disappeared through the gate.

'Well that was brilliant, fucking *Sherlock Holmes*,' she cursed herself aloud.

Next, out came Angela. She looked like she had been crying but was trying her best to put a brave face on it.

That's it, Angela, show the world that you're human, Olivia thought, as she crouched lower still, trying to completely immerse herself into the bush to stay out of the way.

'Oh, Olivia,' she shouted, walking towards her hiding place in the rosebush. 'I'm glad I bumped into you…'

'Hi, Angela, I was… erm, just—'

'Yes, yes. I just needed to know if you were OK for a meeting next week. I've had some great ideas about pushing the IT consultancy side of Paul's business a little bit further afield.'

Butterflies

'Err, oh yes, send me an invite, and I'll be there,' Olivia stuttered trying to untangle herself from her obviously stupid hiding space.

'What are you trying to do in there? You'll cut yourself to ribbons,' Angela said as she walked off, raising her mobile phone to her ear.

Olivia gave her a bemused look and proceeded to unstick herself from the rosebush. It wasn't as easy a task as it sounded.

Her body was scratched and bloody, and she was hot and sweaty from her hiding and her failed extraction. The decision was made to take a shower. The girls would be here in a few hours, and she wanted to look her best for their arrival. There was no way she could handle any more forced sympathy from anyone, not today.

The first thing she did was to check in on Aunt Penny. As the door creaked open, light snores floated through the room as if they were on the wings of butterflies.

This thought made Olivia smile.

Happy and content that her aunt was fine, she made her way towards the guest bathroom at the end of the landing. Olivia had a large en-suite bathroom incorporated into her room, but she always preferred the guest one. It was roomy and airy, and the bath was to die for.

Looking at the large, ornate porcelain bowl, she changed her mind and decided to run herself a bath instead. Penny was asleep, Angela was out somewhere with a mobile phone, the girls were due later, she had nothing else to do but pamper herself. 'Oh yes,' she said. 'Hot bath, oils, headphones. What's the worst that could happen?'

She drew the bath, added the oils and the bubbles, and got herself prepared. Headphones at the ready, a little bit of retro pop music, and she was good to go.

32.

AS SHE UNDRESSED, she inspected the small scratches on her arms and legs from the rose bush. *Next time remind me to think of somewhere better to hide in my own garden*, she thought.

She stripped off and inspected the rest of her body properly for the first time since her accident. She had been incredibly lucky not to suffer any permanent damage. The only visible remnant from it was a long scar down her left thigh. The doctor said that was where she was trapped in the car and they had to cut her out. The act of the cutting had caused a deep gash in her leg. They had fixed it up at the hospital but couldn't do anything else for it aesthetically.

Slowly, she traced her finger along it. Every day since she had been able to, she had rubbed oils into it. The red colour was fading, but the scar itself never would. She didn't mind too much, though, it felt good to have a visible reminder of what she had been through.

She stepped into the deep bath. The water was hot enough to make her skin tingle, but warm enough to allow her to climb in and enjoy the heat.

She left the window open, as it was a beautiful day, and the cool breeze blowing in reacted with the warm steam from the water, making her nipples tighten in a not displeasing way.

Butterflies

She immersed herself, relishing the caress of its warmth touching every part of her body. It lapped at her skin with a delicious ebb and flow. She put on her headphones and relaxed back into the deep water.

Her music took her away to another place, and she drifted off into her own head.

> It's her wedding night. She is still wearing her wedding dress, and they are dancing the night away. Katie and Jan are dancing next to her. Katie's boyfriend is the DJ. He has taken his top off, and his six pack is glistening with a sheen of sweat as he's spinning the tunes and moving his moves.
>
> They are all dancing to some cheesy disco tune.
>
> The dance floor is full. There are some people on it who she doesn't recognise. Aunt Penny is dancing very closely with the vicar from the ceremony. He looks like he wants to be anywhere else but here.
>
> She turns her head towards Jan to indicate what Pen is doing. But Jan is far too busy kissing Anthony, Paul's best man. Katie is at the DJ stand and is passionately kissing him. Olivia is alone on the dance floor, all alone with only the music for company.
>
> The cheesy disco song ends, and the lights dim. A slow, romantic song begins to filter out from the

speakers. A pang of regret rips though her as she is still the only one without a partner. She decides to make her way off the floor, when someone catches her arm and spins her around.

Her heart leaps as Paul smiles at her.

'Paul? But I thought—' she stutters, gawping at him.

He shushes her with a finger on her lips. He smiles that dazzling smile of his and then brings her close to him.

Suddenly, they're no longer in the room, they're in a large bedroom with a huge window. The window is looking onto their garden at home. The only difference is that their garden doesn't encompass Lake Geneva.

They look at each other. Her eyes are half closed, and a familiar, and very missed, sensation fills her senses. Butterflies are taking flight. The big gorgeous blue butterflies are beating their silken wings around her stomach.

He kisses her. *Oh, yes. It's been far too long,* she thinks, as every exposed part of her skin tingles.

His tongue playfully dances with her tongue inside her mouth, and she bites down on it playfully. His hands slide down her back. They plant themselves on both cheeks of her bottom and squeeze. A rush is coursing through her. It's been far too long since she's been touched by a man, this man. Her man!

She opens her eyes to see him again, making sure that it's really him there and not an illusion, some silly part of her brain making up this scenario.

He *is* still there.

She flings her arms around him, hugging him tighter, enjoying the familiar feeling of his erection probing from within his trousers, baying to be freed.

'It's been just as long for you as it's been for me, hasn't it?' she asks, finding it difficult to catch her breath.

'You wouldn't believe how long it's been,' he whispers in reply.

With all the small talk over, it's time for action. She plunges into a kiss as his hands busy themselves, working on her wedding dress zip, fumbling with it. Just not quite able to find the catch.

'Just fucking rip it,' she orders into his ear. 'Get it off me, now.'

As the excitement builds inside her, his hands rise to the back of her dress, grabbing either side of the zip and pulling.

She squeals with excitement as the dress falls from her body. She steps out of it as lies crumpled and discarded on the floor. The breeze from the lake coming in from the open window hits her bare skin, bringing with it goose-bumps… and butterflies.

Stood with her wedding dress in folds by her feet, she is naked except for her lacy white bra, suspender belt over her white French knickers, sheer stockings, and high heels.

He pushes her to arm's length and looks her up and down. The feel of his gaze on her makes her butterflies beat faster. She sees that the sight of her in her underwear has aroused him further; the point is made obvious by the bulge at the front of his trousers.

'Paul, I want you, right now,' she whispers breathlessly, her eyes closed.

The sound of him removing his trousers causes a warm rush towards her stomach. A dull throb begins as she aches in anticipation of what is to come.

Butterflies

He takes her face with both hands and kisses her hard. As he does, she reaches down and finds what she was looking for. It's not hard to find. She wants it right now, more than anything else in the whole world.

He turns her around, roughly but softly, and pushes her onto the thick mattress of their honeymoon bed. The shock of the push takes the wind out of her momentarily as she feels his wandering hands on the back of her French knickers.

Oh, just rip them off, rip them off, she thinks as he applies pressure on either side of her buttocks. She gasps as the silk of the knickers gives way beneath his strong grip. They tear, and she feels the breeze in between her legs, lapping at her with its own refreshingly cool tongue.

'Oh, please fuck me, Paul, please fuck me now,' she moans.

He does.

'Please don't stop, I'm so close,' she says under her breath as she relishes the feel of him inside her.

Just as her untamed butterflies are ready to burst, Paul removes himself from inside her. Her butterflies flock towards the emptiness it has created, allowing the unruly captives to escape.

> She releases a moan. A loud moan. The orgasm is monumental. The sensual ebb flowing from her body releases all her inner tension, and she allows it to run with wild abandon.
>
> It's this moment that she realises she's dreaming. It's a fabulous, vivid, gorgeous dream, but that's all it is, a dream.
>
> She turns to see Paul. He is still in the throes of passion. She knows that she should be feeling the hot deliciousness of his love releasing inside her, maybe even triggering another orgasm; but there's nothing, nothing but the warm lapping of bath water.

She opened her eyes and saw that most of the bubbles in her bath had disappeared. She could still feel the tightness in her nipples as her hand almost involuntarily rubbed between her legs. Her headphones had slipped off her head, and another slow pop song was playing out of them into the echoing, steamy bathroom.

Suddenly, a movement in her peripheral vision alerted her to a presence. *Paul?* She hoped; but stood there in the doorway, looking shocked and embarrassed, was Richard.

Olivia remembered that she was in the bath, and she was doing things to herself that didn't warrant an audience. She was also acutely aware that there were no bubbles left in the water to hide any of this activity, or indeed any of her modesty.

She could feel his gaze greedily drinking her in before it returned to her face. If she hadn't been so shocked, she might have found the change in his facial expression funny. It went from a greedy lust to a horrified stare in one slow movement.

'I, erm. I just… erm,' he stuttered.

'I think you're trying to say that you are leaving, Richard,' Olivia finished for him, now covering any modesty she might still have left with her arms.

'Oh, yeah,' he replied, turning so he had his back to her. 'Olivia, I'm so sorry. I didn't know you were in here,' he spoke with his head facing the ceiling.

'Yet, you're still there?' she answered in mock anger—even though she was embarrassed, she could see the funny side of all of this.

It was her own fault really, she'd left the door unlocked, thinking she was alone in the house except for the sleeping Aunt Penny. She tried to feel angry, but ultimately failed. She even tried to feel upset, but she failed at that too. What she did feel was a little guilty.

Was it wrong to have slightly enjoyed Richard's gaze on her body? The thought of him watching her while she pleasured herself during her dream set just a few of the smaller butterflies off again.

Let's leave that thought right where it is, Ollie, she thought to herself. *You're a married woman.*

33.

'OH MY GOD, Ollie, what did you do?' Katie could hardly breathe; she was laughing so much. She jumped a little as she spilled wine over her skirt. 'You were actually *mid-mastur,* and he was standing there watching you?'

'Well, he wasn't actually *watching*... I think,' Olivia replied, the horrified look spreading over her face. 'OMG! What if he was actually watching?'

Jan was laughing so hard that rosé wine began to stream out her nostrils. She was literally in tears. 'Ollie, did you actually come? Shit, I can't believe I just asked you that.' She continued laughing so hard that she had to put her wine down—for Jan, that was a big thing.

'Yes,' Ollie spat with laughter through her own wine. This caused a massive roar from everyone in the room.

'I don't see that being too much of a bad thing, if you ask me,' Katie said when the laughter had died down. Everyone in the room stopped laughing and turned to look at her, including Ollie, with confused, hysterical looks on their faces.

'Really?' Jan asked.

'Yeah, really,' Katie replied, holding her hand to her chest. 'Are you girls blind? He's a total hottie. Have you seen his body? He's got a great tan, great hair, and big brown eyes. I mean... come on.'

'Well, someone's obviously been taking an interest!' Jan replied with her eyebrows raised.

'When I saw him at the wedding, I liked what I saw, then when I saw that Angela buzzing around, I kind of lost interest,' Katie replied. 'Can't be having that kind of baggage tagging along spoiling the fun.'

'I thought you were with...' she paused, rolling her eyes, 'Was it Jason you brought to the wedding?' Olivia asked, still a little bit in shock.

'Yeah, but he's totally into himself. I'm always on the lookout. You never know, I might have got lucky and had a threesome.'

Jan squealed in delight, and Olivia snorted whilst laughing. 'Would you really have had a threesome?' she asked.

'Well, I've always said I'd try anything once, and if I liked it...' She pulled a face towards them all, as if to say she did like it and had done it again.

Olivia put her glass down and looked at her friend. Her whole face was wide, her eyes, her nostrils, and her mouth. 'Oh, you dirty bitch. Who was it with? When was it? And...' She picked up her wine and put the glass to her mouth, raising her eyebrows. 'What was it like?' This was something that she really wanted to know about.

Everyone in the room quietened so they could hear Katie's story. 'Well, my *first* one—' she began.

'I told you! Total dirty bitch,' Olivia interrupted. Everyone including Katie roared with laughter.

'My first one was when I was in university. Two guys and me. Drunk and also a little high. We started off in the university bar. I really fancied one of them, and the bonus was his mate was fit too. We ended up in my flat because my roommate had gone home for Christmas. They brought a load of drinks and a load of weed and a pack of cards. It all started off rather innocently, but as the drink kicked in, it became more and more… daring. We started to play cards, strip poker, I think, and well… one thing led to another.'

'So, tell us, what were the physics of it?' Jan asked; her eyes were wide, and she had a hungry look.

'Ha! The physics of it?' Helen laughed. 'Trust you, Jan.'

The room roared again.

'Hang on, hang on. I'll just go and fill you up,' Olivia interrupted, and wobbled onto her feet to collect everyone's glasses.

'That's what the two guys said…' Jan shouted.

The room erupted with raucous laughter again. Olivia was laughing so much she dropped one of the glasses, and it smashed on the floor.

'You know what, girls? I've proper missed this,' she said.

Katie grabbed her hand. 'We have missed this, and you too Ollie… but shut up now while I tell you how much of a dirty bitch I am.'

The others cheered.

Olivia went into the kitchen to refresh the drinks and get a dustpan and brush to pick up the smashed glass. While she was in there, she bumped into Penny sitting alone at the table.

'Pen, are you OK?' she asked. 'I was just about to come up and get you, the girls have been asking where you are.'

Penny smiled a wry grin and gestured towards the room. 'Yeah, I can hear that from your stories.'

Olivia blushed. *I wonder how much she's heard?* she thought. 'How long have you been sat here?'

'Oh, long enough to hear all about your escapades in the bath, young lady,' Penny laughed.

Olivia's face turned the deepest shade of red, and a hot flush tore through her. 'Oh, Pen, let me explain…'

Penny looked at her and smiled. 'Do you think you're the only one who has ever had some afternoon delight in the bath? I was young once, you know. Only I didn't display my actions for all and sundry.'

At this, a scream broke out from in the living room, followed by bellows of laughter.

'Do you want to come in? They'll all be so glad to see you.'

'I'll pop in for five minutes, they are, after all, my girls too. I've watched them grow up alongside you all these years.'

Olivia smiled. 'Great, let me just pour these drinks. Do you want one, Aunt Pen?'

'Oh, heavens no, thanks anyway, Ollie. It wouldn't mix with my medication. I'd be swinging from the lights if I had that now.'

'Hey, that's not necessarily a bad thing,' Olivia laughed.

She brought the glasses filled with wine back into the living room just as Katie was finishing her story about another threesome she had, this time with another girl and the girl's partner. When everyone noticed Penny coming into the room, they shushed in respect for the great woman.

'Oh, you silly girls, carry on enjoying yourselves. Don't dare stop on my behalf. I could tell you stories that would make your hair curl. I wasn't always the old lady you see before you now, you know.' Penny looked around the room. 'I've been places and done things you whipper-snappers have never even dreamed about.'

This caused everyone else to roar with laughter once again. Penny turned to Olivia and winked.

34.

THE NIGHT WAS a success. Penny stayed with the girls for about an hour and a half, shocking them with some of her stories. She even managed to make Katie blush, and that was no mean feat.

After she left, they ordered a taxi and then made it out onto the town. They danced until their feet were sore.

Anna lost her handbag, but then found it again in one of the toilet cubicles, minus her purse. If the thief had considered the compartment inside the bag, then they would have found themselves something in the region of one-hundred-and-fifty-pounds better off, their kitty money.

More drinks ensued, followed by late-night Chinese food, and then home.

On arriving home, Olivia had to face one of the biggest obstacles in her life; the front door. She hadn't been so drunk for a long time, and she had totally forgotten how to use a door key. She could see the hole if she closed one eye, and she knew the key was in her hand. *It'll be the middle one,* she thought, as her body completely refused to communicate with her brain. After a good few attempts—she had

Butterflies

given up counting as a fit of giggles overtook her—she hit the spot. 'Bingo!' she shouted in triumph.

Once the key was in and turned, the door decided not to hold her weight anymore. She literally fell into the house. The contents of her bag spilled everywhere, all over the hallway, as the heel of her shoe broke, spilling her through the door face first.

Lying on the floor in the hall, she was laughing as she attempted to kick off her shoes. Eventually, they became detached from her feet, and she kicked out at the front door to close it. She missed a number of times before finally making contact, and the door swung closed with a slam.

She lay there on the wood flooring, sniggering in between hiccups. 'Ah, fuck it,' she said, 'I might as well sleep here.' She sat up and removed her coat, wrapped it up to make herself a nice pillow, and then lay back down.

'Olivia, Olivia! You can't sleep there.' Someone was talking to her, or at her, and they were lightly shaking her. 'Olivia? Come on, get up.'

She opened one eye; the room was spinning, so she closed it again. Then she opened the other one, and the room spun in the opposite direction, so she closed that one too. *Shit, I'm in trouble now,* she thought.

'Olivia, come on now.'

She recognised the voice, it was a man's voice, *and quite a nice voice too,* she thought as she was unceremoniously hauled up onto her feet.

Once up, she gingerly opened her eyes, expecting to see the whole house in a kaleidoscope of shapes and colours going every which way they wanted. She looked on helplessly as three Richards picked her up.

'Why, thank you, young sir. You're most chivalrous,' she giggled.

'You can't sleep there, you'll be as stiff as a board in the morning,' he said, trying to support her.

'Maybe I need something as stiff as a board in the morning. Maybe I need…' she poked him in his chest as she spoke, '…*you* to be as stiff as a board in the morning.' Her words came out in a slur as she tried to stand.

Richard was shaking his head as he carried her up the stairs. As he held her in his arms, she leaned into him and tried to kiss him. 'Come on,' she goaded. 'You know you want to. I saw you watching me in the bath. Come and give me a kiss.'

'Olivia, stop it now, you're drunk.'

'Just a small one. We won't need to tell anyone…'

'Come on. I'll kiss you tomorrow, but for now, let's just get you into bed.'

'Ooh, bed.' She shook her head in delight. 'You're a fast mover. Take me to bed,' she shouted all over the house.

Richard dragged her into her bedroom, but Olivia was already asleep. He started to undress her but stopped. He looked up at the ceiling and breathed out a large sigh. Then he turned her onto her stomach and loosened the zipper at the back of her dress.

He walked out of the room and returned with a light blanket to put over her and a drink of water. She snuggled into the blanket as he watched. Once he knew that she was safe, he turned out the light and exited the room. As he was leaving, she whispered, 'Goodnight, Paul. I love you…'

Richard smiled and turned towards the stairs.

35.

OLIVIA WAS DESTROYED; it was a number twelve on the scale of one to ten of hangovers. Every time she moved her head, it felt like her brain caught up a couple of seconds later. The dizziness made her stomach churn. Worst of all—and this was an affliction she was often plagued with—she was wide awake. Forced to endure every living second of the hell she was currently enveloped in.

There was a knock on her bedroom door. She couldn't even talk to tell the person, whoever it was, to go away. All she could do was moan.

Obviously, whoever it was took her bedraggled sickly moan as an invitation to enter her room.

Her mouth tasted like she had licked the inside of a dog kennel. *Oh, why did I just think that thought?* Her stomach churned again. Then something else to make her feel worse caught her sore eyes and assaulted her nose. The only person she knew who wore the same perfume every day of the week.

'Angela, this isn't a very good time for me. I think I'm about to be sick again.'

'It won't take very long, I assure you. I need to make sure that you are one-hundred-percent behind any decisions I make regarding the business.'

'Yes, you know I am. I wouldn't have made you the CEO if I didn't think you were capable. Can you please get me a cold flannel for my head?'

'Yes, of course,' she said, making her way to the bathroom. Olivia heard the taps run for a few seconds, then Angela returned with a cold flannel. 'Well, good. Because I need to ask your permission for something. I want to take the business into the American market.'

'You want my permission to go to America? If I give it to you now, would you just go and leave me alone?'

'Yes, I'll set wheels in motion, it may mean regular travel there and back over the course of the next few months, all on company expenses. I would travel economy class, of course.'

'Angela, please just go…'

'Yes, I'll go now.'

'Thank you, just thank you, and close the door on the way out.'

As she heard Angela leave, she breathed a huge sigh of relief. She turned over, slowly, in the bed and attempted to go back to sleep. The hangover was showing no signs of shifting.

As soon as she closed her eyes, and the room stopped spinning, she cast her thoughts back to last night.

All the rosé wine, then Katie's confessions, then the confessions from Aunt Pen, a taxi ride, more drinks, more bars. *No wonder my head is bursting,* she thought.

Even more bars, shots, and cocktails, flirting with some firemen. *There was no way they were real firemen,* she mused. More drinks, dancing, losing Anna and finding her again in an alleyway behind the club on the way to the Chinese with one of the firemen—she claimed she was helping him unravel his hose. Then the meal.

'Oh no, I'll never be able to go in there again,' She cringed, hiding her head under her blankets… and it hurt like hell.

The last thing she remembered was falling out of the taxi, then falling into the house, and then trying to kiss Rich—

'WHAT?'

She sat bolt upright in bed. As she did, her brain swam along after her. At this point, she didn't care. The adrenaline that was pumping through her body more than compensated for her sickly feeling.

'Please tell me I never… Please, tell me I NEVER!'

But every time she thought back, she knew she did.

What the fuck was I thinking? Well of course, I was drunk, I wasn't thinking at all. What will I do when I see him? Well, you just tell him you were so drunk last night that you don't remember anything… What if he brings it up? He won't, he'll be as embarrassed as you.

She paced the room a good few times remembering that the first time she had been sick this morning, she had noticed she was still fully dressed. *Well that's some small relief,* she thought, but then she thought back to what he saw in the bathtub. *Getting me into my nightie would have been nothing compared to that.*

Dilemma, dilemma, dilemma!

She sat back on the bed, put her hands to her throbbing head, trying to stem the headache and think straight. She flopped back on her pillows, wondering how on Earth she could have let this happen? 'Oh shit… shit… shit… shit… shit… noooooo… why am I so fucking stupid?'

With that, Aunt Penny popped her head around her door. 'Ah, I thought I heard you get up. Are you feeling OK, sweetie? I've got to go now for my treatment. I'll be home about four.'

'Oh, Pen, I completely forgot. Do you want me to get ready and come with you?'

'No, I told you, apart from the chemo, I rather enjoy the company, always loads of nice people to talk to.' Penny sniffed at the room and her face wrinkled into a grimace. 'Besides, the way you smell right now, I don't think you're fit to drive.'

'Oh, Pen, I'm so sorry. I promise I'll come and get you afterwards.'

'You will not, young lady. In your state, you'd be more likely to kill me than this stupid cancer. No, you stay in bed. I'll get a taxi. I'll see you later.'

Olivia flopped back on the pillows again. 'I know I say this all the time, but there is absolutely no way I'm drinking like that again, ever.'

She turned to look at the clock. It read almost ten minutes to eleven. She put her head in-between the pillows and tried in vain to get back to sleep.

36.

THREE-THIRTY THAT afternoon, after a few more heaves into the toilet bowl, Olivia finally found the strength, and the wherewithal, to attempt the stairs. She slipped out of her hangover pyjamas. *Finally,* she thought, *they were on the verge of crawling off me themselves.* She put them and her underwear in the dirty wash and put on a fresh set.

She had the worst case of bed head she'd seen this side of 1989, and her make up made her look like a reject from the rock band Kiss circa, the seventies. But it was her house, and she could dress and look however she wanted; besides, she hadn't heard anyone else around since Penny left that morning.

With her hairy dog slippers on, her old house robe tied around her, and her pale, pasty skin with the leftovers of last night's flawless makeup, she ventured downstairs, looking like a homeless person shuffling about looking for somewhere to sleep.

She ventured into the kitchen, thinking there might be something that she would be able to eat and drink, something she hoped she could keep down. She settled on a glass of milk and some jam on toast.

Her first glass of the white liquid was freezing cold. As she gulped it down, she could feel it slipping through her tubes all the way down into her stomach. *Bliss.* She put the grill on to make some toast.

As she bent down to get the bread from the bread bin at the bottom of the cupboard, dizziness came rushing back to her head. It was an effort for her not to fall over. She grabbed the cupboard door to steady herself as she fought the urge to bring back up the freezing cold milk. *Not good,* she thought.

Once control was regained, the bread was fetched and put under the grill to toast. She located the butter and the strawberry jam and then poured herself another glass of milk. She flipped the toast over to do the other side and got a plate out of the cupboard. Finally, she rested for a few seconds. She released a deep sigh and had to stifle a gag as the vile smell of stale alcohol mixed with milk on her breath wafted up to her nose. She could also taste it in her mouth…
'Urgh!!!'

The toast was ready. Three pieces. The butter was layered thick and then cut into the bread to let it spread inside. The jam was spread on top of the butter heavily, making a delicious, greasy, sticky mess on top of the hot bread. *I never thought that jam on toast could look so good,* was her most important thought at this juncture of her life.

Standing at the counter, she picked up her first piece and took a huge bite out of it. It was delicious. She hurriedly took another, even bigger, bite.

Disaster struck on her third bite as she knocked the plate off the table. The crockery bounced on the floor, once, twice, before smashing by the cooker. The two hot, delicious, sweet, and sticky pieces of toast fell on the kitchen floor, away from the shards of plate. As fate is so cruel, they both landed jam-side-down on the tiled floor.

Butterflies

Devastated, she dropped to her knees and scrambled around, trying to pick up the stricken, greasy goodness. She wouldn't be able wait to toast more, and as there was no one about, she didn't see anything wrong with just eating her existing pieces straight off the floor. She knew it was clean.

She sat with her back against one of the cupboards and picked up one of the fallen pieces. She closed her eyes and savoured another delicious bite from it.

That was the exact moment that Richard made his way into the kitchen, whistling a jaunty little tune as he entered. He didn't see Olivia sat eating jam on toast off the floor.

Her eyes widened with fright, and she fell onto all fours, crawling in the opposite direction of his sounds, around the island in the middle of the room.

Oh shit, oh shit, oh shit, oh shit, she thought as she did her utmost to stay out of his way. The kitchen was just not big enough to allow her to escape, and her glass of milk on the counter would kind of give the game away that she was around. That and the smell of just cooked toast.

'Olivia. Are you in here?' he asked as he saw her breakfast paraphernalia on the counter. 'I heard a smash, are you OK?' He walked around the island, and his crotch almost bumped into her face.

She was still on all fours, with a piece of toast hanging out of her mouth and another in her hand. The low cut of her pyjama top was giving him another great view right down to her freely hanging boobs. She looked down and attempted to cover herself up with her toast filled hand, only succeeding in smearing jam all over herself.

'Ah, there you are. I was wondering if you were OK. Bearing in mind how drunk you were last night, and the smash I heard a few moments ago.'

She noticed his gaze move to the view down her top. *Oh, you bastard,* she thought, as she removed her hand to stop herself from falling on the floor.

'I'm oh-gay. I just gropped my toast, gat's all.' As she spoke with her mouth full of jammy toast, a huge drop of saliva dripped out of her mouth and landed on the floor.

They both looked at it, and Olivia died a little inside. *Why are you in my house? And why are you looking at me like that? GO AWAY!* she shouted in her head, causing it to throb a little more.

Richard was laughing. 'I'll get the brush and pan and get rid of the mess, and you get yourself back to bed.'

Slightly relieved, she attempted to stand up, using the island as support.

'That's a good look for you, by the way,' he quipped as he walked towards the utility room.

Please, just go away and leave me alone, she thought, as she leaned back against the counter. She finished her toast off in two bites and then angrily threw the other piece in the bin. As she stood up, she brushed all the crumbs and jam off herself, just in time before he walked back into the room.

'Feeling better?' he asked with a smile.

She nodded, more than a little embarrassed, but resigned to her indignity. 'Yeah, I'm a little fragile, but I think I'll survive. If you'd asked me that an hour ago, you would have gotten a different answer.'

Richard smiled and began to clear up the broken crockery.

'Look, I've had enough of you finding me in embarrassing situations. A hat trick now, I believe. Three-nil, to you,' she said with an embarrassed smile.

'OK, let's say that the next embarrassing thing that I do, I'll give you a shout and you can come and witness it. Deal?'

Butterflies

'Deal,' she smiled. 'Now if you'd just get out of my way, I've got a repeat appointment with my pillow.'

He moved out of her way to let her pass, but one of her breasts brushed against his arm. This sent a tingle of unexpected shivers through her and made her nipples go hard.

Damn you, sensitive nipples, she thought, and hurried out before he could notice.

As she got back to her bedroom, she could hear him pottering about in the kitchen, probably still cleaning up after her. She closed her eyes, but all she could think of was that shiver and her throbbing nipples.

Knowing that she had what her and her friends had always referred to as 'hangover horn,' she smiled as she drifted off into guilty dreams.

37.

SHE'S ALONE IN her room, but it isn't *really* her room. Maybe she's back in the hotel in Geneva, or maybe it's someplace else, but wherever it is, she feels safe and welcome.

The room is shrouded in twilight. Through the open curtains, she can see the twinkling lake, or it might be the sea. The stars are just beginning to blink into existence, and the moon is battling the sun in the sky for supremacy; and winning.

She's stood at the window looking out over the breathtakingly beautiful vista laid out before her. Her attire states that she is ready for a night out, and it would seem a lavish one.

Her dress is gorgeous; it has a deep plunging neckline and the beige colour offsets the healthy tan on her skin. She has on a string of pearls with a single gold strand that falls between her breasts.

Butterflies

The necklace screams, 'Look at my breasts.' It is not an overstatement.

The dress is designer; the skirt is short, falling halfway down her long brown legs, it is covered in see-through silk, giving a sexy feel to the whole outfit.

Her legs are naked, and she's not wearing any shoes.

The door to the bedroom swishes open behind her, but she doesn't turn. She can feel that someone she knows, someone she trusts, has just entered the room.

'Hello.' Her voice is deep, sensual.

'Hi,' he replies.

He is on her before she knows it. She can feel his hot breath on the exposed skin of her neck as he trails small kisses over her nape, leading upwards towards her lower ear. She closes her eyes, enjoying every moment of this embrace. Every kiss causes an explosion of flutters in her stomach. She envisions flocks of blue wings, all of them beating to the rhythm of her racing heart.

The scratch of his chin trail is familiar, and she loves the sensation. His strong fingers follow every kiss before resting lightly on her shoulders.

She opens her eyes; the reflection of her mystery man can be seen in the window. His eyes are closed too as he drinks in the scent of her neck and hair.

She is thankful she'd decided to wear her favourite perfume, it makes her feel sexy. Her man, it seems, shares this thought, as he continues to kiss her neck.

Leaning back into him, she reaches for something and is not at all disappointed to feel the hardness of it beneath the fabric of his trousers.

A smile spreads across her face. It is salacious!

His hands find the join of her dress just beneath the nape of her neck and expertly unclasp it. The top half falls away, and the breeze of the room tantalises her already stiffening nipples until they become hard studs, throbbing with sensation. His face is nuzzled into the crook of her neck as his hand reaches slowly around to lightly cup one of her breasts. His fingers slip deftly over her stiff nipple, making her knees buckle slightly as she inhales sharply.

Butterflies

Oh, my word! My butterflies are alive and well. This thought brings a smile to her face as the first real flapping in her stomach commences.

Her man's hands are now around her waist, both reaching around to stroke her flat stomach, toying with the small diamond she wears in her bellybutton. His hands explore towards her lower belly, pushing her dress down a little further.

She brings her arms up over her head to reach back and run her fingers through her man's hair. She can feel the slight rough of his stubble rasp against her hands as she strokes his face.

He finally succeeds in getting her dress to the point of no return. He gives it one final push, and she wriggles her hips to help it on its way to the floor.

Opening her eyes, she realises that it is now almost fully dark outside, and the wide window has turned into a full-length mirror due to the dim, soft lighting behind them.

Her hips are adorned with a laced pair of black French knickers. Their high cut and full behind give her the illusion of the perfect figure. She feels so secure in her body that she allows her inhibitions to dissolve.

Relishing the feel of his hands all over her skin, she closes her eyes again and turns to face him, wrapping her arms around his neck and kissing him fully on the mouth.

He responds in kind.

Opening her eyes, she turns to look at his purple silk shirt. She rips it off in one seductive stroke of violence. The silk tears easily, and buttons fly over the room.

She traces her finger over his well-muscled chest and stomach, leaving a thin white line in its wake. She knows the white line will soon turn red, and she likes the feeling it gives her.

With him utterly at her mercy, she expertly unbuckles his belt and whips it out of its loops. She then undoes his trousers and pulls them down in one quick action.

She kneels in front of him and removes his underwear. She can sense the musky warmth of him in front of her face and does what she knows he wants her to do, what *she* wants to do.

He moans.

Working her head back and forth, she massages him with her lips and her tongue, savouring the feel and the taste of him in her mouth. Loving the pleasure that it's giving him.

Strong arms reach down and lift her from her squat. She feels his mouth over hers and a probing tongue deep inside her. She is roughly turned back around to face the window. There are ghosts of people standing outside the hotel; they are all looking up at the show. A show where she is the star.

She looks at the ghosts and wonders how she must look to these strangers, and a surge of exciting lust begins to spiral through her body. It starts deep before spreading through her butterfly-filled stomach.

A hand grabs the back of her underwear and tears it off. *How many pairs of these expensive knickers am I going to lose?* she thinks, amused. As the lace and silk rip, she feels another tingle, sweet, with a very small amount of pain, just enough for her to enjoy.

He takes her completely by surprise, and she can't help but expel a moan of delight. 'Oh, fuck!' she shouts in shock and pleasure. As he thrusts deeply inside her, she fears it's going release all her butterflies before she's ready for them.

Her eyes are wide, and she is hyper-aware of the crowd watching below. Unperturbed, his rhythm becomes faster as he grinds himself deeper inside her, and her butterflies beat faster.

She puts a hand on the window. The thought of the people below watching her makes her hotter and wetter than she's ever been.

His breath gets faster as he repositions himself, pushing deeper inside. One butterfly flutters free from her belly. It's closely followed by another, then another; before she knows it, there's a flock escaping their confines. Her body tingles as the slow orgasm takes her.

The people below watch her come.

It makes her orgasm harder and faster. She feels naughty. She'd never thought of herself as an exhibitionist before, but this? As she watches her own face flush red, the beautiful ecstasy tears through her. In a moment of clarity, she can see every face of every person below. There are some she recognises, some she doesn't, either way, she couldn't care less.

Then, one face distinguishes itself from the crowd. A man standing at the back of the gathering…

It's Paul.

Butterflies

He stands alone and off to one side. He has a smile on his face.

'Oh, Olivia, that was fantastic,' her man groans from behind her.

She turns to look at him, seeing his face for the first time. She had assumed it was Paul, but with Paul downstairs and outside the hotel, then this could only be one other person…

'Richard, you were fantastic too,' she purrs.

She turns back to the window; the crowd is dispersing. Paul is walking off on his own.

38.

'WHAT?' OLIVIA WOKE with a start. 'What the hell was all that about?' she asked herself. She could still feel a tingle between her legs as she jumped out of the bed.

Guilt covered her in a deep, heavy blanket. *That wasn't Paul?* she thought. *What's going on in my head? What's with all these Richard thoughts? One, I'm married; two, he's married; three, he's married to my husband's sister; four, I hate her.*

She went into the bathroom, still in a haze from her dream, and put the shower on. She took a long gaze in the mirror and felt herself deflate. 'At least that shitty hangover's gone. Time for something to eat.'

She jumped into the shower and attempted to wash away her guilt. It wasn't easy.

Feeling fresher, she made her way downstairs and prepared herself something quick to eat. Once she had washed up, she got ready to go to the hospital. *Another thing to feel guilty about,* she thought, *I haven't seen Paul in nearly two days. I bet Angela has.*

She looked at the clock with her sandwich still hanging out of her mouth. It was a quarter to six. *Shit, I best get going.*

Butterflies

She charged out of the door, slamming it behind her. She fumbled for her keys and got into her car.

As she drove off, she missed the taxi pulling into the driveway, she also missed the frail old lady struggle to get out, and the driver of the taxi helping her into the house.

39.

IT WAS ANOTHER gruelling visit to the hospital. The exercises Paul needed to stay supple were either getting longer and harder, or she was still feeling the effects from her night out. What was really draining her was the fact that Paul was still not getting any better. The doctors kept on telling her they were satisfied with his condition, but she noted that not one of them were mentioning anything about progress.

She did ask, but was only confronted with roundabout answers and half-truth, positive spins. This depressed her even more. If only someone would tell her some truth down the line.

Every time she was with Paul, they were always in the company of machines that hissed, pinged, and bleeped. They were constant reminders of his condition and that he didn't seem to be getting any better.

Driving home, she found herself in tears once again. They were flowing as she reflected on her life with Paul before the wedding day. How they had laughed and loved, made plans, and seen them grow. She thought back to their wedding and how perfect it had been for them. He had never looked as happy, or as excited. She cried thinking about his flashing thong. His special smile he gave her, the love he gave her, his everything. She also cried for her friends, for how they had all been there for her at any given time. She cried for the present Paul gave her, the present that caused this situation they were currently in. She cried for his stalled life, she cried for her stalled life, she cried for her mother, the constant absence, and she cried for her Aunt Penny.

How could everything have gone so wrong, so quickly? As she cleared her eyes, she could have sworn there was a swarm of black winged butterflies flying around in the car.

By the time she arrived home, she thought she was all cried out for the day… but she was wrong.

40.

THE HOUSE FELT empty. There was no sign of Angela or Richard anywhere within, and that was a relief. Olivia had a quick scout around for signs of Aunt Penny, but she couldn't find any. This caused a small worm in her tummy to turn. *She should have been home hours ago.*

Putting her keys and things on the sideboard in the hallway, she continued her search upstairs. 'Penny…' she whispered as she made it to her room. 'Pen, are you in there?'

There was no answer.

'Aunt Penny, is everything OK?' She heard a small whimper from inside the room. Just a tiny, minute little sound, but it was more than enough to turn her whole world upside down once again. She gripped the door handle, her hand—and indeed her whole body—was covered in a thin sheen of sweat. The last thing in the whole, wide world she wanted to do was open the door, it was a Pandora's Box filled with misery and heartache, but she knew she had to.

With her heart racing, she pushed it open.

The room was in complete darkness. Olivia looked at her watch; it was five minutes to ten, and it was fully dark outside.

'Penny,' she whispered. 'Is everything OK, lovely?'

Butterflies

'Oh, Ollie,' was the only reply she got before the sobbing began.

As she sat on the edge of the bed, her aunt almost jumped on her. Her grip was extremely strong for such an emaciated woman. She wrapped her arms around her, buried her head in her chest, and sobbed.

Olivia was instantly transported back to different stages of her youth. How many times had these tables been turned? Millions would be her guess.

Olivia's tears were falling as a small child who was missing her mum and dad, being comforted by her favourite aunt, tears falling because she was scared about the monsters living under her bed, and she was waiting for her aunt to check it out for her. Tears as a teenager over, well, almost anything from boys, friends, exam results, Dynasty on the TV. Tears as a young woman over money, men, clothes, friends. Tears about Paul, her situation, and of course, Angela.

Now here they were, and this was the first time their roles had been reversed.

Olivia had noticed Aunt Penny's recent reluctance to discuss her treatment or her condition. It had caused her concern, but for some reason, this concern had not registered in her consciousness, she'd had other things on her mind.

Right now, it was the *only* thing that registered in her consciousness.

'Hey, Penn. Come on now,' she soothed as she patted the back of the only person in her life who had never once let her down. 'Hey, come on. Tell me what's the matter.'

Aunt Penny could hardly even talk, she was sobbing and crying so hard. 'Ollie! Oh, Ollie. They gave me such bad news today. They told me the treatment isn't working. They told me that they have reason to believe it's spread further than they initially thought. I'm scared, Ollie. For the first time in my long life. This is the first time I've ever been scared of anything.'

Olivia had big fat tears welling in her eyes. She knew that at any moment, they were going to flow over her lids, and then the damn would be broken. Once that happened, there would be no going back.

'Pen, come on now. You know I'm here for you. You know you have a whole army of supporters out there. Everyone is rooting for you. We can beat this,' she reassured.

Penny pulled away from her. She looked deep into her eyes as she wiped the tears away from her own face. 'Ollie,' her tone was in earnest. 'There's nothing left to fight. The condition has won. They told me today that all they can do for me now is make me comfortable. I... I needed a shoulder,' she stuttered, inhaling a shaky breath. 'You have the best one, and the only one I really wanted. I'm done feeling sorry for myself now. I'm resigned to my fate. So, I want to enjoy my last weeks, months together, and let's live... really live. Deal?'

Olivia was shocked. She'd expected frailty and depression. Instead, after her initial wobble, she was getting bravado and courage. She thought that she loved her Aunt Penny even more in that moment than she had in her entire life.

Wiping the tears from Olivia's eyes, Penny looked at her, a small but determined smile appeared on her lips. 'I'm going to bed now; we can start living in the morning. Right now, I'm done in,' she laughed.

'Are you sure?' Olivia asked, still holding the older woman's hands in a fierce grip. When Aunt Penny nodded her head, Olivia squeezed her hand, hugged her, and left her to get some rest.

As soon as she got into her own bed, and she knew Penny was out of earshot, Olivia curled herself up into a ball and cried harder and longer than she had ever cried before. About an hour and a half later, she got herself up, walked around the house turning all the lights off and locking all the doors. She then crawled back up to her bedroom and cried herself to sleep.

Ironically, that night was probably the most restful sleep she'd had in a good long while.

41.

THE NEXT DAY, she slept late. There didn't seem anything much worth getting up for. It was ten forty-two when her mobile chirped, indicating a text message. Flicking the mobile on to see who had sent it, she frowned as the name on the display read ANGELA. Wondering what the hell she could want today; she swung her legs out of the bed in preparation for another battle with her delightful sister-in-law.

> Please meet me at the hospital, we
> need to discuss Paul's treatment.

There was no text speak with Angela; all her text messages were spelt correctly, complete with grammar and punctuation. 'It's the mark of the woman,' Olivia said in a mocking voice.

This was a meeting that she could do without after the depressing news regarding Aunt Penny yesterday. The last thing she wanted was another run in with Angela over Paul's treatments.

As she stepped into the shower, a noise from inside the bedroom made her jump. Wrapping a towel around herself, she peered out, hoping beyond hope it wasn't Richard once again finding her in another compromising position.

It was Aunt Penny. She still looked half asleep, and if it was possible, even rougher than she had the previous night. Olivia's heart dropped in her stomach.

'Aunt Pen... Penny?' she called.

Penny didn't even look up.

'Penny... Are you OK?'

Aunt Penny snapped out of her trance and looked towards Olivia in confusion.

'Ollie... what are you doing in my bathroom?' she asked.

'Penny, you're not in your bathroom, honey. You're in my bedroom.' Olivia's heart broke saying these words.

Penny looked around her, and her face flushed the deepest crimson Olivia had seen on her in a good few years. The poor woman was so embarrassed.

'Oh, Ollie, I'm so sorry. I was... just trying to... erm, I'll go to my own bathroom.' Penny started for the door.

'Pen, no wait,' Olivia almost shouted. 'It's OK, you can go in here if you want to.' She felt bad for addressing her now.

'No. I have to go to the bathroom, and I'll go in my own room.' Penny stormed out of the bedroom. Olivia followed but only in time to see Penny's bedroom door close and to hear the click of the lock.

Olivia stood outside the room, her hand over her mouth. More tears were streaming down her cheeks. She waited there for a few more moments. When there were no more noises coming from the room, Olivia guessed that Penny was back in bed. She then went into her room and got into the shower. As soon as the hot steaming water splashed over her body, she broke down and cried again.

42.

AN HOUR LATER and she was washed, dressed, and mentally prepared for her meeting with Angela, but first she had to make sure Penny was OK. She went upstairs and stood outside her room and put her ear to the door. She was listening for any tell-tale signs that Penny was fine inside the room. She could hear a gentle snoring. Olivia tried the door handle; it was open. Obviously, Penny had calmed down a little and opened it again before having a sleep.

Feeling slightly better about Penny's situation, she went downstairs and looked out into the back garden. Richard was out there tending to some rose bushes.

'Richard, could you do me a massive favour?' she shouted from inside the house.

Richard turned. His shirt was open, and he was wearing a snug pair of shorts. His torso was finely muscled, he had tight pectorals and a slightly fading six pack. He was also nicely tanned. The shorts were a ridiculous bright yellow but were close enough for her to notice his well-exercised bum and muscled thighs.

Olivia, focus, she scolded herself for noticing everything about the man.

'Sure,' he said, flashing his fantastic smile at her again. 'Anything for you, Olivia, you know that.'

This flustered her a little. 'I, erm, I have to go and meet Angela at the hospital; it's about Paul. Could you just keep an eye out for Aunt Penny? She got a bit of, well, a bit of bad news last night, and I think she's feeling a bit confused today. Can you just make sure she's OK? I'm hoping to be back within a couple of hours.'

'Yeah, of course. You know I love that woman too, right? I'll take her a cup of tea up in a few minutes. We can have a chat, she enjoys that…'

'Well, she's sleeping right now, but when she wakes up, I'm sure she'd love such good company. Thanks, Richard, I've got to go. I'll speak to you later.'

With that, she was off, in her car, with the music turned up loud. It was loud to draw her attention away from Paul, Angela, and Aunt Penny, and now—as if she didn't have enough to worry about—Richard.

43.

THE HOSPITAL WAS just as gloomy as it had always been, but today it seemed even worse as she was meeting with Angela.

'I have a meeting with Angela Grantham scheduled here today, it's regarding Paul Martelle, my husband.' Olivia smiled at the receptionist.

'Ah yes, Mrs Martelle, they're in conference room fourteen. It's on the first floor, just follow the signs for the teleconferencing suite, and it's right there.'

'Thank you.' She smiled again politely. Although, today, she felt anything but polite.

Conference room fourteen was bright and airy, not at all like what she was expecting. Inside sat Angela, Dr Polatski, who was overseeing Paul's case here in the UK, and on the video-conferencing unit was Dr Hausen from Switzerland.

They all stood to greet her as she entered the room, even Dr Hausen on the VC.

'Mrs Martelle, we're so sorry to call you here at such short notice, but we feel we have reached an impasse in the treatment of Mr Martelle's condition,' Dr Polatski began.

She looked round the room taking in everyone's gloomy faces. *All except Angela's,* she thought, *I bet that bitch is enjoying this!*

She cocked her head to one side as she removed her coat and hung it over the back of her chair. 'What do you mean *an impasse*?' she asked.

'Well, you see, we've been doing everything we can to try and rouse your husband from his coma, but so far, nothing is working.' Dr Polatski dropped his head a little before continuing. 'We haven't even seen a glimmer of hope that he will wake. There is brain activity, we can see that, but there seems to very little of anything else!'

The hits just keep on hitting, she thought, but did her best to keep a poker face for the meeting. 'So, what's next?' she asked, feeling like she didn't want to know the answer to this question.

'Well, that's where you come in, Mrs Martelle,' replied Dr Hausen. Olivia had almost forgot he was there. 'Mrs Grantham has put forward a rather, erm, radical suggestion. We have analysed it, and we think that it could work.'

'What is it, Dr Hausen?' Olivia asked, shooting her sister-in-law a look. This was something that Angela had wanted for a long time.

'There's a treatment, there are risks, but we think the outcomes may well outweigh them,' Dr Hausen's image on the TV screen continued. 'There's a seventy per cent chance the procedure will work.'

Olivia's face brightened at this news, but the brightness was only temporary.

'But there is also a thirty per cent chance that Paul will not survive the procedure or will become permanently, and irreparably, brain damaged. We are giving you the story straight, Mrs Martelle; we're not going to sugar-coat it for you. We need you—Paul needs you—to make as much of an informed decision as you can.'

Olivia felt helpless as she looked towards Angela. *Help me, Angela, please. If there is one tiny part of you that doesn't hate me, then show me it now. I need you now, more than ever.* 'Angela.' Oliva looked at her sister-in-law with a deadpan expression, only her eyes gave away the devastation she was feeling inside. 'I'd like to know your thoughts on this therapy, please.'

Angela recoiled as if she'd been slapped in the face. She hadn't been expecting Olivia to reach out to her. 'Well, erm… naturally, I brought the idea onto the table, so to speak. Therefore, I, erm… concur with it,' she squirmed.

No, you don't, you don't agree with it at all; you just want control of your brother and everything else, Olivia thought, as she used every part of her being to fight back the tears that were so nearly there.

'In front of you, Mrs Martelle,' began Dr Polatski.

'Please call me Olivia.'

'OK, Olivia. You have before you some notes regarding Mr Martelle's condition and the treatments he has endured. Also included is a complete breakdown of the suggested therapy, including benefits and eventualities.' He paused for a moment before continuing. 'And potential side effects. Please take the time to read it. We would need to start the prep by a week today. Dr Hausen will come over from Switzerland to oversee the procedure.'

Olivia looked towards the screen, her face showing the same mask she had shown Angela, only Dr Hausen saw the fear and desperation in her eyes. He offered her a small, reassuring smile.

Oliva gathered all the papers, shuffled them, and put them into the large envelope in front of her. Inside, she felt dead; outside, she was as cool as anything. 'You'll have my answer within the next two days, I promise. I must leave now,' she said, wiping a rogue tear from her eye as she stood up. 'I want to spend some time with my husband.'

As she stood, so did everyone else. She gave Angela a hard stare, and she stared back just as hard.

Then Olivia left the room.

44.

PAUL'S ROOM WAS quiet. All the doctors and nurses had left, giving her some much-needed privacy. The only sounds were the constant hiss of Paul's breathing apparatus and the occasional ping of one of the machines around him.

'Paul, what am I going to do? I'm being pulled this way and that. I don't know how long I can last. Between you and Angela, and now Aunt Penny.' Real tears were falling now, soaking his blanket. 'I need your help, Paul,' she sobbed, 'I need your guidance. I'm at breaking point. Wake up, Paul, please… wake up.'

More tears flowed. Her sobs were happening in rhythm with Paul's mechanical breathing. She squeezed his hand while the tears fell, holding it so tightly that a nurse had to come in to remove her grip.

'I'm sorry, Mrs Martelle. He can't squeeze back, you see; you could easily break the fingers of his hand. I really am so sorry,' the nurse said.

'I'm sorry, I'm so, so sorry.'

'No harm done, Mrs Martelle. Maybe you just need some rest, eh?'

'Huh!' Olivia scoffed. 'I really think I do, but if I get too much, then I'll start to dwell on things. I don't think I can win.'

'Life's not always about winning. Those people who think it is spend an awful lot of time on the top plinth alone.' The nurse spilt her wisdom as she fussed around Paul's bed, giving Olivia food for thought.

45.

IT'S NOT ALL about winning, Olivia thought to herself on the drive home from the hospital. *It's all about small victories. That's how Angela lives her life, one small victory at a time. She has the control she wanted of the businesses, I don't begrudge her that, and she's beaten poor Richard into submission, now she's trying to regain control over Paul... I can't let her win this one, or she'll control us forever.*

Olivia wished there could be some let up on the attacks. She was currently battling with Paul's condition, fighting with Angela about Paul, and now she'd have to roll her sleeves up and do battle with Aunt Penny's cancer too. *I've got to be strong in the fight with what Aunt Penny is going through. I need to be there for her, like she's always been there for me.*

As she arrived home, the blue flashing lights of an ambulance greeted her on her driveway. Richard was there too, looking grave.

Oh Lord, please give me ten minutes at least, she thought.

'Olivia, thank God you're home. I was just about to ring your mobile,' Richard shouted to her as she got out of her car.

'What is it? What's happened?' Her heart was beating ridiculously as her wide eyes soaked in the chaos happening on her driveway.

'It's Penny. I'm so sorry, but I was out in the back... when I came back in I...'

Olivia pushed passed him, leaving him mumbling in her wake. She dashed into the house and up the stairs. The paramedics were in Penny's room, and there seemed to be too many of them. The walls of the house seemed to be too close for her, and Penny's door seemed too far away.

When she eventually reached the room, two paramedics walked out carrying a gurney. On the gurney was a body. Olivia had no way of knowing if the body was alive or dead. There was no movement.

'I'm her niece, can somebody please tell me what's happening?' she shouted, anger and panic bubbling over in her voice.

A third paramedic took Olivia by the hand and gently pulled her inside. 'You're Olivia?' she asked gently.

'Y-yes. I'm her niece. She's more like a mother to me.'

'Yes, we know. Your husband told us.'

Olivia's heart nearly missed a beat. She looked at the paramedic with confusion. 'My husband?' she asked.

'Yes, Richard, downstairs...'

She felt like her face had turned upside-down, she didn't know what she looked like, and she didn't care. 'Oh, no, he's my brother-in-law,' she told her. *Shut up, Ollie, and let the girl speak,* she thought.

'OK, well this is the situation,' the paramedic continued. 'Your brother-in-law rang us about ten minutes ago. He came back in from the garden and heard a strange sound. He called us straight away, and it's lucky he did. Your aunt has gone into arrest. We think it's a complication of her condition. It seems she hasn't been taking her medication correctly.'

Olivia was shocked. 'She has, I've made sure of it. I've even given it to her personally.'

The paramedic smiled warmly at her and put her hands reassuringly on Olivia's shoulder. 'I'm sure you've taken great care for her, but this has only been a couple of days. All she has been taking are painkillers—a lot of them, it seems.' The girl gave Olivia a compassionate look. 'It looks like a suicide attempt.'

Olivia's vision tunnelled then. Everything became a blur, and she sat down. She didn't even know if there was anything behind her for her to sit on. Luckily, there was. Everything she had been in denial about, things that she hadn't wanted to even think about, came crashing down around her head. 'What? No, never! Aunt Pen is full of life. She's undergoing chemo, and she's responding well to it, she... she told me so.'

'Olivia, whenever we have a case like this, we have to check back to the hospital records. If we were to administer something we shouldn't, then it could kill her. When we reported back, they told us that your aunt was taken off the chemo three days ago. She hasn't been responding, so they sent her home to conduct her affairs. She was then to ring an ambulance or get a loved one to bring her back in. I'm so sorry to have to be the one to tell you this, but your Aunt Penny is dying.'

Olivia put her head in her hands and started to weep. Tears of resignation, tears of sorrow, tears of self-pity. 'I know,' she sobbed. The paramedic put her arm around her to offer what little comfort she could.

'Come on,' she whispered. 'It's time you rode in the ambulance with your Aunt, this one last time.' She guided Olivia up onto her

Butterflies

feet, and slowly, the two of them descended the stairs towards the open front door and the waiting ambulance.

As she climbed in, she stole a look at Aunt Penny's face. She looked so serene and dignified. Olivia smiled, ever so slightly.

She took Penny's hand, careful not to press too hard like she'd done with Paul's. 'It's all OK, Pen. I'm here now, and I'm not going anywhere.' The ambulance doors closed, and she heard the sirens as it pulled out of her driveway.

46.

'MUM, CAN YOU hear me, Mum? You keep cutting out... Mum? What? What are you doing in The Yemen? Married? Married to who? Three weeks?' Olivia was trying to conduct a mobile phone conversation with her mother; a face-to-face conversation had always been hard enough, but a mobile one from Yemen was nigh on impossible.

'Mum, I can hardly hear you. I'm just going to shout it. It's Aunt Penny, she's dying, Mum. Are you still there? Yes. Good. Did you hear what I said? Yes, dying. No, no, she hasn't been lying. The doctors said she only has a few days left. No, *days*. You're going to need to get home, Mum... Oh, bollocks to this, I'll send you a text.'

She wanted to slam the phone down but ended up just pressing END CALL really hard. 'They should make these fucking things with a button that reads 'END CALL... ANGRILY,' she muttered. The frustration of the phone call, her mother, and the whole situation was getting to her.

Fuming, Olivia walked back into the hospital room to be with Aunt Penny, who was lying in her bed, fast asleep. The tubes and machines around were an eerie reminder of Paul, who was lying in a similar state just two floors below. The doctor came in and looked at

Penny's chart. Seeming happy enough with what he saw, he looked over at Olivia and smiled humourlessly. 'Mrs Martelle, I think you need to sit down.'

Olivia did not like being told to sit down. Sitting down was bad, sitting down, in her experience, always meant bad news.

As they sat down, she noticed that the doctor's face was grave and serious. 'I want to get to the crux of this, Mrs Martelle, so I'm going to be as frank with you as I can.'

'Thank you, Doctor, I would appreciate that,' she replied, steeling herself for the worst.

'Ms Britt has days, in my estimation. I'm not expecting her to last the weekend. She's experiencing very small periods of lucidity, and I want you to make the most of every one of them. She is very heavily medicated, but she should be able to understand everything you say to her. Do you understand what I'm telling you, Mrs Martelle? You need to prepare yourself. Say your goodbyes and make your peace with her.'

Olivia was crying again now. 'I know, Doctor. I know. It's just so…' She sobbed and gulped at the same time. 'So, hard.' As the steady stream of tears fell from her eyes, she felt so empty, and so alone.

47.

OLIVIA SPENT THE rest of the night in vigil. She was a constant resident at the end of Aunt Penny's hospital bed, where she sat and watched the nurses come, administer drugs, and leave. She watched the doctors come, check charts, and leave. All through the night, through the dawn of the morning, and right the way into the evening, Olivia was there by the bedside. She dozed in the recliner chair provided by the hospital and refused a room for herself on the grounds that she wanted to be there for Penny no matter what, or when, something happened. There had been quite a bit of guilt about not seeing enough of Paul, but she knew, deep in her heart, that he wasn't going anywhere, whereas Aunt Penny was. *He would understand anyway,* she told herself.

In the small hours of her second night, Penny sat bolt upright in her bed. Olivia had been napping on the chair beside her. Her book was on her lap. The fright she received as Penny awoke sent the book flying off her knee, onto the floor, losing her bookmark in the process.

'Ollie... Ollie, are you there, child?' Penny asked in a tired, drawn out voice. Olivia took solace in the fact she sounded lucid. All

Butterflies

the other times she'd woken up, she'd warbled nonsense, attempting to talk through the drugs, painkillers, and the disorientation.

But this time, she was lucid. 'Ollie, would you please get me a drink of water? I'm parched,' she whispered.

Olivia poured her a glass of the room temperature water—she had been told not to give her it too cold, as her cancer-riddled body could reject it. She walked around the bed and lightly lifted Penny up onto her pillows. *She weighs less than a sparrow,* she thought while fluffing them.

Penny took the water gratefully and smiled at her. A small drip rolled down her narrow chin, and Olivia quickly mopped it up.

'Thank you, child. How long have you been here?' she asked.

She thought about the question for a little while. 'I think this is my second or third night, Pen. You've been a little sleepy and have slept through most of it.' She smiled a pained smile and nudged the frail old lady lying in the bed. 'You party pooper, you,' she finished.

Penny smiled a genuine, million-dollar smile.

Oh, I bet you had your fair share of men running after you in your day, Olivia thought with a tinge of sadness. But the thought of Aunt Penny running around town wearing short skirts, chasing, and being chased by boys made her happy.

'Ollie, I want you to do something for me. Will you?' Penny asked as she beckoned her niece nearer to her bed. She wore a conspiratorial look.

'You know I'd do anything for you. All you have to do is name it and it's done.'

'Thank you, child. Thank you,' Penny laboured. 'I need you to know something, and I need you to keep the secret for as long as I have. Can you do that for me?'

'Penny, you know I can...'

'I know, but this is just such a secret, there's only one other person who knows this… and that person is your mother.'

Olivia was intrigued. She leaned in closer to Penny, desperate to hear the secret.

'Your mother… she's not your real mother…'

Olivia sat bolt upright at this revelation. *Oh, my God,* she thought. *That explains so many things.* Her eyes nearly bulged from their sockets as she looked back at her aunt. She was so filled with shock and excitement at this juicy bit of gossip that she couldn't even get her words out. 'W-well, just who is it then? Who is my mother?'

Penny looked up at her, her face had turned a light shade of grey. Olivia thought that it must have been an effect of her medication wearing off, otherwise, she wouldn't have been able to talk, never mind legibly.

'Who, Penny, who is it?'

Aunt Penny's face broke into an enormous smile once again. As she closed her eyes, Olivia noted there were tears in them.

That was when Penny started to convulse.

Olivia's heart was in her mouth for a second or so. Panic overtook her when she couldn't find the nurse's call button. She stood up and reached over her aunt, hoping the button was somewhere around the top of the bed when she realised Penny wasn't fitting. She was laughing. It looked like it was hurting her to do it, but nevertheless, it was a laugh causing her convulses.

Olivia was more than a little bewildered.

Penny was still laughing. 'Ollie, I'm so sorry…' Penny lost her breath a little and it took some time to get it back. Olivia had her hand on Penny's head. 'I'm sorry. I was joking, I was pulling your leg. Unfortunately, your mother *is* your mother! It's just that I've always had a wish to impart a deeply meaningful bit of information on my deathbed. I'm so sorry, please forgive my indulgence.'

Olivia saw the mirth in Aunt Penny's face and realised that the older woman had made herself feel a bit better with the joke and decided to forgive her, even though it was what she had come to expect from her over the years. She had always been a practical joker.

'Oh, Aunt Penny, the healing power of laughter, eh?' She sighed as relief soared through her.

Penny reached a weak and trembling hand out of the bed. Olivia saw with some horror that it was little more than a claw, and a withered old claw at that.

She reached for Olivia.

'Ollie,' Penny coughed. 'I do have something to tell you, and it's something that I've told you a million and one times before today, but tonight I need you to really understand the gravity of it.'

Olivia lightly squeezed her hand and then wrapped her other one around them. She got up off the chair and kneeled by the side of the bed, so their faces were level. She moved her head towards their entwined fingers and kissed Penny's fingers. She kissed them with a love she didn't even know she had inside of her.

'Olivia, you have been my child all these years. I've thought of you as my own. I've grown prouder and prouder of you in how you overcame all your failings, and in all your triumphs. My only regret is that I must leave you so soon.'

'Oh, Aunt Pen, don't talk like that,' Olivia said, choking back thick tears that were now streaming down her face.

'Ollie, I *will* be leaving you soon. I just wanted you to know. Just being with you has made me the happiest woman alive. You must know that I'm at peace. Please don't grieve for me. Olivia, I love you.'

'Oh, Penny, you know I—'

Penny lifted a finger to Olivia's lips. 'Shush, I don't want you to say anything. Just you being here for me, the fact it's just me and you, says everything I ever need to hear.' The tears began to build in Penny eyes too.

The two women, lives apart from each other in age but bound together with a special bond only they knew and understood, held each other, and cried.

After an hour of holding each other, Penny looked at Olivia with watery, tired eyes. 'Ollie, I need my pain relief. Would you go and get the nurse to administer the morphine? But before you do, there's one more thing I need you to do for me.'

Olivia smiled. 'This isn't another of your tricks, it is, Pen?'

Penny smiled with her thin lips. Olivia could see the herculean effort she had to put into it. 'No, Ollie, it's not. I need you to tell your mother I always loved her too. Please tell her that no matter how wild she was, or how much she tried it on… I still loved her. Would you do that for me, child? Think of it as my second final wish.'

Oliva nodded and wondered what her final wish could be.

'Olivia, I need you promise me that you'll do my final wish, do it without even thinking about it.'

Olivia's vision was almost blurred with tears, but she nodded at the older lady's request. 'You just name it, Aunt Penny.'

'I want you to live for today. Live life like you want to live it. Don't hide away in the past, pining for me, or for Paul. Remember that life is what happens when you're busy making other plans.'

'Isn't that from a song?' Olivia asked, wiping the tears from her eyes.

Penny nodded as she tried to smile.

'Yes, Aunt Penny. I promise I'll live life to the full.'

'Thank you. Now please go and get that nurse for me.'

She patted Olivia's hand, dismissing her.

As Olivia left the room, she glanced back, just the once, to look at her aunt lying serenely on the bed. Olivia wondered how this marvellous woman still had the strength to offer her a little wave and a loving smile.

'Nurse, hi… my aunt in there said she needs some pain relief. I was wondering if you could give her an injection. She mentioned morphine,' Olivia spoke to the first nurse she saw at this late, or was it early, hour.

The young girl smiled. 'I'll just go and check her notes. Give me one minute.' The nurse picked up her board and looked at it. 'She was given a driver earlier today; she has complete control over the doses she takes. She should be free of pain right now.'

'Well, I'm sorry but she has just asked me to get her some relief. Could you come in and see her? Please?' Olivia pleaded.

The nurse smiled another reassuring smile. 'Of course.'

As the two women entered the hospital room, Penny was asleep. Olivia thought that she looked comfortable at last. 'She looks fine now,' Olivia whispered as they made their way to the bed. 'Sorry to be a nuisance.'

But the nurse had seen something that Olivia hadn't. Her face changed from serene to urgent in the wink of an eye, and she pulled the covers away from Penny's chest. She put her two fingers to the older woman's neck, then picked up Penny's arm to check there too.

Olivia watched all of this. Deep down she knew what was happening, but her brain wouldn't allow her to process it. She held her hand to her face, covering her mouth. It was an involuntary action, but one that spoke a thousand words. It told of her grief, her sorrow, and a little of her relief too.

The thought of that beautiful person undergoing the physical changes and the pain that the ravages of cancer brought made her sick to her stomach. So yes, she *was* relieved Penny had been spared it.

'Time of death, oh-three thirty-one,' the nurse said aloud after looking at her watch. She made sure Olivia witnessed her call.

Olivia sat on the reclining chair, wrapped her arms around herself, and broke down.

48.

THE NURSE HAD asked Olivia if she wanted her to call someone, told her she really shouldn't be alone right now. Olivia was confused and slightly dazed. Who could she call at this hour? The only people that she could rely on were right here already in this hospital.

'No, I'm—I'm... I think I'm OK,' Olivia stuttered.

The nurse sighed and cocked her head. 'Well, I don't think you are. Come with me,' she commanded, and gently, but forcefully, took Olivia's arm, leading her towards the nurse's station.

There was another nurse in there already. As they shuffled in, the first nurse mouthed the words, 'Cup of tea.' The second nodded and made herself scarce.

Olivia was still shocked. Her eyes were wide and had a vacant look to them.

'Put extra sugar in them, will you, Pam?' the first nurse shouted to her partner before looking at Olivia. 'Right, there's no way you're going to be alone tonight, so hand over your mobile phone, please.'

As if on autopilot, Olivia did as she was instructed.

The phone was turned off, and after about a minute of fiddling with it, the nurse looked satisfied when she heard the chimes associated with it booting up.

'Right then, how do you work these bloody things?' she smiled, handing it back.

Olivia took the phone, entered her unlock code, and handed it back to the nurse.

'OK then, who do we call?' She started pressing buttons when the phone beeped and vibrated in her hands.

And then it did it again!

'Ah-ha, texts. Let's see who they're off, shall we? We can see if they can be persuaded to come and pick you up at this small hour, eh?'

Olivia just looked at the nurse. She didn't want to talk, she didn't want to say anything, to anyone, ever again.

'OK, we have an Angela Bitch.' The nurse pulled a semi-smiling face towards Olivia. 'I'm just going to assume that you don't want her to come and get you.' She moved on. 'And we have a... Richard.'

'So, Angela Bitch wrote, "Richard I'm off to USA now and I'm leaving in the middle of a fight. It's not because of the sex, or lack of it..."'

The nurse began to blush slightly, then laughed as Olivia's face showed a little interest.

'Somehow, I don't think that one was meant for you. OK, moving on with the next one. Richard writes, "Ollie, I heard Pen is really bad. If you need me just text any time. Thinking of you, Richard."' The nurse smiled. 'I think Richard it is then, eh?'

Before Olivia could answer, the nurse had called the number. It rang out and went to voicemail.

Butterflies

'Hi, this is a message for Richard. My name is Nurse Radcliffe, I'm working at Sister Mary's hospital. I'm sorry for calling so late, but I have Mrs Olivia Martelle with me here. She's had some very bad news tonight. I really think she could do with a lift home. Please ring back when you get this message.'

The moment she pressed END CALL it began to vibrate again. The song *It's Raining Men* echoed all around the ward. It was very loud considering the late hour. As the second nurse turned back up with the tea, she was laughing. 'Great ringtone, I love this one.' She was still laughing as she put the tea down.

Olivia was smiling now as she picked up a cup and took a sip.

'Hello, it that Richard? Yes, no... no, Olivia's fine. It's regarding her Aunt Penny. Yes... unfortunately she passed not very long ago. Yes, oh, she's fine, it's just that, well I don't think she should be going home alone this morning. I was wondering if you, or someone you know, could come and get her? You will? Oh, that's fantastic. Ward twelve. Yes, I'll tell her. Thank you, Richard. Sorry, but I don't know your surname? OK then, thank you, Mr Grantham.'

Olivia was listening intently to the one-sided conversation. As the nurse put the phone down, she was smiling again. 'He's on his way. Said he'd be about half an hour, no later.'

'Thank you, Nurse Radcliffe,' Olivia said, wrapping her hands around the hot mug of sweet tea.

'Oh, please, call me Cheryl.'

49.

RICHARD WAS TRUE to his word. He was there within half an hour to pick her up. He'd brought a thick coat and a pair of pyjamas for her to change into.

'Don't worry, I haven't been snooping through your draws. I got these out of the washing,' he winked as he handed her the clothes.

Olivia and Richard thanked both the nurses for their help and compassion. She was briefed on what would happen next regarding Penny's body, given a telephone number of who to speak to in the morgue tomorrow, and then they were off.

Richard had not had a problem parking his car due to the late hour. It was almost right outside the ambulance bay. He opened the passenger door for her, helped her in, then ran back around to the driver's side. As soon as he had the key in the ignition, Olivia was fast asleep in the seat, snoring lightly.

~~~~

Back at the house, he gently rocked her awake. She was still in the throes of sleep as she grabbed his hand and smiled. 'Oh, Paul, please let me sleep some more.'

Butterflies

Richard smiled before he shook her, a little harder this time, and she snapped out of her doze. She realised she was still holding Richard's hand and did a little jump.

'Come on, Ollie, we're home.'

~~~

The next few days passed in a blur of telephone conversations with undertakers, funeral arrangers, and funeral party organisers (of all things). There was also a whizz of conversations with all her friends. They had all turned up at one point or another. They'd laughed a lot, cried a lot, and drank an awful lot. Katie and Jan were Olivia's constant companions while everything went on around her.

At some point, her mother turned up with a young man on her arm. The man was Asian. Her mother said something about being in love and this was Olivia's new stepfather. Her new stepfather seemed to be younger than Olivia, but she was just glad her mother was home.

Angela was in America and was coming home the day before the funeral, but she said she would have to leave early to catch a flight back that same night. She had mentioned something about negotiations going very well and that Martelle Consulting would very soon have an outlet in Philadelphia. Again, Olivia took little notice, but she did find herself happy that she would be coming home to pay her respects.

Angela also told her they had decided against the shock treatment for Paul, mainly out of respect for the current situation, although Olivia thought she had sounded a little frosty when she reported this news. But on the bright side, Dr Hausen himself was going to fly over to take over the investigation into Paul's condition. Angela told her that he would be in touch with her soon. Olivia saw this as good news, as she'd barely had time to visit her husband over the last week.

~~~~

When she did get moments to visit, they were the only lucid times where she could sit and relax, remember, and reminisce.

She cried as she held Paul's hand. 'Paul, I'm surrounded by friends and well-wishers, people who I love and who love me in return. So why do I feel so alone?' Tears were streaming down her face again. She wondered again about the limit to how many tears a person could cry before they dried up and thought that she must be nearing that limit.

She sat there, enjoying the peace and quiet of the hospital room and the physical connection with her husband.

Doctor Hausen came into the room. 'Hello, Mrs Martelle. It's so nice to see you again. How are you feeling today?'

She wiped the tears from her eyes and rubbed at them, making them red. She tried to smile, but it seemed to give up halfway through. 'To tell you the truth, Dr Hausen, I'm exhausted. I have a house full of people, all doing their best for me, I'm drinking too much, and…' Olivia stopped to gulp a breath. 'I'm missing my best friend and my husband.' Again, the tears fell.

Dr Hausen wrapped his arms around her and gave her a hug. This shocked Olivia into stopping crying. Never, in all the time she had any dealing with him, had he ever shown any real emotion towards anyone. He had always seemed stiff and awkward around others.

'There, there, Mrs Martelle. You'll feel better pretty soon.' He patted her on the shoulders.

Butterflies

Olivia made a brave face. 'Dr Hausen, I'm sorry I haven't had time to thank you for coming over here and taking over this case personally. I'm sure Paul thanks you too.' She turned towards her husband and lightly squeezed his hand.

The doctor blushed a little, 'Ah, you do not have to thank me. This case fascinates me a little.' He patted her on the shoulder again and left the room.

She was left on her own, wondering what the hell had just happened.

50.

THE DAY OF the funeral finally arrived. Olivia was in her bedroom getting ready, both physically and mentally. Today was going to be tough, but she was determined to get through it without having to lean on too many people.

'Don't you worry about a thing,' Jan had said to her. 'If you need either of us, me and Katie, we're both there for you.'

'And if things start to get heavy,' Katie continued, 'I'll punch that Angela in the mouth for you. I'm sure she'll see the funny side of it.'

Olivia had to laugh at that. 'I'm sure she'll understand that it's for me and Aunt Penny.'

With that, both her friends left her to her own devices for half an hour or so. She needed to compose herself before she went downstairs to face the well-wishers. She knew they all meant well and were all here to show how much they loved and respected Aunt Penny, but she just wished they would all leave her alone.

Her purse was on the dressing table in front of her. She reached over and removed the two folded pieces of paper that were inside. She had decided to write a speech. It was the least she could do for such a wonderful person.

She took it out and gave it another once over. She hoped it would make Penny proud to hear the words she had written for her.

Olivia lifted her head after reading it and took a good long look in the mirror. 'How have I not gone grey yet?' she asked herself while inspecting her brunette hair. It was a question that baffled her. Anyone else with the year that she'd had wouldn't only be grey but probably bald by now. She smiled at that thought before getting up to put her dress on, ready to greet her public.

She had been out with Katie the day before and spent a fortune on a simple black designer dress. It had a square neck, and it cut in at her waist. It fit perfectly, and she had quite a bit of wriggle room for all the kneeling and sitting she'd be doing today. A small black fascinator with a sash would cover her face, and it worked perfectly with the gorgeous pearl necklace she'd found in Aunt Penny's drawer. Her black stockings would complement her new pair of, very expensive but very deserved, shoes.

She looked in the mirror; a sad but sweet smile crept over her face. 'You look fucking gorgeous,' she said to herself in a shaky voice, mimicking Aunt Penny's comment to her on her wedding day. A lonely tear slowly tracked down her cheek.

51.

THE FUNERAL SERVICE was moving; it was humbling to see the sheer number of lives Aunt Penny had touched in some way or another. The church was almost overflowing. Everyone wanted to say their last goodbyes to the enormous spirit that was Penny Britt.

Angela was there; she had made it back from Philadelphia late last night, but she would have to leave early as she needed to catch the late-night flight back for another series of meetings. The effort of the long commute for this service was not lost on Olivia, and she thanked her for it.

Richard sat next to Angela.

In a relatively short period, Richard had gone from someone who's name Olivia could never remember, to someone she had grown, not only to rely on, but to almost be her rock.

Of course, Jan and Katie were there too, and the whole host of friends she had accumulated over the years. Olivia felt comfort in all of them.

There were cousins and aunts she hadn't seen in years, and even some she didn't know. There were also a number of 'uncles' she had never met before in her life. At the back of the church, there seemed to be quite a few of them. They were all sitting apart from each other but kept giving each other nods of recognition. These men gave Olivia the biggest lift of the day. It was so obvious that they had been significant in Penny's life. Although she hadn't personally met them, she'd known of their existence. The fact that *all* of them turned up for her funeral spoke volumes about Penny's spirit and her effect on others.

'And now I'm going to hand you over to Olivia, who was the closest of all to Ms Britt,' the priest announced after his eulogy. 'She asked if she could say a few words regarding the force that was the crux of Penny's life. Olivia?'

All eyes were on her as she tried to walk down the aisle towards the altar in her new shoes. An absurd thought came to her that her shoes were literally trying to kill her right now. All she could hope for was that they would not succeed, at least until she had finished her speech.

They didn't, and she made it to the lectern without incident.

She took her notes out of her handbag before looking out towards the congregation; all eyes were looking back at her.

Someone had given her the advice to imagine the congregation naked or at least in their underwear to calm her nerves during the speech. She was a little unsure about the ethics of this practice in a church, though the thought of it gave her a little smile, and enough strength to deliver her eulogy.

'Penny Britt was, and I mean no disrespect to you, Mum, but she was my mother…'

The people who knew Olivia's mother turned to look at her, mainly to see what her reaction to this would be. She was smiling, crying, and nodding all at the same time; she was in total agreement.

'She was there for me when I was growing up. She took me in, much like she took my mother in years before, cushioning me under her enormous wing. There was room under those wings for anyone and everyone. Everyone who knew her knew that she was a force to be reckoned with. If you ever crossed her, wow, talk about passive aggressive...'

Olivia laughed when she said that last part. Most of the audience did too.

'Penny knew how to make you feel guilty. One time when I was a young girl, me and Jan were playing in Penny's front room. We were playing two balls on the wall. We knew we shouldn't have been, but what can you do when it's raining outside, and you're bored? Anyway, it was Jan's turn to pass the balls to me, and as she did, I missed one of them. It smashed an expensive looking vase that was on top of the fireplace. Grey ash scattered everywhere from inside it. We looked at each other, fear spreading across our faces. We were both rooted to the spot, wondering what we should do. Aunt Penny ran in from the kitchen where she'd been making dinner. She took one look at our guilty faces before looking at the smashed vase and the grey ash covering the carpet, furniture, and curtains, not to mention me and Jan. We knew right then that we were in trouble, big trouble. We weren't supposed to be playing with the balls in the house, and now we had broken something—something that seemed to hold significance to Aunt Penny. She quickly checked us over to see if we had cut ourselves. Satisfied that we hadn't, she sat on the edge of the couch and began to cry.'

The people in the audience were enraptured with this story, there was almost total silence. *This is going well,* she thought to herself before carrying on with the tale.

'Jan and I just looked at each other; we didn't know what to do. Neither of us had ever seen Aunt Penny cry before. Eventually, we went to her, put our arms around her, and gave her a hug. I asked her why she was crying, and she told me that the cremated remains of her mother were in the vase that we had just broken, and we'd broken it by doing something that she had expressly asked us not to do. Now her mother's remains lay scattered all over the carpet. It broke my heart... Jan's too, I believe.'

She gestured towards Jan, who was holding a handkerchief to her eyes and nodding, obviously remembering the incident.

'From that day on, I decided that I never wanted to see Aunt Penny upset like that again, and I vowed never to break her heart like I'd done that day. Over the next few rainy days, me and Jan decided to go looking around all the other vases and ornaments around the house, and sure enough, we found the same grey ash in lots of them. Aunt Penny must have been a collector of her relative's remains. Anyway, about a year later, I came home early from school, and walking into one of the rooms, I could smell something funny. As I walked in, there was Aunt Penny on the telephone, smoking a cigarette and tipping the ash into one of the vases by the telephone table! When she saw me, a huge guilty smile spread across her face, and all she could do was shrug at me.'

Olivia sobbed as the congregation burst into laughter at the story. She had to pause and dry her eyes from the tears welling up inside them. She took a moment to compose herself before continuing.

'Her smile spread, and she told the person on the other end of the phone that she had to go. When she hung up, she looked at me. "The remains of your mother?" I asked her. "Your grandmother, and two of your aunts?" She just walked up to me and gave me a big hug.'

Olivia had to stop at that moment to regain her composure once again.

'She was laughing, that great big hearty laugh of hers, then she told me she had to tell me something that would stop me from breaking all of her stuff. I hugged her back, loving her mischievousness and her playful deviousness. From that day on, I never underestimated her, not one bit.'

Most of the congregation were laughing, some were crying too. The atmosphere had lifted considerably.

'So, this is how I remember her. She was there for me after the terrible accident that rendered me in the hospital and put my husband in a coma. She never once faltered in coming forward to offer advice, guidance, support, and of course, love. I'm here today, not to mourn the death of a frail old lady, but to celebrate the life and the strong, mighty force of a *truly* independent woman. My Aunt Penny!'

The congregation was on its feet. Everyone was laughing, smiling, clapping, and crying. The priest looked on a little astonished. He commented to Olivia later that he had never seen scenes like this at a funeral before. He had enjoyed it, a lot.

52.

WHEN THE SERVICE was over, a select few were invited back to the crematorium, while everyone else was directed to the hotel not far from the church. Olivia had paid for a finger buffet and a free bar for anyone who wanted to pay their respects.

The crematorium service was lovely. The crowd had dwindled to just twelve of the closest friends and relatives. The mood was sombre, and as Penny's coffin disappeared behind the red velvet curtain to the sound of Slim Whitman singing 'I'll Take You Home Again Cathleen,' once again there wasn't a dry eye in the room.

Jan and Katie escorted Olivia from the crematorium back to her car.

'That was the loveliest service I think I've ever witnessed,' Jan commented as they got in. 'Are we going straight back to the hotel?'

'You girls get yourselves back there. I need to go and visit Paul for a short while.'

They all agreed, and the rest of the journey passed in a reverent silence.

When they reached the hotel, the two girls got out. 'Are you sure you don't want us to come with you? You know, for moral support and stuff? You've been through a tough day,' Katie said, getting out.

Olivia smiled. 'No, I'm sure. Right now, I need an hour of solitude. I need to see Paul.'

Both girls were leaning into the car and holding her hands. 'OK,' Jan said. 'But you ring us if you want us to come and get you, OK?'

'I hear you. Now both of you go and enjoy that free bar.' Olivia smiled at them as she closed the door and asked the driver to take her to the hospital. As she drove off, Jan and Katie stood by the door and waved.

She waved back.

The hospital was just what she needed; she needed to get these tears out of her. Tears of frustration and grief. She'd felt like a phoney. All day she'd been thinking, 'Poor me. Why is this happening to me? Could anything else go wrong for me?' She had spent precious little time thinking about the triumphs of Penny's life, the people she had touched. She'd also spent a portion of the day thinking about why Paul wasn't here with her to hold her hand and guide her through the tough day. One quick flash of that lopsided smile of his and a quirky comeback or two at the right moment would have been enough to diffuse any sticky situation.

But there had only been her.

She held onto Paul's hand and allowed her tears to fall. She noted, with melancholy that as they landed on his wrist and fingers, there was absolutely no reaction. 'Oh, Paul,' she sobbed. 'Are you ever going to wake up?'

She stood and looked at him, really looked at him. For the first time since the accident, she noticed how emaciated his body had become. His face looked older; his hair had turned grey.

Is this still the man I married? It's been so long; I think I'm becoming confused. A thought occurred to her then, it was the worst thought she'd ever had in her entire life. The fact that she'd had it today disturbed her. *Am I beginning to resent Paul? Am I blaming him for being stuck in limbo?*

She didn't like where these thoughts were going, and she tried to cast them away, as if she'd never had them in the first place. But she couldn't. They lingered on in her subconscious, haunting her. As did Aunt Penny's last words.

'I want you to live for today. Live life like you want to live it. Don't hide away in the past, pining for me, or for Paul. Remember that life is what happens when you're busy making other plans.'

Crying again, she turned on her heels and left the hospital room. Away from the quiet, and away from the artificial breathing. Out of the dim lights and the smell of bed baths. Out into the corridor, right into the arms of Dr Hausen.

'Oh my, Mrs Martelle, where are you going in such a hurry?' he asked. The sight of him made her want to scream. She pushed him away and ran down the corridor towards the exit.

As soon as she was outside, she felt liberated. She bent over, resting her hands on her knees and gasping at the air. She could feel a panic attack was not too far away, either that or she was desperate for a drink.

She climbed back into her waiting car and instructed the driver to take her back to the hotel. 'There is an extra fifty in it for you if you don't mind breaking a few speed limits,' she said. The driver smiled at her in the mirror, gave a little salute, and put his foot down.

They were back at the hotel in half the time it took to get to the hospital. She thanked the driver, gave him his extra money, and entered the hall.

She'd forgot that she'd ordered a disco. It had been something that Aunt Penny had insisted on for years. 'I don't want any of that moping around at my funeral. Oh no, I want karaoke and dancing.

It's all about people enjoying themselves. Remember that, Olivia. Karaoke and dancing.'

Penny got her karaoke and her disco.

When Olivia arrived, there were already people up dancing to 'Dancing in the Street,' the David Bowie and Mick Jagger version, always a crowd pleaser.

Then the karaoke began. Olivia could tell the alcohol had been flowing and couldn't resist a smile at some of the songs. 'I Will Survive,' 'Bat Out of Hell,' 'Going Underground' to name a few. Aunt Penny would have loved it.

Everyone was glad to see her, and she was glad to see the bar. She must have shaken a thousand hands before she could finally utter those magic words.

'A large glass of rosé, please… with ice.'

53.

A FEW WINES later and Olivia was up dancing herself. All the girls had put a tribute on for their lost mother. They were all currently in a circle dancing, and crying, to Janet Jackson's 'Together Again.' Olivia's glass was empty; it was the first time it had been in that state all day. As the song finished, they all broke away, and she made her way over to the bar.

To the left by the exit, she could see Angela and Richard. They looked like they were fighting again. She casually made her way over to their side of the bar and did a little bit of eavesdropping.

'I don't believe you,' Angela hissed at her husband. 'I'm home for one night, a fucking funeral of all things, then another ten-hour flight back to America, and all you can think about is yourself. You are one selfish bastard, Richard.'

'I'm sorry, Angela, but I don't think it's selfish to want to have some kind of fucking relations with my own wife, who I haven't seen in over a week, by the way,' he retorted. Olivia was surprised to hear real venom in his voice.

'Why have I been away? Go on, tell me. Why, Richard? To make us some money, that's why. So, we can get out of that shitty granny flat, so maybe we can have a family.'

'Oh, don't start all that 'family' bullshit on me again, you're not my mother. You can't guilt me with that one. I just want some fucking *FUN,* Angela. You remember what that is, right?'

'Well if you want to have sex, then why don't you go and fuck Olivia, eh?'

Olivia reeled at hearing her name brought up in the argument. She raised her eyebrows and leaned onto the bar, getting comfortable for the long haul.

'What the hell are you talking about?'

'I've seen you looking at her, don't you think I haven't. I'm onto you.'

'You're crazy, Angela. You're living in cuckoo land; do you know that? You're fucking twisted in the head.' He tapped his temple to emphasise his point.

'Yeah, well, you're a prick. I'm off back to America, and you choose this time to start a fight?'

'No, Angela, you started this last night. All I wanted was a kiss, just some acknowledgement that I was there, you know, and what did I get? *I'm going to bed, big day tomorrow. Goodnight.*'

There was a quiet beep from outside, and the audible ticking over of a taxi engine.

'Right, well that ended well. I'll call you when I get back to Philly.' She stretched to give him a kiss on his cheek, but he turned his head away from her reach.

'Yeah, well have a safe flight.' Richard walked off in the direction of the gent's toilets. Angela collected her small flight bag, which she had left by the door. She gave a cursory glance in the direction her husband had walked off in, then lifted her head and walked out of the door.

54.

THE REST OF the party was great. The disco played on until midnight, which considering that they began at two that afternoon was a good stint. Olivia had paid for the bar all night; it was the least that she could do for all the people who'd turned up for Penny.

She, however, had not counted on drinking most of the bar tab herself. But this she did.

The whole drama of the last few months poured out of her. Penny, Paul, the wedding, the funeral, Angela... the lot.

She was rotten drunk.

As the evening came to a natural end and the taxis were called, Jan and Katie took Olivia to one side and sat her down at a table. Jan, a little worse for wear herself, went off to get them all drinks of water. As she returned, they sat down together. 'Ollie, will you be all right? Tonight, I mean. On your own.'

Olivia regarded her with a glazed look, then she smiled. She leaned in and gave Katie a huge kiss on the cheek, then on the forehead, and then on the other cheek. She then flung her arms around her and Jan, pulling them both in towards her. 'Do you know, you two? Eh? Do you know that you guys are my very best mates in the whole world? Did you know that?' she slurred. 'Listen to me,

I'm not just saying this. Seriously I'm not. I love you guys, and I don't care who knows it.' Olivia gestured towards the whole room, hiccupped, and then covered her mouth.

A man walked in the door and shouted, 'I've got a taxi outside here for a Miss Howarth... Howarth, anyone?'

Jan got to her feet. 'That's us, Ollie. Listen, come with us if you want. I don't know where we're going, but I bet it'll be good.' She giggled and nearly fell over. She would have if Richard hadn't swooped in and caught her from out of nowhere.

'Whoa... are you OK?' he asked, setting her straight.

Jan giggled and put her hands to her forehead in a theatrical gesture. 'I am now,' she slurred.

Richard blushed.

Katie stood up. 'Is it my turn for you to save *me* now?' she asked, fainting theatrically into his arms. Richard blushed again but caught Katie just before her pretend fall became a real one.

'My hero!' she sighed.

'Right.' Jan tried to focus on Olivia, missing ever so slightly. 'We're off now, you ring us first thing in the morning, or not, you know what I mean, and then we're all going for lunch, right, you two?' She widened her pointing arc to encompass Katie, who was still trying to untangle herself from Richard.

'What? Oh yeah, lunch,' Katie slurred. 'Come on, Jan, our taxi will be going in a min if we don't get a wiggle on.'

They both kissed Olivia and gave her a hug, then Katie kissed Richard, going just a little too far, and Olivia and Jan had to pull her off him.

'I'm OK, I'm OK!' she shouted as Jan dragged her towards the door. 'Call me tomorrow,' she shouted towards Olivia, and a little towards Richard.

Butterflies

Olivia watched them leave with a smile. Then she looked at Richard and raised her eyebrows. 'Looks like it's just you and me, kid,' she said. 'Shall we leave? My little white knight.'

'Yeah, the taxi's booked; it should be here soon. You need to get home and straight to bed,' he said with a bemused look.

'Ooh, is that an offer?' she laughed. 'If it is, then it's got to be the best one I've had in the last few months.'

Richard's mobile phone rang; it was the taxi company calling to say the taxi was outside. 'Come on, you, let's go.' He picked her up underneath her arms and stood her up. 'The taxi's here,' he said, pointing her in the direction of the front door.

'Well lead on, McDuff,' she slurred, and began walking. He walked behind her and slipped his arm through hers, making sure she didn't fall. She turned to him with drunken eyes and smiled; he smiled back. 'Do you know, you're the only person I have now who I can depend on?'

Richard blushed again.

'And I just love the way I can make you blush.' She turned away from him and concentrated on the taxi. They got there safely, and Olivia conked out as soon as she sat down.

Richard told the taxi driver the address, and they sped off.

'You do know if your girlfriend there throws up, you're gonna have to pay for it, don't you?'

'Yeah, she'll be OK,' he sighed. 'It's just been a tough day.'

~~~~

Back at the house, Richard had to drag Olivia out of the taxi. As he turned to pay the driver, she took the time, and opportunity, to complete the falling over that she had started about an hour earlier in the club.

'Whoa, you look like you got your hands full there, mate. I'd offer to help, but you know how it is.' The taxi driver proffered a shrug and drove off.

Richard turned to find Olivia laughing and rolling about on the grass outside the front door. He rubbed his forehead before beginning the process of coaxing her into the house. After a short while, he managed to get her upright and sensible. 'Right, we need to be quiet now, we're going into the house.'

'Shhhh!' She put her fingers to her mouth and tried to stand up straight. Richard had to help her do this, otherwise there would be a repeat of the rolling about from earlier.

'Richard,' she whispered loudly. 'Why are we being quiet?'

'Because it's late,' he replied.

'But there's no one in. Just me and you.'

He hadn't even thought about that. In his struggle to get Olivia into the house, he had completely forgot they'd been out for Penny's funeral. Angela would be languishing in an airport lounge right now, and Paul… well, Paul was in the hospital. He took the key out of Olivia's purse and opened the door. He then guided her in with his other hand on her back, frog-marching her into the house.

She heard the door close behind her and decided this was her cue to start undressing. Making her way up the stairs, she started to unzip the back of her dress, all the way down to the seam of her underwear. Richard was walking behind her, looking rather embarrassed. She reached to undo the clips in her hair, and she shook her head so her long brown hair cascaded down her back.

Suddenly, she stopped. Richard nearly bumped into her as she did. Grabbing hold of the bannister to steady herself, she lifted one foot and prised it out of its shoe. When it was free, she flung it down the stairs, barely missing Richard by inches. She then repeated the process with the other foot. This time he was ready for it and ducked well in advance, and it whistled safely over his head. She then resumed her climb.

Richard looked down the stairs at the discarded shoes lying at the bottom. He wondered at how much they must have cost her, remembering how fond of them she'd been all night. He looked up at the top of the stairs just in time to catch Olivia lift her dress high over her head and throw it onto the floor of the landing.

She had opted not to wear tights for today's funeral, as the weather had been quite warm, and had gone for black lacy French knickers, stockings, and a black bra. As she reached the top of her climb, she turned the corner towards her bedroom. He could see her arms wrap behind her back to unhook her bra. With a sigh, he watched her discard the bra to the floor just as her naked leg disappeared around the corner.

He had stopped halfway up the stairs.

His body was telling him to carry on, but his heart was telling him to stop. Even though he'd not drunk half as much as she had, he was still a little drunk, and he knew this situation could go horribly wrong.

That was until he heard the crash, a bang, and the tinkle of broken glass.

He ran up the remaining stairs two at a time, his heart pounding, wondering what had just happened. His head was filled with gruesome scenarios in the short time it took him to get to the bedroom. He half expected to see her lying in the middle of the room with a massive head wound and broken glass everywhere. He envisioned puddles of claret on the carpet, and a veritable fountain of the stuff pouring out of her.

He was relieved to find her sitting on the edge of her bed in her nightgown, completely blood free, but soaking wet all down her front. The smashed glass and pool of water around it gave an insight into what had just happened.

He couldn't help but steal a furtive glance as the wet fabric of her nightgown traced, and clung, to the curves of her breasts and her hardened nipples. Feeling slightly embarrassed for his lingering look, he busied himself collecting the larger shards of glass lying on the floor.

Olivia was sat on the edge of the bed, still holding the plastic bottle of water in her hand—she hadn't managed to drop that. The incident seemed to have sobered her up a little.

'What was the bang?' he asked as he went about his work.

Olivia smiled. 'I dropped the glass. I tried to catch it but banged my head on the chair.' She pointed to a chair in the corner of the room. It looked like a big heavy one, but she had somehow managed to knock it over onto its side.

'Are you OK? Have you cut yourself anywhere?' He walked over to her and removed the bottle from her hands. He sat next to her and put his hand around the back of her head.

'What are you doing?' Olivia asked through the hiccups she had just developed.

'Don't panic, I'm just checking for any bumps.' His hand slid through her hair. As they did, he felt a nasty little bump rising from the side of her head. 'There is it. I'm afraid, Olivia, that I'm going to have to keep you awake for at least another hour. Can't let you go to sleep with that.'

Suddenly, and surprisingly, she began to cry. Deep, loud sobs emanated from her as tears suddenly burst and began to stream down her face. She wrapped her arms around Richard's waist and began to cry into his stomach.

He was surprised, and a little disturbed, given the location of her face, but he lingered to offer her a reassuring hug. 'Hey, come on,' he whispered to her. 'Don't you think you've done enough of that today? And the last few months. Come on, you need to get out of that wet nightie and into something dry.'

He lifted her from the edge of the bed, into a wobbly standing position, and Olivia kissed him. It wasn't an ordinary kiss on the cheek, or even on the lips, of someone you know well; this was a full, mouth open, tongue in, kind of kiss.

~~~~

Richard jumped back from her with a jolt. She, however, had other ideas. Her head was whirling, she knew where she was, she knew who she was with, she knew how... wrong this was. But she was helpless to stop it.

Yes, she was drunk; yes, she was a little bit vulnerable; but she was firm in her conviction of what she was instigating. Regardless of the guilt, regardless of the consequences for tomorrow morning, what she wanted right now was to be held by someone, and that someone was Richard.

Undaunted by his jolt backwards, she pursued his mouth with hers. She was hungry; hungrier than she'd felt in months. She knew, however, that it wasn't food that would fill the void she was feeling.

Richard resisted her advances, pushing her away, but it dawned on her that he wasn't trying too hard. She advanced again. Her kisses, this time, were returned. Only tentatively at first, and then with increasing vigour. Olivia's eyes were closed, but her mind was very much open.

Is this wrong? Is this wrong? Oh... Oh, please tell me if this is wrong! The thought travelled around and around and around her head, while the kisses got stronger and stronger.

His tongue was probing her mouth deliciously. He was kissing her like a man who knew what he was doing, and was very good at it, but hadn't done it in a long while.

She was kissing him like a woman who knew it was wrong but could not stop herself from doing it anyway.

His hands were on her face, his fingertips tracing the delicate curves of her chin and cheeks. Wherever they went, they left behind traces of tingles, almost as if they had magic in them. She was longing for those magic fingers to make their way further down and quench her thirst, the longing that she had down there, but she couldn't rush this.

She was not going to rush him.

She did make the second move, though. Her hands moved down, from around his neck, and spread across his broad shoulders. As they did, his breathing became rapid. She knew he was enjoying this just as much as she was.

Her hands came around to his chest, finding the seam were the buttons were located on his shirt; she pulled at it. The sound of the fabric tearing and the *pop! pop! pop!* of the buttons pulling away made her giggle.

Richard pulled away from the kiss. 'Are you sure?' he whispered. 'Are you perfectly sure you want to do this?'

Olivia raised her hand to cover her mouth, her eyes were holding his. 'Yes, I am,' she whispered.

That was all he needed, and before she knew it, he was kissing her again. He kissed her lips, her cheeks, her forehead, and her neck. He pushed her back on the bed. She went without any hesitation. One part wanted to delight in the kisses on her skin, another part wanted to give him access to more of her.

She was wet now, and not just from the water on her nightgown. As his fingers trailed behind his kisses, she felt the heat beginning to swell in her stomach. It was a heat she'd known very well not so long ago, but one that had since been denied to her.

She'd missed it.

Bring on the butterflies, she thought.

Richard was on top of her, still kissing her neck. She had a feeling that he was maybe a little too shy to take the next step.

So, once again, she made the first move.

She slid her hands inside his torn shirt, over his shoulders, and removed it from his back. He lifted his arms to take the sleeves off, and she could see the power in them. When the shirt was off, she marvelled at his physique. Sure, she had seen him with no top on many times, but never this close, never this… intimate.

As he leaned in to resume his kisses, she decided that enough was enough. She rubbed her hand up his thigh and stopped when she reached the enormous muscle between his legs.

She almost gasped as she wrapped her hand around it through his trousers. She couldn't tell if it felt like the biggest one she'd ever felt, or if she was just imagining it because it had been so long since she'd had hold of one. Either way, she wanted it out of its confines, now.

Richard gasped, and she felt him move away from her slightly. Inwardly, she smiled. *I think he nearly came then,* she thought, slyly marvelling at the effect she had over this mountain of a man.

Before she knew it, she was fumbling at his trousers, and he was leaning in, kissing her. This time, the caresses were light, but with more passion than she could have imagined him ever possessing.

When she finally had his belt and button undone, she giggled as the sheer weight of what was inside caused his zip to undo of its own accord. Hungrily, she grabbed at it. She wanted to marvel in the size of his manhood. Once it was freed of its prison, she knew instantly that it *was* the biggest one she had ever seen.

This excited her even more, and the butterflies in her stomach intensified their flutters. The liquidity of their wings spread all the way through her, preparing her for this next, huge in every way, adventure.

His magic fingers had moved to her breasts. Her nipples, already hard and sensitive from the water on her nightgown, were throbbing at his touch. What was that he was doing? How could his fingers make her skin feel so... so, tingly? Whatever he was doing was working, and her nipples were poking through her wet nightgown. She was almost praying for him to grab them in those strong fingers. She wanted him to pinch them, to twist them. She needed a small amount of pain to reduce the sensitivity that their throbbing had caused.

It was his mouth that made it to them first.

He kissed and bit them playfully. She could feel his frustration as the fabric of her nightgown came between her skin and his tongue.

'Rip it off me,' she gasped.

He didn't need telling twice!

His powerful hands were at the neckline of the nightgown, and she felt his strength as he pulled the fabric apart, effortlessly, almost as if it was a paper bag. She felt the tear and the rush of warm air over her wet body as he continued to rip the gown down the middle. The sheer exhilaration of having her clothes, literally, torn from her body sent tingles across her skin, causing her butterflies to beat even faster.

Her own hands moved up her body, feeling the goose-bumps on her stomach as the warm air caressed the moistness of her skin where the wet nightgown had previously been.

Her hands finally made it to her breasts. Her own fingers caressed her throbbing nipples. She had no choice than to tweak them herself, she needed to release the pressure building up inside. As she took one between her forefinger and thumb, Richard's eyes widened. She looked at him, surprised to see his reaction as he drank in every minute detail of what she was doing.

He groaned and swore under his breath.

Absently, she wondered if he'd ever watched Angela pleasure herself in front of him like that, then quickly cast the thought from her mind. If he liked her playing with her nipples, she wondered what he would do if she began to pleasure herself another way. She wondered if this might be too much for him. She decided she wanted to test her theory.

She traced her fingers around his cheeks and then across his lips. He parted them, and slowly, she inserted two of her fingers into his mouth. His tongue wrapped around them, wetting them. She removed her glistening digits and placed her other hand on his muscular chest, gently pushing him back into an upright position.

As she did, she marvelled once again at his enormous manhood. It might have been ten inches in length. It scared her a little, but in a good way.

Her moistened fingers traced their way down her stomach towards the black lace of her French knickers. They slid beneath the elastic waistband before finally reaching their destination. When they did, she found that there wasn't any need for them to be moistened anyway.

She noticed Richard couldn't look away from what she was doing.

This fascinated her.

She expected her butterflies would make an appearance anytime soon. She held her breath in anticipation.

All the disappointment was blown away as she looked up at him, kneeling above her, mesmerised by every visual treat of her pleasuring herself. His more than obvious excitement at what she was doing turned her legs to jelly, and she had the overwhelming desire to have him, all of him, inside her. *If he'll fit,* she panted.

His puppy dog eyes were looking down at her, and she knew, deep inside, that anything she asked of him right now he would gladly, willingly, do.

'I want you inside of me. I need you to fuck me,' she whispered. She felt his body relax ever so slightly as she slipped her hands around the back of her underwear and pulled them down over her legs.

He climbed off the bed, kicked off his shoes, and slipped off his trousers in almost record time. Olivia lay back on the bed, offering herself to him.

'Come here,' she whispered.

He did.

He mounted the bed; his bulk made the mattress buck and roll as if they were on a ship at sea. She felt his muscular arms leaning next to her head as he held his position over her, and the buffeting stopped momentarily.

Her butterflies raced and danced inside her, tickling the places that needed to be tickled. The anticipation of what was about to happen was all consuming, she could think of nowhere else in the whole world she would rather be right now.

It's been TOO long... too fucking long!

As he began to push himself into her, it became obvious that he was just too large for her to accommodate all at once, and just as it was all about to go wrong, something delicious happened.

She felt his head in-between her thighs. She opened them a little wider, giving him her permission. With no pretence, he began to moisten her more than she already was. The tremors that ripped through her body were amazing, like electricity, causing little shocks to buzz through her with every thrust of his tongue, every caress of his lips.

Suddenly, he pulled away, and she felt the loss almost instantly. 'Don't stop,' she gasped.

'I've got no intention of stopping,' he whispered. 'I just think it's time we did this properly.'

Olivia felt his arms back either side of her head. She felt the heat of him hovering over her. This time she knew she was ready, and she angled herself to accommodate his size. The excitement of the moment, coupled with the expectation, made her heart beat faster—she could feel its rhythm in her throat.

She braced herself for his thrust, but he surprised her by lightly easing himself instead. As he entered her, she lost her breath. Aware now that she hadn't breathed for a few moments, she exhaled, and the involuntary action of her hips allowed him to slip another inch or so deeper. Not knowing if she could, or even should, take anymore of him, he twisted his body in a slow arc over her.

He was smiling a devil's grin as he looked down on her from his elevated position. 'Olivia,' he whispered. 'Are you OK? Your face is bright red.'

She tried to speak, but all that came out was a hoarse whisper. 'I'm fine,' she croaked, sucking in a deep breath. 'Just carry on.'

Oh fuck, she thought. *I'm not going to be able to walk in the morning.*

Rough hands grabbed at her shoulders, and she allowed herself to be turned over onto her stomach. He guided her to the edge of the bed, so her stomach was supported by the mattress. He gently, but firmly, took her by the waist and guided her body into a position that she was not completely used to. He pushed her upper body down onto the bed and raised her bottom, then shifted her a little to the left.

'I don't want to hurt you,' he whispered into her ear.

She was too lost in her abandon to care.

This time, there was barely any resistance at all. Her body knew what was coming and it was ready for it. His thrusts were so light it was almost a rocking sensation. This, she was glad of, as she believed that he may well have done her some internal damage if he'd gone for the full thrust.

Her eyes closed, the familiar feeling in her feet began. The tingling of her toes, spreading up through her legs, widening its heat throughout her body.

Butterflies, she thought.

This would be her first orgasm, the first one not of her own doing, for God only knew how long, and what a fantastic way to get it.

His breathing had sped up. There was an inhale for every inward thrust, and an exhale for every outward one. He was getting faster; she was getting closer.

Her orgasm began in her lower belly and rushed through her limbs, her torso, her head!

She felt Richard pull out of her, and she could feel, and hear, the result of his orgasm.

The effect was everything she had wished for.

55.

SHE WAS WIDE awake; despite the physical exertions she had just endured and all the drink she had consumed earlier in the day. Richard's heavily muscled body was lying next to her, snoring lightly, as they both lay on the bed.

Olivia picked up his arm and moved it from around her. She edged out of his embrace, slowly laying his arm back onto the duvet before sitting up. She looked down at the sleeping man. The sudden realisation that she'd just had sex with her brother-in-law caused her to stand up, collect her robe from off the back of the door, and exit the room as quickly as she could. She entered the bathroom at the end of the landing, slamming the door closed and locking it.

Sitting on the edge of the bath, she thought her tears would be close, but surprisingly, they didn't come. The whole emotional side—the whole guilty side—that she'd been feeling seconds before was gone. Replaced with a strange realisation.

Putting her rational head on and ignoring the guilt, and possible ramifications, of her actions this evening, she thought about the sex, or more importantly, about the lack of something within the sex.

Yes, Richard had been tender, as tender as someone with so large an... *appendage* could have been. And yes, she had made all the moves.

The physical act had been amazing... So, what was it that had been missing?

She didn't kid herself that it was the 'love' aspect that was absent. She knew it wasn't love, just lust and a physical needing on both sides. 'So, what was it?' she asked aloud. Her voice sounded like she'd shouted through a megaphone through the silence of the bathroom.

A noise beyond the door made her heart begin to beat faster. Thankfully, it passed the bathroom, travelled down the stairs, closing the back door behind it.

She said a silent prayer of thanks to whoever was the patron saint of adulterous women that she didn't have to engage with him again tonight.

She didn't think she could look him in the face again.

'Oh fuck, fuck, fuck...' she scolded herself. 'Why do I get myself into these situations?'

She turned the shower on and waited for the room to get misty before putting a menthol scent on the showerhead and breathing in the steam. It helped to clear her fuzzy head. She removed her robe and stepped into the shower. The hot water coursed down her aching body, making her feel alive again.

For almost ten minutes, she stood in the shower—it was as if she was trying to cleanse herself of the sin she'd just committed.

The answer to her question came to her completely by surprise, and she shouted out, 'Butterflies! *That's* what was missing.'

She turned off the shower and towelled herself dry. As she dried the top of her legs, she winced. She was more than a bit tender there from the workout she'd just had. She dressed herself in a clean nightdress, sighing as the material caressed her body. Now the water and steam had gone, the alcohol in her system reinforced itself and she felt sleepy again.

She went back to her, now empty, room and flopped onto the bed with an enormous sigh. As she lay with her head on her pillow, she closed her eyes. *It was fantastic sex, no doubt about that, but the butterflies didn't soar.*

That was her last thought before a deep and dreamless sleep took her away for a few hours.

56.

THE NEXT DAY was bright and sunny, a gorgeous October morning. The sun was streaming through the windows in glorious shafts of bright light. Inside the shafts, millions of small dust motes performed their tireless dance within the gentle and invisible eddies in the air.

All of this was annoying Olivia considerably, as one such shaft was shining right on her face. She turned over in bed to avoid it, but the light was just too bright.

Her head was throbbing from the alcohol.

As she lifted it off the pillow, she felt the horrible, yet familiar, feeling of her brain following roughly half a second later. 'Oh, for fuck's sake,' she shouted at no one in particular, which was good because there was no one there to shout it at. She grabbed the pillow and stuffed it over her head. That was no use either, she could never sleep with anything on her face. She put her head underneath her blankets, but it was just too hot and stuffy. There was only one thing for it, she was going to have to get up and close the curtains.

She kicked her blankets off and felt an agonising pain rip through her abdominal area and reach all the way through her crotch and down the back of her thighs. It took a minute or two to realise what it was. Her *exercise* last night.

Oh great, she thought as she tried to sit up. It felt like she had either broken the world record for sit ups or had been in the ring with a heavyweight boxer. *This is not good.* She struggled out of the bed and waddled over to the curtains. *Is this for real?* she thought, trying to put her legs back together and realising she couldn't. 'I can't go through the day walking like I've just ridden a Grand National winner,' she groaned.

With the curtains closed, she returned to bed. A couple of seconds later, after her brain had caught back up with her, she fell back asleep.

~~~

She awoke around mid-day, feeling groggy, tired, and sore. The guilt that was so glaringly absent last night had returned from its holiday and was refreshed and ready for business.

How could I have been so stupid? she thought. *At Penny's funeral too!*

When she was younger and just starting out in the world of drinking and nightclubs, Olivia, Jan, and Katie used to call this kind of guilt *a cornflake head*. The reasoning behind it was that you always got the flashback of the embarrassing things you did while sitting eating your cornflakes the next morning. Olivia was having the mother of all cornflake heads right now.

She decided that she needed to go downstairs and get something to eat. She only got as far as outside her room when she was confronted with the first insult from last night: her discarded bra. It looked at her accusingly. Olivia looked back at it guiltily. She decided to brave the stairs. Her black designer dress lay crumpled halfway up, and she cringed as she passed, trying not to look at it.

There was more humiliation when she got to the hall and found one shoe by the front door and the another lying underneath the occasional table against the wall. She sighed as she crept past them and into the kitchen.

The kettle was still warm, so was the grill. Richard had been here, and not so long ago by the looks of things. She hobbled over to the fridge and opened it. She stared absently into it for almost a full minute before reaching in and grabbing milk and bacon. As she closed it, she jumped, very nearly dropping her items. Richard had chosen that moment to walk into the kitchen.

He was up and dressed, almost as if he was on his way out of the house for the day. As he saw her, he stopped. She was standing with milk in one hand and bacon in the other, not knowing what to do. They both stared at each other for the whole duration of the awkward moment. Both looking vacant, both looking guilty, and both looking slightly rough too.

Olivia watched as his eyes went from hers, down to her breasts, then she realized that she had erect nipples poking through the nylon of her nightdress from the open fridge.

You bastard, she thought, moving her arms up to hide them from his gaze before realizing the futility of it. As she remembered where his head had been last night, she decided erect nipples were the least of her worries.

'Um, mornin'' he said tentatively. 'Did you... sleep all right?'

'Oh, yeah. Like a baby. I always do after... err, after I've had a drink,' she laughed. It was a totally forced laugh, and it sounded that way.

'I was just...' they both said at the same time.

'Oh great, well I think I should...' he continued.

Butterflies

They both remained, just looking at each other. Somebody should have laughed, if only to have diffused the situation, but neither of them did.

She lowered her head and walked past him towards the stairs, cursing her abdomen for hurting so much. As she waddled comically, almost penguin like, out of the kitchen, she could feel his gaze burning into the back of her neck.

Halfway up the stairs, she realized that she was still holding the milk and the bacon. She carried on regardless, slamming her bedroom door behind her.

~~~

'Shit, fuck, shitty shit, shit!' she screamed as she stood with her back to the closed door, still holding her refrigerated items. *What the hell am I going to do? I can't live with him here now. What happens when Angela...* She didn't finish the thought. Sliding down the door onto her haunches, she put the milk and bacon down and her head into her hands. *What happens when PAUL comes back?*

She banged her head against the door. The thought of Paul and what she had done behind his back sickened her. It brought back fresh tears.

The bang of the front door snapped her out of her internal melee. Then the gunning of the engine of Richard's car on the driveway brought almost sweet relief to her. At least now she'd have some time to think about a strategy to survive the situation.

A quick jump into the shower, she thought, *to liven myself up, and just maybe forget this stupidity for a short while.*

Putting the milk and bacon aside, she made it to the bathroom and turned the shower on. The steam coming from the hot water brought her another wave of relief. As she stretched her leg to step up into the shower, it all came flooding back to her. The lactic acid buildup in her thigh muscles screamed at her, as did the small of her back. *OK, forget the shower I think it's time to run myself a bath.*

She ran the bath and poured enough bubbles in there to sink a small luxury liner.

When it was full to her limit, she removed her robe, braved the pain stepping over the side, and sighed as she eased herself in. The heat was glorious as it lapped at her tender parts, caressing the pains away. Her thigh muscles relaxed, her lower back relaxed, and the area that had been assaulted and stretched so much last night?

That relaxed too.

She lay back and enjoyed the, much needed, peace and serenity.

57.

OVER THE NEXT few days, Olivia and Richard danced a merry dance of avoidance around each other. The prelude to the dance would begin by listening out for each other's movements. A casual observer would be highly amused to see the lengths they would both go to avoid bumping into the other.

If Richard was in the kitchen and Olivia was wanting to go in, then it wouldn't be unusual to see her crouching behind one of the couches in the living area. If Olivia was in the living room watching the television, then Richard would climb over the fence into the back garden to get to the flat at the end of the garden, rather than open the front door and go through the house. If they both needed to leave at the same time, either one of them could be seen rushing like an Olympic sprinter to get to their car, as if they had an important meeting and were late, when in fact, neither of them really had anywhere important to go to.

Things settled into an unsettling routine.

Then Angela came home!

58.

OLIVIA WAS AT the hospital visiting Paul. These normally reflective periods had changed lately. She felt that the doctors and nurses were almost avoiding her direct questions. 'Is there any progress at all?' she asked a substitute doctor, Dr Rose, as Dr Hausen had taken leave to go home and see his family.

'Well, I'll be honest with you, Mrs Martelle, Mr Martelle seems to be stuck in a status quo. The good news is that he's not deteriorating, but over the last few weeks, we've not seen anything that would lead us to believe that he'll be coming out of this coma any time soon.'

Although she appreciated the honesty, it was not the news that she'd wanted to hear. 'What are you saying, Doctor? That he may be stuck like this for a while yet?'

'It's difficult to say. He's not responding to any stimulus we introduce. The only thing we know is that his brain swelling has receded and it is back to its normal size. We'll be looking into the issue of bruising; we may well also look into electric shock treatment.'

Olivia reeled at this. 'What treatment?'

'Electric shock treatment. Don't worry, we're not in the dark ages now, Mrs Martelle. It simply means that we put electrodes along his spinal column and make a small incision into the back of his head. We then treat him with a series of electric jolts. It's quite painless. It's designed to kick start his brain functions.'

'Oh, thank God for that,' Olivia replied, fanning herself with a magazine she had been reading. 'When you said electric shock, I envisioned all sorts of things. Is this therapy different than the one you wanted to do a few weeks back?'

'It's nowhere near as harsh as that, and it's far too late in the day to start that off now anyway. If we get your permission, we can look to begin this as soon as Monday morning. Would we have your permission for this procedure, Mrs Martelle? We already have Mrs Grantham's.'

Olivia pulled a face. 'Whose?'

'Mrs Grantham's, Mr Martelle's sister.' The doctor looked a little sheepish now, like he'd put his foot in his mouth and began to chow down.

'Why would you need her permission? And *how* did you get her permission? She's currently in the USA on a prolonged business trip.'

The doctor looked like he wanted to be somewhere, anywhere else right now. 'Err, no, she isn't, Mrs Martelle. She came home last night. She was here until gone ten o'clock. She also had papers to show that you'd given her power of attorney over yours and Mr Martelle's estate.'

'Our estate? No, you must be mistaken, Doctor, she has power over the business dealings but nothing to do with our estate.'

'Right, well you might want to have that conversation with her. I'm no legal genius, but the papers did look legitimate.'

59.

WHEN OLIVIA ARRIVED home, she noticed a brand-new Porsche 911 on the driveway. This built quite a bit of kindling under the fury-fire that was already roaring inside her. She slammed the door of her BMW and stormed into the house. 'Angela... Angela, are you here?' she shouted.

Angela was home. She was in the kitchen, at the island sipping a large cup of tea. Richard was sat next to her, looking sheepishly towards Olivia as she bounded in. The first thing she noticed was that Angela looked good. She'd had her hair tinted; it now had blonde highlights and had been styled. It was quite a change from the tight ponytail she usually sported. She'd lost weight too, and gained some in the right places, obviously from gym use while away. And she had a tan. Angela had always been more than a little pasty; she had never worn makeup, that Olivia could remember, but today... full facial.

'Hi, Olivia, how's things?' she beamed as Olivia walked in.

Olivia also noticed her, and Richard, were holding hands too.

'Don't give me that *hi, how are you* crap, Angela.' Olivia was furious now, not only because of the legal papers, but because Angela now looked so fucking good. *You cow,* she thought, before continuing. 'What's all this power of attorney thing, Angela? You don't have power of attorney over our estate. I gave you control over the business dealings, and that's all.'

Angela smiled. There was precious little humour in it. 'I don't have power of attorney over your estate, Olivia. What I do have, as you quite rightly just pointed out, is power over the business assets. The business is called Paul Martelle Consulting; therefore, Paul Martelle is a business asset, and I have a certain say over what treatment he does or doesn't get.'

'No, no you don't. He's my husband, you have no legal holding over him.'

'I think you'll find that I do. You signed all control of the business over to me, so I no longer work for you.'

Olivia stormed towards her and was glad to see a little of her cockiness flinch away, and that she was no longer holding Richard's hand.

'You know I'm going to contest this, as I have an inkling that you're wrong, and even if you are right, the hospital should have notified me of any changes. What's wrong with you, Angela? Why are you so adamant to get control of Paul?'

'I'm not, I'm just a concerned sister. I'm not trying to take anything away from you. I wish you would stop fighting me on this.'

She slammed her hand on the kitchen island and stormed out.

As she walked away, Angela shouted, 'Oh and by the way, it's good news from Philly. We got the contract. As of next week, Paul Martelle Consulting will be trading in the American markets. We'll need to have a meeting to discuss this.'

As Olivia was walking away, she raised her middle finger. 'Discuss this, bitch!' she snarled.

60.

THE VERY NEXT day, the first thing Olivia did was call up her solicitors. She needed to know what rights Angela had. She got an appointment to see Miss Rathbone that afternoon. Until then, she'd just have to do her best to avoid the happy couple all together, both of them. Wishing she had the counsel of the one person who could always give her the right advice, Aunt Penny, she decided to go shopping.

She checked off her schedule mentally. At twelve, meet Jan for lunch, one-thirty, shop, shop, shop! Four o'clock; solicitors. Five-thirty; evict Angela and her husband. It seemed like her day was rather full.

She hopped into her BMW and drove into town.

The traffic was horrendous, and she was stuck at roadworks. This gave her time to think dangerous thoughts. *You know what?* she thought in a particularly spiteful moment. *I'm glad I fucked her husband!*

She instantly regretted it, and her mind took her to Paul's hospital room. She winced at the vision. Banging her hand on the driving wheel in frustration, she forgot that the horn was placed in the centre of it. The short little blast caught the attention of nearly everyone around her in the queue, including the two burly workmen who were busy digging up the road. They looked up at her, smiled, and waved.

She put her head down and willed the cars to begin moving along.

They didn't.

'All right, missus, if you wanted a date, you could have just asked,' one of the men shouted to her; the other just laughed.

Olivia got her mobile phone out of the holder and pretended to talk on it just so they would leave her alone. Finally, the traffic started up again. She had never been so relieved to drive in her entire life. As she drove away, she looked in her rear-view mirror to see the two men shouting for her to come back.

By the time she got to meet Jan, she was a nervous wreck.

'Jesus, Ollie, what's the matter with you?' Jan asked as her friend entered the wine bar. 'You look like you've just seen a ghost.'

'Oh, Jan, I've just had the worst week, ever. Well, since Penny's funeral anyway.'

'You hang onto that thought, girlfriend. I'll get us both a cup of tea.'

'Thanks. I'll have an Earl Grey.'

She came back a few minutes later with two large cups and one even larger teapot with a label sticking out of the top of it. 'Right, tell me all about it, Ollie. I'm all ears.'

'I slept with Richard!' Olivia burst out.

Jan never missed a beat. 'Hang on a minute will you,' she said. Standing up, she walked away from the table, leaving Olivia looking confused, and a little angry too.

I just told her my most intimate secret and she left, just like that.

About two minutes later, she returned with two large glasses and a bottle of rosé wine. She removed the pot of tea and the cups to the next table and then sat back down. 'Right, what were you saying about Richard?'

Olivia spilled the lot, right down to the size of his manhood and the fact that it took her nearly three days to walk properly again.

'I can't believe you,' Jan said as she finished off her second, large glass.

Olivia drained her glass and looked at her friend—her brow was ruffled, and her eyes looked hurt. 'Do you think I'm a heartless slut?' she asked, as more tears welled in her eyes.

Jan frowned. 'No way, I think you're one lucky fucking bitch. Ten inches? Jesus, Ollie. It's a wonder you can walk even now.'

During a break in their laughter and whispering, they ordered another bottle of wine. Olivia then remembered that she had a meeting with the solicitor.

'Oh, just cancel, they aren't going to bill you. You're probably their biggest client anyway. Sort it out for another day. I want to hear more about Mr Big Dick!'

'There isn't any more, honest. Angela came home from America yesterday and started off on the heavy about Paul being an asset of the firm's and as such, she has power of attorney over his medical treatment.'

'She's just trying it on,' Jan reassured her. 'Are you forgetting I know a little about the law?'

Olivia laughed out loud, a little too loud for the time of day, but not loud enough for the two large glasses of wine that they had drunk in the last... what? Olivia looked at her watch. Two hours had passed. She did feel loads better after her talk. Jan was a solicitor who specialized in business law, but they had always insisted that friends and business don't mix.

Olivia's phone beeped. She picked it up and grimaced at the name on the front.

Butterflies

'Who is it?' Jan asked. 'Bitch tits?'

'Yeah,' Olivia replied with a grimace, confirming it was Angela.

'What does she want? Blood?' Jan asked, trying to pull a vampire face. They both laughed again, drawing more disapproving looks from the 'Ladies What Lunch' brigade sitting opposite them.

'Go and get another bottle while I read it,' Olivia ordered.

As Jan came back with another bottle of the same wine, she saw that Olivia's expression had turned from dour to almost sunny. 'What are you smiling about? You look like you just got some good news,' she said, putting the wine on the table.

Olivia smiled. 'Angela has to go to Glasgow for four days and wanted to know if we could put off our meeting until then.'

'Great news, that'll give us time for me to look over the papers concerning her role in the company and what sort of legalities she holds over Paul. It also means that we don't have to hurry back home.'

The girls clinked their glasses together and both took large swigs.

61.

A FEW HOURS later and a good few glasses of wine, the friends separated, and Olivia took a taxi home. She'd have to worry about getting her car sometime tomorrow, and maybe think about that shopping trip at another time too.

She paid the driver, got out of the taxi, and looked at her house. It was a nice house with a bit of land. The drive was spacious and private with a lot of landscaping done to it. All her windows, and there were quite a few of them, were dark. *Of course, they are,* she said to herself. *You live alone now, Ollie.* With this melancholic thought running through her head, she opened the front door and entered.

There was a noise coming from the living room, and a glowing flickering light told her that the TV was on in there. 'Hello?' she shouted as she dropped her bag onto the hall floor. 'Hello! Richard, is that you?'

Richard appeared in the doorway, he was wearing a pair of shorts and a t-shirt, holding a bowl of ice cream. 'Oh, Olivia, I'm sorry I didn't think you'd be back anytime soon.'

Butterflies

She looked at him, offered a fuzzy smile. Just him being here in her house, eating her ice cream in those shorts... *Oh no*, she thought through her wine addled brain. *Not again.*

Before she knew what she was doing, she walked over to him, leaned up onto her tiptoes, and kissed him. It gave her a strange sensation, deep in her belly, where she knew her butterflies lived.

She willed them to fly.

As she kissed him, she brushed one of her jeans-clad thighs against the front of his shorts and was not disappointed at what she felt there.

It was like an iron bar.

Richard was kissing her back now, with surprising passion, while still holding his bowl of ice cream. She could feel the cold of his tongue exploring her warm mouth. She could taste the sweetness of the vanilla ice cream he had been eating.

Her hands moved from his face and traced their way across his torso, enjoying all the muscles from his shoulders, to his pectorals, to his abs. Still her hand continued to move downward, until it found its intended destination.

The feel of him through his shorts filled her with a desire she had not felt for months. Sure, she and Richard had sex about a week ago, but that had been more to do with grief.

This was drunken lust.

He took in a lung full of air as she wrapped her fingers around his bulge. It felt good; she loved having this level of control over him— well, over anyone really. Knowing that with just a kiss, she could get a man like Richard hard.

That was real power.

She pulled away from the kiss, still with him gripped firmly in her hand, and looked at his face. He looked in shock. His eyes were wide, as if this was all going to be some elaborate joke and she was going to pull away from him any moment.

I'm not going to pull away from him, she thought. *I'm going to do something, though, something stupid. Something I've never even thought of doing before.*

She took the bowl of ice cream from him. *Good,* she thought. *Nice and sloppy, but still cold.* She took a great big spoonful of the desert into her mouth, then she dropped onto her knees in front of him.

Putting the bowl down on the floor, she hurriedly went to work on the front of his shorts. It was hard to pull them down in one movement, mostly due to the sheer size of his manhood.

Finally, she managed, and the monster that he had been hiding sprung out at her. She was sure that if it had hit her, it would have left a bruise. *Imagine trying to explain a massive, cock shaped bruise on my face,* she laughed to herself, as she grabbed at him.

At this point, she realised that she had miscalculated something. In order to get this thing into her mouth, she was going to have to open it wider than she had ever before, therefore spilling the ice cream. *Ah, fuck it,* she thought, and continued with her naughty idea.

He flinched as his member entered her freezing mouth, but it soon warmed up.

'Come up here,' he whispered after a while, as his strong arms slipped underneath her armpits and lifted her off the floor. They stood, looking at each other. 'Do we really want to do this? Again?' he asked.

Until that moment, she hadn't thought about it, she had been acting on pure drunken impulse; but now that the question was out in the open, hanging in the ether between them, she gave it some serious, or semi-serious—due to the copious amount of wine she had consumed—thought.

Butterflies

Eventually, she came to a conclusion.

'Oh fuck, yes. Let's do it.'

Richard smiled and swept her into his arms.

For some reason unbeknown to either of them, they ended up in the kitchen. Richard deposited her on top of the kitchen island, and she wrapped her arms around his neck as they kissed. It was a fast, furious, and lustful kiss. One that said, 'I want to fuck your brains out,' rather than saying, 'Oh please come over here and make sweet love to me.'

This was fine with her. She wanted—no, needed—to get her brains fucked out.

Richard fumbled with the buttons on her shirt. He was messing it up quite a bit, so Olivia decided she'd repeat the favour she'd done to him last week. She pushed him away and ripped the front of her shirt right open. The buttons went everywhere, but it was worth it just to see how his face brightened, either from the ripping or the exposing of her black lacy bra. Either way, she didn't care.

She put both her hands up to the centre of her bra and unhooked it. As she did, she felt both the cold air of the kitchen and the intense heat of Richards gaze on her at the same time. She could never fathom men's obsessions with boobs, but she wasn't going to start analysing it now, she was just going to enjoy it. Shrugging off the remains of her shirt and bra, she began to work on her boots. Richard had begun to remove his t-shirt, having already lost his shorts in the hallway.

As his t-shirt stuck over his head in his haste to remove it, she took a moment to appreciate him. He was truly an Adonis. He was deeply muscled, although she'd never really seen him work out, and he was tanned. She put both of these down to the fact he was a gardener by trade. But the most remarkable thing about him was his huge, thick…

She never got to finish her train of thought, as he lowered her down on the island in the centre of the kitchen. He clawed at her jeans, pulling them off, taking her panties with them in his haste.

Why the hell did I wear Winnie the Pooh socks under my boots? she thought.

Richard's head was between her legs, doing what he needed to do last time, something that she enjoyed very much, *maybe too much?* the pragmatic side of her thought. It was only a quiet voice right now, but no doubt it would be in full tenor mode tomorrow morning.

In one movement, Richard hopped onto the island and rotated her. He now lay on top of her with his whole body in-between her legs.

Olivia was shocked at his swift movements but was too excited at the thought of him inside her again to care. Gently, he pushed himself inside her. Her fingernails sunk into the flesh of his thick arms as she raised her head and bit him lightly on the shoulder.

After a few moments of tenderness, he lifted her, effortlessly, and brought her around to straddle him. Very slowly, and very deliberately, he lowered her down onto him. He guided her, allowing her to accommodate his width. It was obvious that he'd done this before.

He was so gentle and so thoughtful.

He rocked her lightly again, like last time. She honestly believed if he decided to thrust into her hard and fast, she wouldn't survive intact. He really was that big.

She could feel butterflies stirring inside her; she knew that they were the large blue ones with the fantastic, fluttering wings.

He continued to rock back and forth. Her nipples were rubbing against his chin, his neck, and occasionally, his lips and tongue. Her orgasm was close, but for some reason, she didn't want to risk it with him inside her. She was scared that if she came—and she felt like it was going to be a big one—with that thing inside her, she might tear something.

But for now, she was content just to rock.

She was desperate to come; she needed her butterflies to fly. *No,* she thought again, *I need them to soar.*

Richard continued to fuck her, or more accurately, rock her. She felt like she was going to come. For some reason, she knew that there was not going to be a chorus of butterflies, but the orgasm was rising anyway. *Are they shy?* she thought. They certainly seemed shy; maybe they feared the huge thing inside her?

Her stomach flipped. Her skin tingled. Her nipples stiffened to the point of being sore.

She was on the precipice. *Just hang on Richard... One more thrust...*

Then it was there. Her senses heightened and a delicious shiver coursed through her entire body. It shook her like a lightning bolt. The effects were visible all over her body as goose-bumps raised on every inch of her exposed flesh. She felt like someone was twisting at her nipples as their sensitivity rocketed.

She couldn't help herself from shouting, moaning aloud.

All of this was too much for him, and with an almighty yell—or was it a roar—Richard came too.

Then, almost as quickly as it came, it passed.

She was out of breath, and so was he. That whole few minutes had been an emotional rollercoaster for her. She did something then, something she thought she'd never, ever do again. She wrapped her arms around his shoulders and kissed him.

62.

THE NEXT FEW days flew by. Olivia spent them in one of two places: she was either found in the hospital at Paul's bedside being the dutiful wife to the stricken husband, or at home being the slutty mistress to her well-hung brother-in-law.

The sex was fantastic; the more they did it, the better it got. It seemed her body had grown to accommodate Richard's size and was becoming accustomed to it. She was glad about this, but the guilt was killing her. She could tell it was affecting Richard too.

Tonight, they had decided to go out of town for a meal. They needed to address this attraction thing between them. As Angela was due back home from Glasgow tomorrow, they'd both thought that tonight would be the best time to do it.

'So, I'll meet you at the restaurant at eight-thirty, OK?' she shouted to Richard as she was making her way to the front door. 'Don't be late. I don't fancy sitting in a strange place on my own.'

'No worries, I'll be there about eight, just to make sure,' he replied to her from the kitchen, where he was washing up the breakfast dishes.

Butterflies

Olivia got into her car and drove off. *We're like an old married couple,* she thought. *Him washing up after breakfast, arranging to meet for dinner tonight. We* have *to put an end to this.*

But then she thought about last night. How Richard had surprised her in the shower. She'd been hoping he would. He was already naked and as hard as iron when he got in.

Oh, for fucks sake, she thought, angry with herself as the more she thought about it the hornier she became. *I need to talk to someone about this...*

The naughty thoughts were not going anywhere, and she couldn't forget the feeling of Richard with the hot water of the shower.

She was now lost in her own little world—a world of well-hung gardeners satisfying her within the hot spray of a shower—when a horn blared. It snapped her out of her reverie, and she had to over steer the car in order to avoid the stopped car in front of her. Unfortunately, she'd been going too fast and the crash was inevitable. She felt a jolt, then she heard the tinkle and pop of a smashing side light as she hit the car.

She steeled herself for possible flashbacks to the accident in Geneva, and the horrible predicament she found herself in because of it. *What the hell did I think I was doing?* she thought, relieved when she realised there was no damage to herself, *or to Paul,* she thought, sparing a glance over at the empty passenger seat.

She flicked on her hazard lights and got out of the car. The white car she had collided with looked OK, and she breathed a sigh of relief. Her car, too, looked undamaged, which was another relief; all she waited on now was the angry driver to get out and tear a strip out of her. She envisioned a thuggish, skinhead, aggressive type, and her heart sank as she watched a scruffy looking type, with a hoodie pulled over his head, get out of the driver's side door.

'Look, I'm so sorry, I had a moment of distraction there...' she began, '...and I didn't see you. It was my fault. Totally.'

The man looked at her and lowered his hoodie. She was dismayed, fearing the worst, when the skinhead stared back at her.

She winced, expecting a tirade of abuse... but it didn't come.

She looked at the man, really looked at his face, and was instantly relieved! 'Oh my God, Anthony? Anthony! How are you?' she shouted as she recognised Paul's best man and oldest, best friend. 'I haven't seen you since the...' She trailed off for a second. '...since the wedding.'

Anthony smiled a genuine beam of a smile. 'Olivia?' he replied, blinking his eyes. He then rushed forward and wrapped his arms around her.

He held her out at arm's length for a moment or two before pulling her back in for another hug. 'I was just on my way to the hospital. I was going to see Paul.'

'That's where I'm going too,' she replied, grinning.

Anthony looked good, a little rugged maybe, but good. His hair had been cropped into a skin head, almost to the bone, but he'd always been fair haired anyway, so it looked a little worse than it was. He had a scruffy beard, and he was dressed in khaki shorts and a green fatigue style t-shirt. He looked a little thinner than he had at the wedding.

'Where've you been? I was wondering why you hadn't been to see me and Paul.'

'The day after the wedding, I had to fly out to Thailand. I'd signed up for a Doctors Without Borders course. I was already in the air when the...' it was his turn to pause, '...the accident happened. I had no way of getting back, or even getting a message out. How are you after it, anyway?' He pushed her away from him again to give her another once over. 'You look really good.'

'Yeah, I was lucky. Paul protected me during the collision. The impact should have killed him, they said.'

'Look, there's minimal harm done here with our cars. Let's go to the hospital and we can chat in Paul's room. I want to know everything they've done with him, and I want to know how you are too.'

Without further ado, they got back into their cars and drove towards the hospital.

63.

AN HOUR LATER and the pair of them were sitting in the subdued ambiance of Paul's hospital room. Anthony looked shocked to see his friend tied up to all the machines, and to see him so emaciated. Working with sick people all over the world apparently hadn't desensitise him to seeing his oldest friend looking so fragile. Olivia held out her hand to him, knowing instinctively that he would be having a problem seeing Paul like this.

She was like an old pro.

Anthony and Paul had been friends since they were boys together, in school. They'd grown up like brothers, almost inseparable their entire lives. As she looked at him, she noticed a tear welling in his eye. She squeezed his hand and pulled him in close. As she did this, Anthony's dam broke.

The tears flooded down his face, and his mouth turned down in a grimace. His soul was bared to her, and she could empathise with his feelings.

Suddenly, she felt like a phoney. *Why don't I cry for Paul like that anymore? Am I such a bad person?* she chastised herself. *Yes, you are! And sleeping with Richard behind Paul's back proves that point.*

Butterflies

They both stood in the dark of the room and hugged, seemingly not able to let each other go. Anthony was crying for his lost friend; Olivia was crying for her lost husband, and her lost soul.

~~~~

THEY HEADED TOWARDS the café to get a cup of tea and have a catch up, away from the noise of the machines and the gloom of the hospital bed. Anthony came over carrying two cups and sat facing her. His eyes were still pink from his crying, but other than that, he had done a sterling job of composing himself. 'So, tell me what happened. I already know little snippets, but being away, and incommunicado too, I never managed to get the whole story.'

'It was all over so quick. Paul had bought me a new car, and we went for a drive. The lorry came from out of nowhere. Apparently, Paul must have dived over to my side of the car to protect me, and that was how he sustained his head wound.'

'And he's been in this coma ever since. How long is that now? About six months?'

'Seven in two weeks,' Olivia replied without any hesitation. *See, she thought to herself. You do care, you know exactly how long he's been out of action.*

'Seven months... jeez, that's a long time to be out. Have they mentioned muscle dystrophy?'

'Yeah, very early on, after the brain swelling went down. We entered into an intense regime; he's exercised twice a day. I do it myself most days.' *Except for just lately, when I've been busy with 'other' things,* she scolded herself.

They sat for a long while and talked. They talked about him, about what he had been up to in the Doctors Without Borders programme, what his plans were now he was home. They talked about what he thought about Paul's condition. They also talked about Aunt Penny, and how Olivia was dealing with the situation with the added mourning for her beloved aunt. They talked about Angela. Although Olivia refrained from calling her a bitch, and from telling Anthony that she had been fucking her husband.

All these thoughts shocked her so much; she really didn't realise that there was so much self-loathing happening inside her.

Tonight, was definitely the night she and Richard were going to call a halt to their stupid affair.

'Look, Olivia, I really have to be somewhere. It's been fantastic seeing you here. Can I get your number, and we can meet here again? I really want to get involved in this situation.'

'Oh yeah, right. Here, type it into your phone and ring it; that way, I'll get your number too.'

She relayed her mobile number, and he pressed dial. Olivia was a little embarrassed when The Spice Girls 'Wannabe' blasted out into the hospital coffee shop.

Thankfully, Anthony flicked his phone off.

He smiled a little, and she looked at him, red-faced.

'Thank you,' he said. 'Thank you for bumping into me, literally! Thank you for being with me today. I don't know if I could have done it without you. But most of all… thank you for what you are doing for Paul.'

They stood up, embraced, and Anthony departed, leaving Olivia alone in the hospital with her thoughts and her conscience.

Butterflies

64.

OLIVIA WAS RELIEVED that Richard wasn't about when she got home from the hospital. He had told her that he had some things to do before they met and would be meeting her directly at the restaurant. She had about an hour before she needed to start getting ready. She decided to make full use of that hour and mope about in her bedroom, or maybe even have a nap.

Between the accident, the meeting with Anthony, and seeing Paul's condition anew, she was drained. She took off her shirt, skirt, and boots, and lay on her bed in her underwear.

Within a minute, or two, she had fallen asleep.

> She's in her wedding room. It is dark, the low lighting is creating quite a romantic atmosphere, but it's also a little intimidating.
>
> The big window is a mirror again, as it's dark outside and the dim light in the room is reflecting everything. She can just make out the image of the lake through it. It's a deeper dark than the rest of the exterior, and

there are lights bobbing along the waves, like fireflies going about their business.

She is looking at herself in the window. All she is wearing are the skeletal remains of her wedding dress. Her bodice and veil cover her top half, white lacy French knickers, white stockings, and suspenders cover her bottom half.

She is still wearing her high heeled shoes too.

She smiles at her reflection.

From the corner of her eye, she notices the door open. Her heart begins to pound, she can feel it in her throat. *Paul*, she thinks.

Olivia turns as the door opens wide. In walk two men she knows very well. They are both dressed in morning suits, ready for the wedding.

Although expecting Paul, and maybe even expecting some pre-wedding delights with her groom-to-be, the sight of these two men excites her.

Richard and Anthony stand side by side, silently surveying her, enjoying what they are seeing.

She remembers that she is semi-naked, but instead of trying to hide it from these two men, she embraces it.

Butterflies

She smiles and nods, as if understanding why they are here.

Turning to face the window, she walks to the ledge, completely aware of the view both men are receiving. She delights in their appreciative gazes as their expressions reflect in the illuminated window.

As she arrives at the ledge, she leans forwards, putting her head to the glass. She wants to see if there is a crowd below, here to watch her, like last time. She is not disappointed. She searches for Paul and finds him standing at the back of the crowd. He smiles and waves at her. She waves back before opening herself up to the two men.

Looking up into the glass, she sees Anthony and Richard have made their way across the room and are behind her. Although still fully clothed, their excitement at this situation is more than evident.

Olivia is leaning onto the window ledge; her pert derriere raised into the air for their delectation. Richard is the first to make his move. Anticipation is causing her heart to pound. She swallows at the feel of a rough hand on her bottom. Her eyes close as she feels someone else working at the back of her wedding bodice. They are unhooking the hooks; fumbling in their haste to expose her flesh.

The hand on her bottom is stroking her soft skin. Her bodice falls away onto the floor, exposing her naked back and white lacy bra.

Before she knows it, hands are working at the strap of her bra, while others are working on the suspender belt around her waist.

Olivia closes her eyes, enjoying the feeling of two men on her body.

Her bra finally unhooks. As the garment falls to the floor, warm hands hungrily cup both her breasts. The fingers head straight for her stiff nipples. The thumb and forefingers dance around her areola, teasing the sensitive skin, causing them to tighten and become even harder.

As her suspender belt falls around her ankles, the hands—she doesn't know whose they are as her eyes are still closed—slowly trace up her inner thigh. She opens her legs wider, allowing access.

Still with her eyes closed, she turns. Although almost naked, she feels more exposed as the hands leave her skin. Opening her eyes, she notices that both the boys are naked too. Richard's huge member is hard and at attention, Anthony's, although smaller than Richard's, is also ready for action. Both have their own, individual attractions to her.

Butterflies

She leans back on the window ledge. Richard is standing next to her; his strangely electrified hands once again cover her breasts. Wherever they go, they leave a tingling sensation, especially around her nipples.

Leaning in, he kisses her, and she pre-empts the kiss with her tongue.

Meanwhile, Anthony is on his knees before her. His hands are tracing up her thigh, and he is following closely behind with light, delicate, kisses.

The sensation of two men caressing her whips her butterflies into a frenzy in her stomach. The added fact that they are both forbidden fruit makes it all the more intoxicating.

Her body is tingling, her mind is blown. Never, not even in her wildest dreams, has she envisioned herself with two men devoting themselves to the act of pleasuring her.

Anthony slowly lowers her underwear. As he does, he traces their descent with kisses and light, tingling bites. He then retraces his kisses all the way back up her thigh, until he can go no further.

What he does then delights her.

Richard's attention has fallen onto her breasts, or more precisely, onto her nipples. His tongue curls around them before he takes a playful bite.

She can't believe her luck, and a small sigh of pleasure escapes her. She turns her head to look at herself in the reflecting window.

She likes what she sees.

Reaching down to where Anthony is kissing her, she pulls his head away. The tingle is still present, almost lingering, as if his tongue is still there. She looks at him; he can't remove his gaze from her.

His lustful look causes a fresh longing, and she can't wait for something deep inside her, to quell it.

He stands up and kisses her. Richard backs off a little, allowing Anthony some of the fruit.

As he kisses her, he reaches down to her breasts. Her hand does its own exploring and takes his erection within her grip.

She isn't disappointed.

Smiling, a thought passes through her head. *One is built for brute force, the other is built for stamina.*

Butterflies

She turns her head and looks out of the window. The crowd below are looking up at her, they are cheering. She scans for Paul. She knows he's at the back somewhere, but she can't find him. Feeling disappointed, she turns again to give all her attention to the job at hand.

Both men are stood in front of her naked; both of them are excited and waiting for her to make a move.

She does.

She closes her eyes and moves her head forward. Her mouth is open, and she is salivating in anticipation of the feel, and the taste, of Anthony. Once again, she is not disappointed. Anthony's legs buckle as she takes him into her mouth. The moan emitting from him spurs her on.

Her other hand is wrapped around Richard's erection, and she slowly massages her hand up and down the thick shaft.

You dirty bitch, she smiles to herself. *Two gorgeous men at once. I must have been a good girl in a past life.*

Suddenly, she feels lifted. Both men are holding her underneath each arm as they carry her over to the bed and lie her down.

At last, she thinks, ready to finally get something deep inside her, something that just might stop her incessant ache.

Turning onto her stomach, she is gently pulled to the edge of the bed. Acutely aware of the sight they are both witnessing right now, she is excited to ponder on which one of them will be the first to enter her.

Secretly, she hopes it will be Anthony, as if Richard entered her first, she might have a problem even feeling Anthony inside her.

All four of their hands rub up and down her back, occasionally venturing to her buttocks, pulling them apart, exposing her most intimate areas. She closes her eyes again, enjoying the sensual attention.

She felt, rather than saw or heard, the door of the room opening and closing again. There is a third man in the room.

Panic begins to rise in her stomach as she wonders who it could be.

Her heart leaps, it feels almost as if it has missed a beat, as she turns and sees who it is.

It's Paul, he's awake, he's alive… and completely naked too. A third player has now entered the Olivia Martelle show.

Butterflies

This one is the top bill, the main event.

Her butterflies swoop and swirl in expectation of Paul, her husband, the man she would love until the very end.

She sits up and tries to move towards him. She is desperate to hug him, to kiss him, smell him. But he moves away. He puts a finger to his lips to shush her.

She knows what he intends to do, and she wants it, is longing for it. She turns away, closes her eyes, and waits.

Her skin tingles, aware of every throb in her body, every beat of the butterfly wings inside her. She is ready for Paul's love.

Her stomach feels like it is erupting with life. Ten! One hundred! One thousand! One hundred thousand…

Butterflies.

Large and blue… bright and beautiful.

Paul has not even entered her yet, and butterflies are soaring everywhere. They're fluttering through every nerve ending in her body, coursing through every vein, every bone, batting against her skin…

She is close now. The butterflies have brought her orgasm with them on their silken wings. She feels Paul enter her. It is beautiful, it is right.

His whole length slides deep within her. She remembers his feel, her body reacts.

There is an explosion of wings…

The orgasm tears through her body…

It woke her up.
She was lying in bed, her underwear was pushed aside, and wet. Her eyes were wide, and although she was smiling, and red faced from her exertions, a small tear trickled down her cheek.

~~~~

'What is going on inside my head?' she asked, sitting on the edge of her bed, gripping the duvet in her fingers. 'That dream was fucked up.'

She tried to convince herself that it didn't mean anything, but it kept coming down to the same thing. Richard had gotten into her head, period.

But what was all that about Anthony? And Paul? The thoughts kept coming, hard and fast. There must have been some meaning to the dream. Something in her subconscious maybe? *Yeah! I'm drinking too much and having far too much sex.*

Tonight, was the night she would get her life back together. She needed to finish this, whatever it was, with Richard, and get back to focusing on her husband's recovery. Once he was back in the safety of their home with her at his side, then all this craziness could be put behind her. Richard could go back to being her brother-in-law. No one would ever need know what passed between them. She could go back to avoiding Angela because she hated her and not because she was having sex with her husband.

Everything would be as it should be.

'And it all starts tonight,' she told herself in the mirror as she started to get ready for the meal.

65.

OLIVIA ARRIVED AT the restaurant about ten minutes later than she'd arranged. As it was an out of town restaurant, no one in there would know who she was, or more importantly, to whom she was married, so she entered without hesitation.

The Maître d' approached her. 'Mademoiselle, can I be of assistance?' He had a charming smile, but Olivia could see that there was very little charm in his eyes.

This man sees all and forgets nothing, she thought, noting this for when she came to pay the bill.

'I'm here for the table. I think it was reserved under the name Smith,' she replied. As the Maître d' looked at her, she noticed the twinkle in his eye, and she noticed that he noticed that she noticed... *This could go on forever,* she thought.

'Ah, yes, the *Smith* table. There he is over there,' he pointed to Richard, sat alone at a table drinking a bottle of beer.

'He's my brother-in-law... we're fucking.' She whispered the last part and winked at him.

He looked shocked, but delightfully so, then he winked back at her. 'Don't worry about it,' he whispered back at her in a Northern accent. 'I'm not really French.'

Butterflies

They smiled at each other as he ushered her in. He took her to the table, where Richard was already stood, waiting for her.

'Monsieur et mademoiselle, I am so sorry for any inconvenience caused to you, but you see, there has been a terrible mistake. This table has been reserved for another patron; one I cannot deny. If you would follow me, please.' They walked around the room to a nice table in a shadowed area of the restaurant. He clicked his fingers at a waitress, and she scurried off behind one of the bars. 'For your inconvenience, please accept this, our top table and a complimentary bottle of our best Champagne.'

'Why, thank you very much,' Olivia replied, tipping him a wink.

'Of course, my lady. It is my pleasure,' he winked back.

The lighting was subdued, and the candles were lit. *Not the ambiance I was hoping for, given what I have in mind,* she thought, whilst thanking the Maître d'.

The waitress came back almost instantly with a chilled silver bucket containing a bottle of Krug Champagne sitting on ice. Two large flutes were produced. 'With the compliments of the house,' she said, and popped the cork of the expensive bottle.

The flutes were filled with the bubbling amber fluid, and the bucket was placed at the end of the table. 'If there is nothing else?' she asked, before leaving the table. As she went, an awkward silence descended upon them.

'So, erm, do you want to order?' Olivia asked.

'Yeah, I was thinking of having the Whitebait for starters and the chicken supreme. What about you?'

'Yeah, that sounds good to me too,' she replied, gulping down the last of her first glass of sparkling wine. *Oh God, this is awkward,* she thought, and then she poured herself another glass and topped his up too.

'Right, shall we get right down to it? What exactly is happening between us?' Richard asked, pulling at his collar. She noticed there was a sheen of sweat on his forehead.

Oh, thank the lord, she thought. *I was thinking I was going to have to be drunk before this conversation started.* 'Richard, I've… enjoyed our times together, believe me I have, but I'm feeling—'

'Guilty?' he interceded.

Olivia laughed. 'Yeah, exactly, guilty. How about you?'

He smiled and took another sip from his flute. 'Olivia, I can't deny that I've got feelings for you, but I think they're more physical than emotional. You're a gorgeous woman, any man would be lucky to hold you, and I count myself as very lucky to *have* held you.'

'I know what you are saying.' She was becoming more animated as she talked. 'Physically, you're… impressive.' She noted that he'd blushed. She really liked his humility; it was one of his most endearing features. *Well, that and his great big cock,* she thought. The thought embarrassed her, and it was her turn to go red. *This isn't going well...* This last thought kicked her back down to earth, and she began to compose herself.

'But…' she continued, '…you're married to my husband's sister, and I'm *still* a married woman. Paul could wake up tomorrow. He is, and will always be, the love of my life.'

Richard smiled and looked down at his drink. He topped up Olivia's, and then he did his own.

She looked at the nearly empty bottle lying in the ice bucket. A bad thought ran through her head. *Oh no, how long have we been here, and we've nearly drank that whole bottle already.*

'You probably won't believe me when I tell you this, but Angela is the love of my life too.'

Olivia must have screwed her eyes or made some sort of gesture with her face as Richard began to laugh.

Butterflies

'See, I told you that you'd never believe me.' He signalled the waitress to bring another bottle of Krug.

He composed himself a little. 'She is, though, that's the funny thing. When we first met, she was wild. I mean, she had a pure lust for life. We'd have sex in the strangest of places. She'd run out of restaurants without paying, just for fun.' He shook his head in a melancholic gesture. 'I really don't know what happened to that free spirited, fun loving person.'

'She sounds a lot like Paul,' Olivia replied with a bittersweet smile.

Richard looked down once more, towards his almost empty glass at the mention of Paul's name. 'I've known the family since he was about twelve. You'll never meet a sweeter kid in all your life. He really used to look up to me. I used to take him to the football, to the cinema. When me and Angela got together, were good to him, including him in everything we did.'

'What happened to their parents? Neither of them has ever mentioned them to me,' Olivia asked, leaning into the table, wanting to know more.

'It wasn't long after I met Angela, well maybe about two years or so. As a family, they never had much. They lived in this small house on a council estate. Their dad was the only one in the street who had any money because he had a job in the Post Office. He'd start work at five finish about two, then go and work in the grocery shop on the corner. Their mother had major complications while having Paul and was always sickly. Whatever they had, they shared with their neighbours; it was a nice community, neighbourly.'

'What happened?' Olivia asked.

The waitress turned up with the bottle of Champagne. 'Are you guys ready for your starters?' she asked.

'Oh, yes please,' Richard replied.

She left to get their food.

'Carry on,' Olivia prompted.

'Well, a new family moved into the estate, rough as anything. They had six kids in tow ranging from five to sixteen. They got wind of the money the grocery was taking in on a weekly basis and decided that they wanted it. Typical of some people, not wanting to work for a living and thinking they can just take what they want by force. Anyway, they went into the shop, masks, shotguns, the lot. The oldest kid thought Paul senior had recognised him. He shot him, there and then.'

Olivia covered her mouth. 'Oh my God, he never told me anything about any of this.'

'Their mum, Nicola, withered away and died. It took about two years. It turned out she had cancer, but everyone who knew her knew she'd died of a broken heart. Angela was seventeen at the time, so was I. We decided to get married, that way we could become legal guardians of Paul.'

Olivia reached across the table and grabbed Richard's hand, wanting to let him know that he was a good man.

'Paul and Angela were close before, but afterwards, they were nigh on inseparable. I was working as a gardener and bringing in some money, Angela went to college, and Paul stayed on in school. It was like they'd made some sort of a pact between them, a pact to make something out of their lives to honour their mum and dad, you know? Paul got straight A's in school, went to university, came out with a first. He started his consultancy business, and well, you know the rest.'

Their glasses were topped up again, and Olivia took a long gulp out of hers. She needed to prep herself for the next question she had.

'So, tell me, why does Angela hate me?'

Butterflies

Richard laughed and took a long swig of his drink too. At that moment, the waitress turned up with the starters. The whitebait stared up at her. Fifty or so black, fishy eyes looking at her—it freaked her out a little. When she'd asked if she could get them anything else, they both thanked her and told her they were OK. She took the hint that they wanted to be alone and smiled as she walked off.

'Angela doesn't hate you, she's just too protective of her little brother.'

'OK, but why is she like what she is now? It's like she has to be in control of everything.'

'You just answered your own question. She saw you as someone she couldn't control, and that you could take away the control she had over her brother.' Richard laughed humourlessly. 'Then she turned all of her control over onto me. We haven't had any intimacy for about two years. She won't drink, she won't let her hair down. I was almost relieved when you put her in charge of Paul's affairs because things were getting to breaking point, but now, I don't know. It seems like we're different people, drifting apart. The business, and the control of everything that comes with that, are her husband now. I need to let you know that in the twenty years we've been together, you're the only person I have ever.... Well, you know.'

Olivia loved it that he turned red at this point, even though she knew she shouldn't.

She finished the rest of her glass in one swallow, pushed her plate away from her, having not actually eaten any of it, and held her breath for a few seconds. She couldn't believe that she was going to tell someone this, but she just had to get it off her chest. She had to tell someone, it may as well be Richard, otherwise it would be Jan or Katie—both her best friends, but a little flaky in their own way.

Aunt Penny would know what she meant. Was Richard a surrogate Aunt Penny? With benefits?

'I think I'm losing him!' There, she'd said it. She couldn't take it back now, even if she wanted to.

Richard looked shocked.

'What?' he asked looking exasperated.

'I have to look at the evidence that's in front of me. He's not had a change in his condition in over six months. Dr Hausen keeps giving me the 'hang in there' speech; he's given it to me so many times that I think he's come to almost believe it himself.' It was her turn to look down at her glass. 'He's not coming back to me, is he?'

As she asked this last question, tears welled up in her eyes. The dam broke, and they trickled down her cheeks. Richard wiped them away. He got out of his seat and came around to sit next to her. As he wrapped his arm around her, she buried her head into his strong embrace.

66.

THE PLAN THAT night was to finish off their little affair. Angela was coming home from Glasgow tomorrow, and they needed to have their house in order. The last thing either of them needed was any suspicion.

So, the best-laid plans of mice and men did not take into account four full bottles of Krug Champagne and not a lot to eat. They also did not take into account sob stories, rising emotions, strong arms, hugging, and the removing of panties in the ladies' toilets.

But all of this happened.

67.

THE NEXT MORNING, Olivia awoke in her bed. Her head was aching so bad, and the throbbing was in tandem with the pulsating ache coming from somewhere further south, somewhere that she had come to associate with sleeping with Richard.

Opening one eye, she peered over the other side of the bed. There, fast asleep, was Richard. Inwardly she groaned. *Didn't we sort this out last night?*

She got out of bed. Apparently, she was sleeping naked these days. She hated doing that. She must have been very drunk. She also had the taste in her mouth that told her she'd been drinking vodka and engaging in oral sex. She kind of remembered both; at the same time.

With her head in her hands and a deep sigh, she made her way gingerly towards the bathroom. *It must have been some strenuous sex last night,* she thought, *judging by the way I'm walking this morning.* She looked at the clock in her bathroom. Twelve forty-five p.m. *Oh well, judging by the way I'm walking this aftern—*

She didn't finish her thought.

Twelve forty-five?

'Oh shit!' she shouted. Angela was coming home today. She was on the nine-thirty train, that would get her into London for around one o'clock.

'Richard, Richard, get up. Get up. It's nearly one o'clock,' she shouted as she just about managed to run back into the bedroom.

'What?' Richard's head popped out of the duvet. 'What are you shouting for?' he asked groggily.

'It's nearly one o'clock. Angela said she'd be in about one-ish. Where's your phone? See if she's rang.'

Richard lifted his head. 'I haven't got a clue,' he said and then registered why Olivia was in such a panic.

'Fuck! Oh shit.' These were just some of the expletives that came out of his mouth as he jumped out of bed and ran around the room looking for his phone and his clothes. He looked at Olivia when he'd found his trousers.

'What the hell happened last night? I remember messing about in the toilets, then I remember... Oh no.' He stopped and put his hand up to his face, his eyes widened as the rest of his face fell.

The colour drained out of Olivia's face too. 'What?' But she knew exactly what he was going to say.

A small smile of remembrance crept over his face. 'I remember you giving me a blow job in the taxi on the way back here.'

Olivia feigned shock, although she was now having complete 'cornflake head' recall of the incident. She remembered the taxi driver's reaction, and how he refused his tip as he thought he'd been given enough for the journey.

'Oh fuck! Just get dressed and find your phone. I'll jump into the shower and make myself scarce while you bring Angela home.' *I am NEVER drinking again, and I mean it this time.*

Richard was now frantically looking all around the room for the rest of his clothes. So far, he was without a sock and his underpants, and most importantly, his mobile phone.

Olivia had her phone on the table next to the bed. 'I'll ring it,' she said, panic dialling. 'There, it should be ringing now.'

They both stood still and silent, Richard in his trousers and Olivia naked with her mobile phone to her ear.

Very faintly they could hear the theme from Mission Impossible coming from somewhere downstairs. The relief in both their faces was almost comical.

'I'll keep on ringing it, then when I'm in the shower, you can get dressed and get Angela,' she shouted as he left the room on his quest.

About a minute later, he answered. 'Why was my phone in the fridge, covered in cream?' he asked with genuine concern.

'I don't know, and right now you shouldn't care, just go and get Angela.'

When she heard the front door slam, she jumped into the shower. The water felt like it was blessing her skin in small, beautiful drops. As she immersed her head into the downpour of steaming water, she had another recall of some of the things they were doing last night.

They had come in from the taxi ride. She remembered giving Richard head by the front door. She remembered him lifting her up and turning her upside down, he was so strong. As she was upside down, he returned the favour. She remembered giggling about never having somebody go up on her before. She felt a little dizzy at that thought.

Clothes were strewn all over the room. Richard must have had most of his on as they made it to the bedroom, but he was missing his underwear.

Butterflies

Her eyes opened wide under the spray of the water. 'Oh no, his undies.' She jumped out of the shower, towel dried her hair, and dabbed at her underneath to dry herself. She was still very tender.

She'd just had a flashback. The fresh cream! Richard had tried to whip the cream with his penis. It had been the funniest thing in the world last night, and she'd enjoyed licking it off, and then him repaying the favour. But that meant that his underwear must be somewhere in the kitchen.

Olivia dressed quickly before her phone chirped. *Text*, she thought. As she ran downstairs, she opened the text it was from Richard.

> Undies in kitchen. A due in at 1:35.
> Will just make it.

Olivia looked at the clock. It was one-twenty-seven; it would take him about twenty minutes to drive her back from the train station.

Undies, undies... Where do you find undies in a kitchen?

She looked over the floor, she looked by the bin, *in* the bin, but there were no undies to be found.

She stopped to think for a moment. If his phone was in the fridge with the cream, would it stand to reason that his underwear would be in there too? As she opened the fridge door, a massive flashback of last night opened itself up to her. 'Oh, for fuck's sake,' she muttered. This was bigger than the missing underwear.

Her phone now read one-thirty-seven. Would Angela be in yet? She'd have to risk it. She rang Richard's phone; it rang once and then went onto voicemail. Her heart sank and sweat began to bead on her brow.

She opened the freezer and removed the underwear from the ice tray. She carried them to the utility room and put them in the dirty wash basket that Richard and Angela used. Then she put her hair in a ponytail, put on a pair of sandals from the downstairs closet, grabbed her car keys, and left the house.

In the car, she looked at her phone. No calls or texts. 'Shit!' she exclaimed. Her phone was one of those with a million and one functions, most of which she never used, or even understood. It took a couple of flicks and she was staring at her photograph gallery.

Her phone also had a very good camera. And it seemed she was not a bad photographer either.

She sat and flicked through about twelve photographs of her and Richard indulging in various sexual exploits. In some of them, she could clearly see Richard was taking photographs of her at the same time.

This was very, very bad!

68.

OLIVIA SPENT THE day at the hospital. She and Paul went through their rigorous exercise routine. Dr Hausen came around and told her that everything was fine; Paul, although showing no signs of waking anytime soon, was doing fine; everything was fine; the hospital was fine; her fucking life was fine...

In her mind, nothing was fine.

Through teary eyes, she looked at her husband. How could she do what she was doing behind this beautiful man's back? With her head in her hands again, she shivered. Was she resenting herself for her inexcusable actions, or was she resenting Paul for not being there with her? She hoped and prayed that it was the former, but her life had become one huge shade of grey.

It would be Christmas very soon. She'd be alone, alone with her guilt, and possibly alone with her sister-in-law's husband, even though she knew that his wife was still the love of his life. Everything, everything that she had believed at the beginning of this year had gone sour.

Aunt Penny had left her too. It was difficult to get angry with her because she was the nicest, most pure person Olivia had ever had the good fortune to know and love; but she was gone.

'I don't even know who I am anymore,' she sobbed. 'I'm such a horrible person.'

She sat in the hospital room alone and cried. She cried for Paul, for his situation, and for what she was doing behind his back.

~~~~

Dr Hausen was standing outside the hospital room. He watched, biting the inside of his cheek, as Olivia cried. He needed to speak to her. There were things that she needed to know, things she needed to ready herself for, but he couldn't bring himself to tell her, not yet anyway.

It could wait until she was in a better place.

Butterflies

69.

BACK AT HOME, Olivia saw Richard's car on the path. That meant the wicked witch of the west was back at home. Which also meant there was a good chance she might have seen his phone at some point. Which meant there was an even better chance Olivia might be murdered as soon as she stepped inside.

She opened the door and looked into the hallway. It was empty, but she could hear Angela's voice calling to Richard from somewhere upstairs.

They sounded convivial; this came as a relief to Olivia. *So, no viewing of those pictures yet,* she thought.

'Hi, I'm home,' she shouted. There was no reply.

'Hello?' she shouted again.

Richard popped his head around the doorway into the kitchen. 'Hey, Olivia. Angela's home,' he said, pulling a little face.

'Oh yes, I forgot that was today,' she replied out loud. Then she mouthed, 'Where is your mobile phone?'

Richard looked at her as if she was daft. 'What?' he mouthed back.

'Your mobile phone. Where is it?' This time she put her thumb and little finger to her ear and shook it.

He looked at her and shrugged.

She shook her head and whispered aloud. 'Where is your fucking phone?'

'It's here, in my pocket.' He tapped his pocket, and then pulled a face, he tapped his other pocket, nothing in there either. He shrugged. 'I don't know where it is right now. Why?'

At that moment, Angela decided to pop her head out of the kitchen too. 'Hi, Olivia, how's my brother? I hope you don't mind us in the kitchen. This big lummox here didn't get any food in.'

'Hey, no! Me casa es tu casa!' she replied flapping her hand. 'I've just got back from the hospital now,' she shrugged. 'There's not much change, I'm afraid. We're doing all the exercises we can, and they're trying to stimulate his brain, but he's still deep in the coma.'

Angela pulled a sad face. 'Right. Listen, we need to talk about all this 'asset of the company' stuff I was talking about. Please forgive me for all that, Olivia, I really don't know what I'm doing sometimes.' As she walked out of the kitchen, Olivia noticed she traipsed her hand around Richard's hip.

'I've had time to think about our relationship, and I don't think I've been very fair towards you. You didn't have to give me the permissions to act on Paul's behalf in all of the business dealings, and I do thank you for it, also, you didn't have to give us a roof over our heads either…'

And I didn't have to keep your husband warm for you while you were away, Olivia thought forcing a smile her body didn't want to perform.

'But you did, and I'm so grateful.' She held her arms out to give her a hug. Olivia was so stunned she couldn't think of anything else to do but hug her back. As they embraced, she looked back towards

Richard and shot him a quizzical look. He shook his head and shrugged.

'Listen, I'm glad we're all here together. I need to ask you two a favour.'

Olivia and Richard swapped awkward glances.

'I know I haven't been here lately, leaving you two to your own devices. Richard, neglecting our relationship, and Olivia, neglecting my responsibilities towards Paul.' She paused and looked right into Olivia's eyes. 'And I know I've been a bit of a bitch about it too.'

Olivia had to look away. *Maybe the guilt hasn't completely gone away,* she thought.

'Anyhow, I know how hard it's been for you both.' She looked at Richard. 'I know it's been especially hard for you. So, what do you think about the next time I have to go to America, that you two guys come with me, and we make a little holiday out of it?'

Richard's face lit up. 'Yeah, that's a great idea,' he enthused.

Angela turned towards Olivia. 'I do have a little confession to make though, Olivia. It'll be a little bit of a busman's holiday for you. There'll be a few people I'll need you to meet, and we'll need to sign some papers, but other than that, it'll all be ours. What do you say? It'll give us a little time to bond. Don't worry about Paul while we're away, we'll be gone for five days, tops. I'm sure you could do with a small break away from your duties.'

You don't know how much of a break I need, she thought, smiling at Angela. 'Yeah, I think it would be a great idea. When do we go?'

Angela smiled at the two of them. 'Well, I know it was a bit of an expense, but I thought *to hell with it.* If we're going, were going first class.' She reached into her bag and produced three aeroplane tickets. 'I booked them for anytime within the next two weeks.'

70.

OLIVIA NEEDED TO get some time alone with Richard. She needed him to delete whatever photos might be on his phone. That, as it turned out, was easier said than done.

Angela had become a constant companion to him, and if she wasn't shadowing him, then he was following *her*. She worried, almost constantly about the content of the photographs. She didn't know how often he checked his gallery, and she hoped Angela *never* checked his phone, but knowing how much of a control freak she was, Olivia could not guarantee she wouldn't, especially after her being away so often.

'Why, oh why do I get myself into these situations?' she scolded herself.

It had been three days since Angela had been home, and Olivia had not yet had a decent night's sleep. She'd thought about sneaking into their house at the end of the garden during the night and getting his phone. She'd thought about hiding it every time she saw him put it down. She'd even thought about smashing the horrid little thing into a million pieces, but she'd never had a chance.

'Olivia, are you OK?' Angela's voice, coming from behind her, caused her to jump a little.

Butterflies

I'm so jittery... she thought.

'Oh, yeah, I'm fine,' came her stuttering reply.

'Oh, you just looked a little, I don't know, zoned out there for a moment,' Angela replied with a smile.

'I'm just worrying about this America trip, you know, not seeing Paul for five days. I'm also worrying a little about Christmas too. It's only six weeks away. I don't think I've ever been alone at Christmas before... the first one without Paul, and Aunt Penny.'

Angela did something then that Olivia thought she would never, ever witness in her whole life. She walked over to her and wrapped her arms around her, giving her a hug.

Olivia's eyes were so wide they nearly popped out of her head.

'Hey, listen. You'll have Richard and me here for you this year, and you always have your friends too. It'll be hard for both of us not having Paul around, you know how much he loves Christmas.' Angela pulled herself out of the hug and looked into Olivia's face. She wrinkled her nose at her. 'Don't worry about it; I'll make sure Richard sees to your every need over the holidays.'

Olivia smiled at her and shifted her eyes away as soon as she could.

Angela gave her a big smile and moved away.

Olivia made for the door, as quickly as she could. 'Speaking of Richard, I haven't seen him all day. Where is he?'

'He had a number of jobs to do, I think he was doing some gardening... why?'

'Oh, no reason, I just got used to seeing him around.'

She saw this as an opportunity to ring him and get him to sort out the pictures on his phone. 'Well, I'm off to the hospital to see Paul for a while. What are you doing?' Inwardly she cursed herself for asking, even to her, it sounded obvious she needed time alone to contact Richard.

'Do you know what? I think I'll come with you. I didn't get a chance to see him yesterday. It might do him some good to see the two ladies in his life getting along for once, eh?'

Olivia, over the years, had become adept at a few things, one of these talents related directly to Angela. She had evolved an inward groan while smiling on the outside! She exercised this talent right now.

'Excellent,' she lied. 'Let's go.'

71.

THE TIME SPENT in the hospital was unbearable, not just because she was spending it with the new and improved Angela, but because she was trying to get away to either call or text Richard.

The ward sister was being a cow regarding the mobile phones. To be fair, she had never allowed the phones to be on while in Paul's room, but then, she had never had such a pressing reason to use one before today.

'Angela,' Olivia whispered, and they were both sitting in the room. 'I'm just nipping out to the toilet; I'll be back in a moment.' She was readying herself for Angela to decide to come with her.

'OK, see you in a min,' she replied.

She tried her best to supress her relief and almost ran to the ladies' toilets, one floor down from where they were now. As she got inside, she locked herself into the cubicle furthest from the door and fumbled for her mobile phone. It seemed to take an age to boot up into the welcome page.

'Hurry up, you fucking thing,' she whispered, gripping it tightly in her sweating hands. Eventually, it booted. She rapidly chose Richard's number from her contacts and dialled it.

Beep, beep, beep, beep…

'What? No!' She wanted to scream. There was no signal in the toilets. She very nearly threw the device against the wall.

With her high heels balancing on the rim of the seat, she climbed up onto the toilet, waving the mobile phone in the air, relentlessly searching for the elusive one bar of signal. A bar flashed momentarily as it was waved over the cubicle next to the one Olivia was occupying. To utilise it would involve the tricky business of stepping off the toilet in her heels without slipping into the bowl.

Somehow, she managed it.

Running into the next cubicle, she discovered the signal was just as bad in this one as it was in the last. Her expensive high heels were straddling precariously on either side of another bowl. As the phone was waved in the air again, the signal bar flashed to two.

'Yes!' she shouted in victory. The battle of the signal had been won!

'Ahem... excuse me!' came a small voice from somewhere below her. 'Can you wave that thing somewhere else, please?'

Olivia looked down from her elevated position. There was a woman sitting on the toilet in the next cubicle, looking up towards the mad woman towering above her.

Olivia, in her obsessive madness to find a signal, had failed to even notice the other cubicle was occupied. The shock of seeing her there caused Olivia to fall back and rock on her heels. The lack of grip on her expensive shoes was brought home to her as she slipped. She emitted a small yelp as her foot fell, shin deep, into the murky water of the bowl below her.

'Err, thank you,' came the voice from the next cubicle, along with the flush and the door being unbolted, rapidly, as the woman exited as fast as she could. She didn't even wash her hands in her haste to leave.

Butterflies

'Shit,' Olivia muttered to herself as she dragged her sodden leg out of the toilet. 'Why did I not flush that thing before standing on it?'

Her trousers were dripping with questionable water, and she had some used, sodden toilet tissue clinging to her shoe.

Disgusted but still undaunted, she opened her stall and danced around the whole room trying to shake off the soggy paper and look for a phone signal at the same time.

In the end, she conceded defeat, realising it was a choice to either climb back up onto the toilet bowl or go outside where she was bound to get a signal. Looking down at the mess of her trousers and her nice shoes, the decision was made to take it outside.

The line of smokers, all dressed in their dressing gowns, was large, and the blue smoky haze they were causing was fogging out most of the landscaped reception garden of the hospital. Retreating to a safe distance away from the passive smoke, Olivia finally got her three bars. Richard's number was on the last number redial, so she pressed it.

It rang.

'Thank God,' she muttered.

It rang, and rang, and rang, until finally; 'Hi, you have reached the voicemail of Rich…'

'JUST ANSWER THE FUCKING PHONE, YOU FUCKING FUCK, FUCK BASTARD!' she screamed down the handset at the top of her voice. Everyone stood outside the hospital stopped what they were doing and turned to see the mad woman with the wet leg and the toilet roll on her shoe, screaming and raving.

Then she saw the woman from the toilet. She was leaving the building at the same time as Olivia's tirade. She turned to see what the hullabaloo was. Noticing that it was the same mad woman from the toilets, she hastened her pace towards the car park, looking back, just once, over her shoulder, presumably to check that Olivia wasn't following her.

Embarrassed by everyone staring at her, she slipped her phone back into her pocket, lowered her head, and squelched back into the building.

Everyone watched her as she hobbled past.

~~~~

'What happened to you?' Angela asked as she took one look at Olivia coming back into Paul's room.

'Oh, the erm... the toilets were broken,' she replied, acting calm even though inside she was reeling. 'I just needed to make a phone call, I had to go all over the world to get a signal.'

'You should have just asked. I got a new phone the other day, I've got a full signal.' She showed Olivia her phone, there in the top corner were five full bars.

'Does the sister know you have that on in here?'

'Yeah, they only ask you to turn them off because of the annoyance of the ringing and the talking aloud, if you let them know you have it on silent and will take the calls outside, then they're OK.'

Olivia turned on her phone. It beeped quite loudly, attracting the attention of the ward nurses, she muted the ringer and looked at her display. Five full bars. Inside, she cursed harder than she had ever cursed in her life.

Butterflies

72.

THE NEXT TWO days were hellish, between trying to get a message to Richard without Angela becoming suspicious and Angela trying to be her new best friend; Olivia felt she was losing her mind.

And now there was a holiday to America to look forward to. She truly couldn't think of anything worse. She would sooner claw her own eyes out. The thought of going away with her awful sister-in-law and the brother-in-law who she has been sleeping with filled her with dread and dismay!

'Have you been to see Paul today?' She jumped as Angela crept up behind her.

'Yeah! There's no change. Although I did get the suspicion that Dr Hausen wanted to talk to me about something. He said it could wait until we got back from America, so it can't be that important.'

'Did he not even give you an inkling of what it could be?' Angela asked, her curiosity piqued.

'No, I did press, but he kept waving me away. It can't be anything to worry about, otherwise he wouldn't have let it go.'

'I suppose not. Anyway, I'm just letting you know the taxi will be here in about an hour. I'll send Richard up to get your bags in about twenty minutes, is that OK?'

More than OK, Olivia thought while giving Angela an 'Uh huh.' *At last, I'll be able to talk to him on his own.*

She eventually finished her packing. Angela had given her a little bit of an itinerary, so she'd have an idea of what she'd need.

Philadelphia is cold in November, but the hotel they were staying in had a gorgeous indoor swimming pool and spa, so a costume or two wouldn't go amiss. There would be at least two formal dinners she'd have to attend, so something nice and classy, and then the rest of the time, walking shoes and jeans would be good.

Two suitcases later and she was ready to go.

'Richard, could you please come and give me a hand with these bags?' she shouted downstairs. *At last,* she thought. 'They're just in here in my room.'

As he walked in, she grabbed his arm and pulled him to one side. She had her phone in her hand.

'Richard,' she whispered. 'Have you got any photos on your phone?'

He pulled a funny face, as if to say, 'I don't know what you are talking about,' and shrugged.

Olivia clicked her phone into life and passed it to him, she watched as his face slowly recognised what it was. The image on Olivia's phone was taken from the point of view of someone lying on the floor.

The image was of a large, erect penis just about to enter into someone's mouth. That someone was naked.

That someone was Olivia.

Butterflies

The owner of the large erection also had his mobile phone raised, about to take a picture.

Richard's face went from titillation to colourless in less than five seconds when he realised it was him taking the picture of the event.

She tried to convey that she wanted him to go downstairs, take his phone into another room, and delete any photographs that he may have on there. She needed him to do this now, without any further delay.

She tried to convey this by just using her eyes and twitching her mouth, but it just seemed to wash over him. He was still stood there gawping at the picture. She snatched the phone from him and made an exaggerated show of deleting the photo. This sprung Richard into action. He pulled an 'Oh yeah' face and left the room.

Shaking her head, she popped her head around the corner of the doorway and witnessed him making his way downstairs. She waved her arms towards him to grab his attention; he turned to face her with a quizzical look. He watched as Olivia pointed rather vigorously towards her suitcases that were still in her room. He pulled another 'oops' face and came right back for them.

As she followed him down the stairs, they found Angela waiting by the front door.

'Taxi's here,' she shouted as Richard raced past her with Olivia's suitcases. He put them in the boot and returned for Angela's suitcases, and then his own. Finally, all ready, they got into the taxi. Richard was in the front seat, with Angela and Olivia in the back.

'Heathrow airport, please, mate,' Richard instructed the driver. 'Terminal two.'

'Right-o,' the driver replied, and drove off the driveway.

73.

TWENTY MINUTES INTO the journey and even the driver had shut up. He'd done nothing but waffle on about some football club doing something else to another football club. He took the hint that no one was really interested and eventually stopped talking.

Richard was sleeping in the front seat, and Angela was reading a magazine. There was a chirp from Olivia's bag as her phone informed her that she had received a text message. Eager for something to do, she dug around in her large handbag and finally located the phone.

The text was from Anthony. He wanted to know if she was going in to see Paul today and whether he could meet her for lunch. Disappointed, she texted back to tell him she was on her way to Philadelphia for five days and she'd give him a call when she was back in England. She asked him to check in on Paul as much as he could over the next few days and send her any updates. He said he would. He told her he hoped she enjoyed her break, that he was jealous, and he would get into the hospital at least every other day.

Anthony was now working as a casual consultant on Paul's case; he couldn't get on as a full-time consultant due to his personal relationship with the patient.

Butterflies

Olivia knew he would keep her apprised.

As she clicked the text message from Anthony away, she accidently clicked on her phone gallery, but she did not just click on a picture, she selected a video file that was residing on there. At first, she didn't notice that she had activated it, until, at top volume, she heard her own recorded voice saying, 'Oh come and fuck me with that big hard dick.' Then there were heavy panting noises and a scream as, evidently, someone must have put his 'big hard dick' inside her.

Olivia went pale. She didn't remember videoing any action from the other night, but then she hadn't even remembered taking photographs. It amazed her in an abstract way as she didn't even know how to use the video function on the phone. Sweating, she fumbled at every button and every icon on the touch screen. Somehow, she managed to turn the video off. As she did, she could feel the flush of embarrassment rising over her face.

The taxi had stopped at lights. As Olivia looked up, the driver was looking at her with an amused face, Angela was looking at her with a mixture of shock and a little moral high ground. Richard was the only one not looking at her, and that in itself was a bad thing.

She smiled at them all. 'That was… Jan,' she said shaking her head and smiling. 'She was sending me a video of her and… erm, her and some guy she met the other night… I've—I've deleted it now.'

The taxi driver winked at her and turned his attention back onto the road. She could see Richard's head slowly shaking left to right in the front seat. Only Angela kept her eyes on her. 'She's a bit of a goer, that Jan, isn't she?' she said with a sly looking smile.

Olivia had no love for the way she was looking at her, none at all.

74.

AFTER THEY ARRIVED at the airport, Angela went to look in the duty-free shop for some new perfume. Olivia took this time to talk to Richard.

'Did you get those photos off your phone?'

'I haven't had a chance; I'll do it now.' He started to search around his pockets. 'What happened in the car?'

Olivia's face went white all over again. 'Richard, I don't know. We must have filmed some of what we were doing too. I don't even know how to use the video function while sober, never mind as drunk as we were that night. What are you doing?'

He was still searching all around his pockets. 'I think I've left my phone at home. Shit, I'm so stupid, how could I have done that?'

Olivia was shaking her head in frustration. 'So, you didn't delete them before we left?' Olivia asked with rising panic in her voice.

'Did you see me with any time on my own since you told me all about them?' Richard snapped.

'Great, that's a no then, isn't it?'

'It's worse than that,' Richard replied still whispering in a sharp tone. 'Have you seen Angela's new phone?'

'Yes.'

Butterflies

'Did you not notice it's the exact same model as mine? Same colour, same picture on the home screen?'

Olivia's heart sank. 'No, I didn't.'

'Well it is, and now I'm worried she's picked up mine instead of hers.'

'I'm going to ring it. I'll pretend that you're at the bar and I'm changing my mind on what drink I want.'

'Good idea.'

Olivia called his number on her phone; it rang for about six rings and then went to the answerphone.

'Well that proved nothing. I'll ring her number.'

Richard was stood next to her nodding. Olivia dialled again. The phone was answered after two rings.

'Hello?'

'Err... Angela, sorry for ringing you, but Richard's going to the bar. He wanted to know what you wanted to drink. It looks like he's left his phone at home.'

'Trust him to do something as idiotic as that. Err, I'll have a Black Russian with loads of ice please. Do you want me to get you anything from here?' she asked.

'No, I might go and have a look a bit later. I'll let Richard know about that Black Russian. We're over by the bar now when you're done.'

'Right, I won't be long.'

Olivia turned to Richard, who was stood next to her with a stupid look.

How did I ever get mixed up with you? she thought, then she remembered his gentle loving and his huge... sympathetic shoulders.

'You best get to the bar. One large Black Russian, I'll just have a bottle of beer. You haven't forgotten your wallet, have you?' she asked sarcastically. She noticed this sarcasm was lost on him as he frantically began searching around his pockets again. Olivia fished out her purse and handed him a twenty-pound note.

Blushing, he accepted it and disappeared off towards the bar.

Olivia found a table for them to sit at. From her vantage point, she could see him being ignored as the young bartender flirted with two girls who looked like they were off on a hen weekend somewhere. She could see Angela arguing and pointing her finger at one of the women at the perfume counter in duty free.

'What a week I'm in for,' she said.

Her phone chirped again. On checking it, she felt a peculiar sensation of her heartbeat raising its tempo as Anthony's name flashed up on the screen.

Maybe a little bit of normality to help me get through this hell I appear to have found myself in, she thought.

She opened the text. It was not what she was hoping.

> Ollie, been to see Dr H. There's something he's not telling me. He wants to speak to us and Angela at the same time. I'll look at records to make sure everything is OK. Don't worry while on your jollies, I got everything covered back here. Love Ant xx

Her phone chirped again then, twice this time, indicating that she has received two texts. One was from Jan, the other from Katie. Both of them alluded to her having sex with Richard while Angela was asleep, neither was really funny, but they did both wish her a wonderful trip and a promise of a large night out on her return. Katie also hinted she had something to tell her, but it could wait until she got back from America.

Two people now who want to see me on my return. This holiday is going to drag, she thought as Richard returned from the bar with a bottle of ice-cold beer. Just what she needed. She took a gulp, nearly draining half of the bottle before letting out a loud involuntary belch, just as Angela returned from duty free.

'I hope you're not going to do that when we meet our business partners,' she said with a smile that said, 'I'm joking... but not really.'

'I got you both a little something,' she announced taking a little sip of her Black Russian. 'Aw, Richard, you know I don't like strong drinks.' She flashed him an annoyed face, then returned to her announcement. 'Olivia. I got you a bottle of the good stuff, because I know you like it. Richard, I got you this aftershave, because I like it.' She tipped him an exaggerated wink making sure Olivia saw it too.

He didn't even notice. He was too busy fishing about in a pocket halfway down his leg in the combat trousers he was wearing. 'Here it is,' he announced triumphantly.

Olivia had half a hope he was talking about his mobile phone. She was disappointed when he produced his wallet and held it over his head, grinning from ear to ear.

75.

PHILADELPHIA WAS COLD.

It was very cold. Olivia saw it as an excuse to shop more, to buy herself a new, warmer, wardrobe.

The first day and night went by without a hitch. The hotel was beautiful and was situated in the Logan Square region. This was only a short stroll from the main shopping strips, the bars, and the restaurants.

The first day of the trip was spent together. It was not as horrendous as she had expected. By the time they had arrived at PHI, retrieved their bags, cleared customs, got their transport, and checked into the hotel, they were all exhausted.

They met up for a bite to eat in the restaurant of the hotel, had a quick drink, and then an early night.

The next morning, Olivia was up and awake at four a.m. Jet lag had already set in. She could see no point in lying around in bed wide awake and on her own, so she got up and went to the gym on the top floor of the hotel.

There were already a number of people in there, mostly Brits doing the same as her, trying to burn off their jet lag.

Butterflies

After half an hour of running on the treadmill and cross trainer, she went to relax in the spa pool and steam room.

She was surprised to bump into Angela in there.

'Can't sleep either?' Angela asked as Olivia walked into the hot, steamy room. They were the only people inside.

'Nope, never can when I get jet lag. I always have this great idea I'm going to get up at five every day and do an hour in the gym. It never quite works out that way.'

Angela offered a lazy smile, 'Ha, yeah, that's a pity, isn't it?'

'So, what's on the agenda today?' Olivia probed.

'I have a ten-thirty meeting with our partners that should last about an hour, two at the very tops. Next, they'll want to meet with you. I've briefed them on the fact that all your business transactions will be going through me, and that you are, don't take any offence here, just the figure head.'

Olivia laughed. 'None taken. Will I need to get dressed up for this meeting?'

'Nope, they do all their work in smart-casual. Jeans and nice shirts, that sort of thing.'

'I may need to do a bit more shopping before I go then.' She smiled as she relaxed back and enjoyed the steam opening every pore in her skin and clearing out her sinuses.

I can't believe I've just had a proper conversation with Angela and not wanted to rip her eyes out afterwards, she thought as she closed her eyes, letting the steam embrace her. *Maybe I'm warming to her after all.*

76.

AFTER A PLEASANT morning shopping on her own and a light bite for breakfast, Olivia returned to the hotel to get ready for the meeting. With a new pair of designer jeans and another pair of expensive shoes, she felt more than ready for whatever could be thrown at her today.

As she was getting dressed, there was a knock on her hotel room door.

It was Richard.

'Hang on a minute,' she shouted as she struggled into her new blouse and fastened the buttons on her jeans.

'You look fantastic,' was Richard's salute to her as he entered the hotel room.

She smiled at him. 'Don't start all that again,' she scolded him. 'You know where it got us last time.'

He pulled a face; it was amused, but slightly disappointed.

'We did have a laugh, though, didn't we?' Olivia said. 'I just can't seem to get my head around where this new Angela has come from. I actually had a conversation with her today and didn't want to rip her head off after it.'

Butterflies

Richard laughed. 'Well if it makes you feel any better, she still seems to be in the refrigerator section of the sex store.'

She couldn't help but laugh. Richard only ever seemed to be fidgety and awkward whenever Angela was about. When *they* were together, he was witty and charming. But all that was in the past now. When they got home and he had removed all evidence from his phone, then she'd broach the subject of them moving out of the flat at the bottom of the garden. She'd miss them in a way, but the arrangement was always only supposed to be temporary anyway.

'Right, I just came down to let you know that the taxi is booked for half an hour. I'll meet you in the lobby then, OK?'

'Yeah, I'll be ready. I'll see you there.'

He winked as he exited from the room.

There's no way he would have ever winked at me like that if Angela was around. What sort of hold does that woman have over him? she thought, as she watched him leave.

77.

THE MEETING WAS arduous. The person who was to work the USA side of Paul Martelle Enterprises was a man named Aaron Mitchell. He was mid-fifties, in great shape for his age. *If he was a bar of chocolate, he'd eat himself,* Olivia thought with a secret smile. Twice, she caught him eyeing her up in her skinny jeans and tight black blouse. On the second occasion, he had the audacity to wink at her. It was a wink she could imagine a crocodile giving a small girl stuck in a stream, right before it ate her whole. She shivered.

At the end of the meeting, the papers that had been drawn up were presented to Olivia. Angela had apprised her that they'd been waterproofed by their solicitors and were OK to sign, so she did. Aaron stood up after the signature was secured and began to applaud. Apparently, this was considered the common practice in America, and she was cajoled into joining in.

She felt more than a little foolish doing so, but customs are customs.

After the backslapping was complete, Aaron rounded off the proceedings. 'I would like to extend my thanks to our British cousins for coming all this way and signing this joint venture. I'd like to

Butterflies

thank you all for a job well done and take everyone out to lunch at my favourite restaurant, then for cocktails in the bar above it. How about that?'

Everyone cheered a little. Most were in total agreement. Olivia was of two minds, but then she thought it might look rude if she didn't turn up for at least one or two drinks.

'Well all right then, let's go, shall we?' Aaron boomed.

He waltzed over to Olivia and took her by the hand. 'If you don't mind, I'd like you to accompany me as my guest.' He lifted her hand to his mouth and kissed it. As he did, he offered her another one of his reptilian winks. She tried to smile, but only succeeded in producing a death grimace. Aaron didn't seem to notice as he whisked her out of the room.

'Martha, order my car for the front lobby, would you please? We're going to need taxis too, three of them,' he shouted as he sped through the reception to his office. A harassed, but pretty, young woman hurriedly picked up the phone and spoke into it.

By the time they'd reached the lobby, the car was already waiting for them. Without further ado, Olivia was whisked into the stretched limo with Aaron and another lady who had been introduced to her, but whose name she couldn't remember.

'Tom, take us to Aldo's please.'

Tom the driver turned to look into the back, gave Aaron a nod, and pulled out of the street into traffic. 'No problem, Aaron. We'll be there in about ten minutes,' came Tom's reply.

'I like everyone who works for me to call me by my first name, and I get to know everyone else's first name too. It gives work that little 'not work' feeling to it. Don't you think?'

Olivia just smiled at him, not really taking anything in. She'd only just caught her breath from the whirlwind of the meeting.

'I was thinking we could have a couple of steaks and then go have ourselves a party. What do you say, Olivia?'

She was beginning to get the creeps. The way this man was fawning over her was making her skin crawl. He had to know she had a husband, his business partner, and he had to know that he was still alive, surely? Then she thought about Angela, and about how eager she'd been for her to attend this meeting.

I wonder what she's been telling him about me? she thought, sitting uncomfortably close to Aaron, who was still wittering on about something or other.

She was quite relieved to arrive at the restaurant at the same time as the other taxis turned up. She had never been so happy to see Angela in her whole life. Her heart lifted as she saw Richard get out of the taxi too. She was glad to see people she knew.

Aaron had booked the best table in the house; the Maître d escorted them to the back of the room where a large table was already prepared. There were twelve places set in all.

All through the night, Angela cringed at the brashness of the Americans, but to be fair, they *were* nice people. For all his brashness and pushiness, Aaron seemed to be nice too. He was polite to all the staff, he seemed to know them all by their first names and made it his business to get to know the ones he didn't.

The food was excellent as was the personally chosen wine that seemed to flow the whole night.

Olivia felt like she was trapped in some sort of whirlpool. Maybe it was the wine or the fast-talking, or the idea this deal would make her comfortable for the remainder of her life. Either way, she was beginning to relax and was actually having a good time.

At least, she was until the end of the night.

Butterflies

78.

'I'LL ORDER MY car around and give all of you a lift back to your hotel,' slurred a drunken Aaron. 'It'll give us a chance to talk a little about our business deal, eh?'

Olivia had finished a good few drinks. But, despite the wine, she still had most of her wits about her.

'Are Richard and Angela coming too?' she asked, thinking this was a great idea as she didn't trust a taxi this late, and she was getting tired.

'Yeah, of course they are. Meet me in the lobby in five minutes.'

Aaron had a look about him, a look like the cat who had gotten the cream. Olivia hadn't noticed; although not completely drunk, she was still a little merry and caught in the merry-go-round of the night. She went to the ladies to powder her nose and look for Angela to let her know they were getting a lift back to the hotel. She couldn't be found anywhere, neither could Richard for that matter. She assumed, or hoped, that they'd both be in the lobby waiting for her.

As she entered the lobby, the car was idling outside the restaurant. She walked over to it and opened the door. Inside, Aaron was alone.

This sent alarm bells through her, and she hesitated to get in, until she realised, he was on the telephone. 'Yeah, she's here right now, just getting into the car. Are you guys coming or what?' It seemed he was talking to Angela.

That was when Olivia made her mistake. She *assumed* that he was talking to Angela, waiting for her and Richard to come down to the lobby and get into the car, so she got in.

As she closed the door behind her, she heard Aaron conclude his conversation. 'OK, so you and Richard are going to get a taxi? Are you sure? OK then, I'll drop Olivia off and ring you in the morning.' As he hung up, he turned to Olivia and smiled. 'It looks like it's just you and me, sweetheart.' The doors to the car locked, and they began to move.

'Whoa, hang on a minute, what's happening here?' she asked with a shake in her voice.

'I'm dropping you off at your hotel,' Aaron replied, once again flashing her his reptilian smile.

'No, I want out of here right now,' she said, trying her best not to sound as scared as she felt.

Aaron looked hurt, and a bit amused. 'I'm only offering a little bit of hospitality.' He smiled. 'Angela did say you would be, erm, how did she put it? Responsive? To a little hospitality.' As he said this, his eyebrows raised, and a lizard smile equal to his reptilian wink intensified.

Olivia's eyes widened. 'What did you say?'

'I said…' He moved closer to her on the long settee. '…Angela said you would be responsive to my hospitality.'

Olivia felt the first real pangs of panic at this point. She looked around the cabin of the car for some way of escaping the advances of the creepy, drunken letch before her. The only thing she could think of doing was pushing him back away from her. Her heart was in her mouth, and she was afraid that her voice would come out shaky. 'Oh, she did, did she?' she asked with a sass that she knew she didn't possess. 'Well listen, Aaron. I'm not 'responsive,' and I don't think that this is appropriate behaviour.'

Unconcerned with her rebuff, he continued to move closer. She could smell the bourbon on his breath and could see a sheen of sweat across his top lip. He put his hand on her lap and his crocodile smile returned. She moved his hand away. Her heart was now beating so fast, she had never been so scared in her entire life.

He put it back on her lap, with a little bit of force.

With an involuntary gesture, Olivia smacked him across the face, catching his cheek and the bridge of his nose with a loud snap.

The force of the smack knocked his face away from her. When he turned back, there was already a welt in the shape of her hand beginning to redden on his cheek.

'You fucking bitch!' he said, and lunged at her.

Without thinking, she brought up her knee as he loomed over her, catching him, but not in the place she was hoping. She caught him in the thigh. It made him squirm in discomfort, but it didn't do much to deter his advance. His hand was back on her thigh and it was sliding up her tight jeans. She clamped her legs together, trapping his hand between them, but his other was on her chest in a mere second.

Both her hands were behind her, trying to stop her from falling back on the long seat. She knew that if she did, then this struggle would be over. He yanked his hand out from between her legs and kneeled over her, leering a drunken, evil looking smile. He then slapped her hard across the face. The shock and the power of his slap sent her reeling back.

She knew now that she was all but helpless.

Her legs were kicking out at her attacker but failing to make any impact. He was now in a dominant position.

His hands were scrambling at her belt and the buttons on her jeans as she tried to turn away. She needed to free herself to be able to put up any resistance.

She looked towards the driver's window, hoping that Tom would put a stop to this. But the partition was up.

This was obviously a situation they had been in a number of times.

Aaron was fumbling with his belt and trousers, and she could see that he was enjoying this struggle. His face was wet with sweat, he stunk of alcohol, and he was sporting a maniacal grin. It was also more than apparent that the alcohol in his system was having no detrimental effect inside his trousers. The bulge at the front told her he was fully loaded and was expecting more than a little business.

Olivia was petrified by how this man had gotten the upper hand on her so quickly. It was obvious he'd done this before. An unaccompanied woman, plied with alcohol, gets into his limo for a *ride home*.

How could she have been so stupid?

She felt his hands move from her opened jeans and grab, hungrily, at her chest; his fingers pinched mercilessly at her breasts and nipples. They caught purchase at the neckline of her blouse, and she felt his muscles tighten as he ripped it down. As the buttons popped, the blouse opened, exposing her black bra, and the sight sent him into a frenzy.

She could do nothing as he leaned into her and began to bite her neck.

The cold, slimy skin of his lips touched her, and she recoiled, her skin felt dirty. She screamed, hoping to alert the attention of

Butterflies

Tom, but it was to no avail. She resigned herself to what was happening, or to what was *about* to happen.

As his mouth and teeth did their filthy work on her neck and ears and his fingers began to probe where they should never probe, she fought him every step of the way. She was not going to give it up without a fight.

She could sense his frustration, and also his enjoyment as he frantically tried to pull her jeans down.

He sat up, raised his hand one more time, and brought it down hard onto her face. This slap knocked the fight out of her. He caught her on the bridge of her nose, instantly sending her into a world of strange colours and stars.

Then, without a moment's hesitation, he was back on her.

This time she couldn't do anything to help herself, except cry. She wasn't aware the car had stopped, and she wasn't aware of the raised voices outside. Neither was Aaron. His trousers were around his ankles now, and he was rubbing his naked erection against any part of her exposed flesh it could touch, all while still trying to work her tight jeans off her legs.

'Come on, give it up, you British whore. You fucking slut!' This was his mantra now as his frustrations were mounting at his inability to remove her clothing.

Olivia's eyes were closed. He had her pinned to the seat, and she couldn't move her legs. Her fear, and her refusal to accept this situation, caused her to miss the doors to the limo unlocking themselves.

Aaron was also unaware as one of the doors was yanked open. He was too preoccupied to notice when a large hand reached through the door and grabbed him by the back of his neck. Even as he was effortlessly lifted off Olivia, his bared teeth were testament to his sexual frustration and heated lust.

She could only watch as her oppressor was unceremoniously dragged out of the car. It took a moment for her to realise what was happening, why she wasn't being attacked anymore.

Aaron was standing outside the car, his trousers around his ankles, his formerly proud penis beginning to wilt as he obviously realised the gravity of his situation.

Olivia hurriedly pulled up her trousers, bunched up her blouse in her hands to cover her modesty, and made her own exit from the limo.

They were in the parking lot of the hotel. The driver, Tom, was sat, leaning against a giant wheelie bin, there was blood over his face. He looked dazed, and his nose looked broken.

She turned to see Richard. He had taken Aaron in a headlock and was now punching him in the face. Aaron's nose had burst, and there was blood over his suit jacket. His trousers were still around his ankles, but his flaccid penis was now no-where to be seen.

A cry came from behind her. Fearing the worst, she turned on her toes to see who was there. The sight she saw filled her with rage and hate.

It was Angela.

She was standing on the other side of the limo holding a shawl around her as if it was going to save her life.

Olivia looked at her and a red mist descended over her vision. 'Oh, you fucking BITCH!' she screamed. Then she went for her.

'Olivia, I'm sorry, I'm so, so… so…' Angela never got to finish her sentence before Olivia was on her. She slapped her hard in the face, then scratched at her and pulled her hair.

Not once in the attack did Angela even try to defend herself. Olivia was too incensed to notice, or care.

Butterflies

'Why, Angela?' she shouted as she pulled her down by her hair. 'Why do you hate me so much that you would do this to me? Why? WHY?'

Angela was on the floor, sobbing hard. Olivia was standing over her, her fists balled, wanting her to say something, anything, to give her another excuse to hit her.

Richard dropped Aaron onto the floor in a bloody mess and walked over to where the girls were fighting. 'What's going on here?' he asked, looking between the two women.

'It's her,' Olivia spat. 'She told Aaron I'd be a willing participant to his lecherous advances. Didn't you?'

'What? You set her up to get attacked and raped? Angela?'

Angela was sobbing now. Blood was drooling down her chin from Olivia's attack. She was looking towards the floor, not able to meet anyone's eyes. 'I never set her up to be raped or attacked. I just told Aaron she might be up for a little fun. I never knew his idea of fun was... was this!' She swept her arm around the parking lot.

Aaron had got up from Richard's beating and was trying to get his driver up from his seated position. They both clambered into the limo. Aaron was limping and bleeding quite badly from a number of cuts. 'You, you fucked up here, man. You'll be hearing from my lawyers. Assault and battery, that's what this is.'

Richard turned to face him, and the man cowered back into his car. He pointed up towards a CCTV camera that took in the whole of the car park.

Richard spoke softly to him. 'Do you think that camera up there has any footage of you being dragged out of this limo with your little prick dangling between your legs? And do you think it'll have any footage of my friend jumping out in a state of panic with her clothes torn and ripped? I'm willing to bet a twenty-year stretch for assault and battery that it has. What are you willing to bet?' The malice in his voice was accentuated by the spittle coming from his mouth and landing on Aaron's face.

Aaron got into the car after glancing up at the camera, and the limo sped away, tires screeching as it went.

Richard turned back to the girls. Olivia was sitting on the asphalt next to a crying Angela.

'So, come on now, what is all this about?' he asked.

'Aaron was on the phone to her. She told him I was up for it. How the fuck could you tell him that, Angela? Why?'

'Because,' she paused, attempting to catch her breath. 'Because, I know about you two.' There was a low grumble in her throat. 'I know all about you two and the sordid little affair you're having behind my back. I KNOW YOU'RE FUCKING MY HUSBAND!' she screamed.

Richard's face told Angela everything she needed to know. He was almost crimson and was shaking his head in denial, but his eyes were as guilty as anything. Angela opened her dropped bag and removed her phone. To Olivia's horror she realised it wasn't hers, but it just looked like hers.

This one was Richard's.

She handed the phone over to Olivia who accepted it in her shaking hands. 'You'll find what you're looking for in the photo gallery,' Angela spat.

Olivia, shamefaced, opened the phone gallery and looked at the pictures. She understood how Angela could be so angry. The pictures were rather graphic. There was no way of denying that it was either of them.

Richard was stood above the two women; his head was hung low.

'So, you'll excuse me if I'm seen as the bad guy here, won't you,' Angela growled as she glared at them.

Butterflies

Olivia sat back on her hands. She had buttoned up her jeans, but there was nothing she could do about her ripped blouse. She looked up to the sky and sighed.

'Angela, I—' Richard began.

'Don't you bother giving me your excuses. You both went behind my back. My husband and my sister-in-law. Getting up to God only knows what while I was away trying to build a foundation that would keep us all afloat. If... if...' She couldn't say what she wanted to next, it just wouldn't come out of her mouth.

'If Paul dies... that's what you're trying to say isn't it?' Olivia finished for her. 'You're trying to build a foundation for us for if, or when, Paul dies.'

Angela looked away from them both. 'Yes, that's exactly what I was about the say.'

'Angela, I cannot and will not try to explain my deplorable actions. Yes, what we've done is wrong, I'll not deny that fact. We called it all off when we realised there was a bigger picture.'

'A bigger picture?' Angela asked grasping back at the anger in her voice. 'A bigger picture? What do you mean? Like my brother lying in a coma in hospital?'

Olivia took that blow on the chin, and simply looked at her sister-in-law. She was drained of fight now, she felt empty. 'Yes, like my husband lying in a coma in hospital, like the only mother figure I've ever had and my best friend dying before my eyes. Like the only confidant I could find whose best advice was not to get pissed was living in the same house as me. And that confidant was going through his own personal agony.'

'Agony? Agony? What are you talking about, Agony?' Angela rasped.

'The agony of being ignored and bullied and ridiculed by the one person in the whole world I love,' Richard cut in.

Angela's face fell. As she turned to look at him, Olivia saw the fight drain out of her too. Richard's one sentence had cut a swathe through her.

'What?' she whispered. Her eyes were almost closed, as if she couldn't quite believe what she was hearing.

Richard looked at her. The sweet innocence of his face right then shocked Olivia.

He really does love her, she thought.

'You heard me right, Angela. When was the last time you had anything nice to say to me? When was the last time we had any intimacy? I'm not even talking about sex; I'm talking about sitting together in the same room and holding each other as we watch the telly or read a book. You take great pride pointing out my clumsiness to everyone, never once trying to help me. I sometimes can't even talk when I'm in your presence, I'm too nervous I might embarrass you, or myself. I become clumsier.'

Angela was sitting on the damp asphalt listening to him. Tears were welling in her eyes. Olivia thought that it was the first time she'd ever actually seen Angela take any notice of what her husband was saying to her.

'I've been on my own for the last, I don't know… three years. All that time I've watched you from afar, loved you from afar, not even daring to come anywhere near you for the fear of rejection.'

Richard was crying now.

'I know what I've done. I know it's unforgivable, but…'

Angela tried to interject. Her eyes were red and wet, although there was still anger in them, it seemed to be abating.

'No, Angela, you can hear me out. I know what I've done is horrible, but I've been needing some human interaction. I let all my friends go for you because you didn't like them or didn't like me being with them. I was so in love with you I just let them go. I was left with no one, just you, and in the end, even you rejected me.'

As he paused to wipe the tears away from his eyes, Angela looked at him, her face ashen. Her red eyes were wide, and her cheeks were wet with tears.

Olivia felt like a voyeur in this conversation. She felt like she shouldn't be here. She should leave these two to get on with whatever was happening between them. She stood up on her shaky legs, wiped her jeans down, straightened her ripped blouse and began to walk towards the front of the hotel. Then she realised that she still had Richard's phone in her hands. Turning to give it back to him, she watched as they embraced each other. A small smile crept across her face.

She went to leave the phone on the floor beside the couple, then she remembered the photographs and videos on there. Scrolling through, she permanently deleted any evidence of her and Richard. As they deleted, it felt like a weight lifting from her chest. It wasn't just because they no longer existed in the world, but because it felt like a new start; definitely for them, and maybe even for her.

79.

AS SHE GOT into her hotel room, she felt better about her life. Tonight had illuminated quite a few things. She knew she was vulnerable, but she also knew that sometimes, the worst of times can also be the start of the best of times.

She picked up the hotel phone and rang through to reception. She asked them to book her onto the next flight to the UK. She was informed that there was a flight tomorrow morning at nine-thirty.

'Could you book me a seat in business class, please? Yes, just the one. I'll be checking out first thing in the morning. No, no, there's been nothing wrong with your service, it's just a personal matter. Thank you, yes, goodnight.'

She hung up and lay on her bed. She thought she might cry, but no tears came. In fact, she felt… happy.

Her peace was broken by the sound of Whigfield singing 'Saturday Night' and the screen of her mobile phone illuminating the room.

Butterflies

80.

OLIVIA LANDED AND collected her things. She walked out to the meet and greet area of the arrivals lounge, and there among the crowd were her two best friends.

Both of them were sombre as they approached her. Katie wrapped her arms tight around her and gave her a massive hug, then Jan did the same.

'You look done in,' Jan said with a small smile. 'Come on, let's get you home.'

Katie drove. It took them about an hour to get out of the airport and onto the motorway. 'Rush hour traffic!' Katie complained. 'I'm sorry, Ollie, we'll be out of it soon.'

Olivia hadn't even noticed. She was sat in the back seat of the car with her head on a pillow. She wasn't asleep, but then she wasn't really awake either. She was just in a small, lost space in-between. She no longer had time for any of the bad stuff that had happened to her this year, that was all in the past.

D E McCluskey

81.

'DO YOU WANT me to wait for you?' Katie shouted up the stairs after her.

'If you don't mind. I'm just going to jump into the shower; I won't be long,' Olivia shouted back.

Jan and Katie were sat in the front room of Olivia's house. All her bags were stacked haphazardly in the hallway. They both sat in the opposite chairs to each other. Both uncharacteristically silent. They heard the shower being turned on.

'What do you think happened in America then?' Jan asked, leaning into towards Katie.

'I haven't got a clue, but it must've been bad. She said she got the phone call *after* she'd booked her flight. Something must have happened.'

'It's a bit strange that Angela never came home with her, or Richard for that matter,' Jan replied.

Katie leaned in even further towards Jan. 'You do know she'd been sleeping with him, don't you?'

'Yeah, she told me. Do you think it's got anything to do with that?'

Butterflies

'Could be, but we won't know for sure until after,' Katie shrugged.

'Yeah. After.'

Both friends then fell silent again as the listened to the spray of the water from the shower upstairs being turned off.

82.

THE THREE FRIENDS were in the car. Olivia was in the back seat again, and all of them were silent for the majority of the short journey.

When they arrived, Olivia got out of the car, looking tired, downtrodden, and a little depressed. 'Hun, do you want us to come in with you?' Jan asked, holding her hand out of the passenger side window.

Olivia grabbed the offered hand. She looked at both of them, really looked, and then smiled. 'No thanks. I appreciate the offer, but this is something I have to do alone.'

'Should we wait? Or do you want to give me a ring a bit later when you need picking up?' Katie asked, peering through the open window opposite her.

'Listen, you guys, I love you like sisters, but I'm OK. I'll get a taxi home. I don't know how long I'll be here. I'll ring both of you if I need anyone, deal?'

'Deal,' they both agreed.

Olivia turned and walked into the hospital.

83.

DR HAUSEN'S OFFICE was on the fourth floor. Normally, Olivia would take the stairs for a little bit of exercise, but today, she chose the lift. As she rode up, she remembered the last time she was in a lift with Paul. It was the day after their wedding, and they'd shared it with that lovely old couple. Thinking about them made Olivia smile. But it was short lived when she remembered what the woman said to them as they got out of the lift, something like, 'Goodbye, and I hope you have a long and healthy life…'

Olivia sighed. *Fat chance of that,* she thought as the doors opened and she exited onto the fourth floor.

She knocked on Dr Hausen's door and felt her stomach sink to the pit of her belly.

'Come in, come in, Mrs Martelle. I hope you had a pleasant journey home from America?' he greeted her in his Germanic accent.

'It was…' She paused as she thought about her next word. '…pleasant. Kind of, anyway,' she finished.

'Please, sit down, we have much to discuss, much to discuss.'

Olivia could tell he was just as nervous as her, mostly by the way he was flittering around. She just wished he would get to the crux of what she was here for, then she could leave and have some time alone.

'Mrs Martelle, your husband has been under my care for a little over seven months now...' he began, fidgeting with his pen and a small note pad before him.

Olivia leaned over and put her hand on the pad, settling it onto the desk. Dr Hausen looked up at her, surprised, but also a little relieved.

'In those seven months, all we've been able to do is to reduce the swelling on his brain and make him comfortable. Along with the exercises, there has been very little else we could do.' He stopped to clear his throat and wipe his glasses.

Olivia could sense a 'but' coming along.

'But now,' he continued. 'The swelling has resumed. We don't know what is causing it this time. We noticed it start just about a week ago. We thought it was nothing at first, maybe a little infection that we could treat with antibiotics. We did treat it, but it was all to no avail. We were going to tell you before you went to America, but we didn't want to worry you unnecessarily if it did indeed turn out to be just an infection.'

'Doctor, what are you telling me?' she asked, the question muffled from behind her hands.

She already knew the answer.

'I'm telling you, Mrs Martelle, to prepare for the worst. The swelling accelerated yesterday, that is why we were compelled to call you while you were in America. It has continued to swell at an accelerated pace.'

Olivia looked at him. She was surprised that there were no tears in her eyes. She felt odd receiving this news. It was like she was watching a drama unfold from the other side of a TV screen. Very soon, she expected a handsome neurosurgeon to walk in and demand he operate on the beautiful lady's husband. But deep down, she knew that this *was* happening for real. Deep down, she'd been expecting this for the last, what? Two, maybe three months?

'Are you OK, Mrs Martelle? You look a little distant, do you want a drink or something?'

'No thank you, Doctor, please continue.'

'I'm afraid the swelling has already reached the point of no return. Even if we could reduce or even stem it completely, I'm afraid there would be over an eighty per cent chance of irreparable damage.' He looked down at his hands, and they moved towards the pen and pad that was still before him. He managed to stop himself before he looked back at her very slowly. She could see the sorrow in his eyes. 'We have seen no indication that reduction is going to happen. If it continues to swell at its current rate, I do not expect Paul to live past tomorrow, maybe the day after at the very limit.' As he said this, his eyes dropped back down to his desk, and this time, he did begin to busy himself with the pad and pen again. 'I'm so very sorry, Mrs Martelle. We've done all we can.'

84.

ANTHONY ALREADY KNEW the situation. 'I'm so sorry about not being able to tell you. Dr Hausen wanted to tell you himself. The poor guy is taking this personally. I found out late last night. I wanted to ring you, but I didn't know if you were on the way home or not,' Anthony said over the phone. She could hear the waver in his voice as he spoke. He'd been Paul's friend since boyhood. 'Where are you now? I'll come and meet you. It'll give you someone to talk to, share your feelings with. I know I could do with it?'

'Yeah, that sounds good. I'm in the hospital now. I thought it might be best to spend as much time here as possible. Hausen said Paul doesn't have much time left,' Olivia replied.

'OK, I'm at home, but if I leave now, I'll be there within the hour.'

'Can we meet in the restaurant? I've spent quite a bit of time in his room already.'

'That's no problem. Can I get you anything?'

'No, I'm OK; but when you get here, I do have a favour to ask.'

'Right, I'll see you within the hour.'

Butterflies

85.

OLIVIA HUNG UP from Anthony and stepped into Paul's hospital room. The familiar feel of the room was gone, instead it felt like a mausoleum, a shrine to the person her husband had been.

This is what defines him to me in the end, she thought. All the happy times and good memories they'd shared prior to the accident were all still there, but this sight would be etched into her memory for the rest of her life.

A single tear trickled down her cheek.

She felt strange about the tear.

Inside, she knew it was more for her than for her husband. She felt like she'd used up all the tears she had for Paul, and for his accident. 'Why do I feel like this? Why can't I grieve like a normal person?' she asked aloud, but ultimately, to herself.

She jumped a little as a small, female, voice from behind her replied in an Irish lilt. 'That's because you've been grieving for him for the last seven months. Almost non-stop.'

Olivia turned to see a small woman. She looked in her late fifties. She had short cropped white hair that had a kind of blue tinge to it and was wearing the scrubs of a ward nurse. Olivia had never seen her before. 'Oh, I'm sorry, you scared me a little there… I'm…'

The woman smiled at her, 'I know who you are, Mrs Martelle. My name is Poser, Marie Poser. I'm here to look after Paul. To ease him through this last part of his journey, and, if you'll let me, to ease you through it too. Please sit.' The diminutive woman gestured towards the couch at the back of the room. Olivia looked towards it and having never noticed it before, was a little surprised to see it.

The woman saw her reaction to the couch and smiled. 'There's a lot of stuff in this room that you'll not remember seeing. When you look back over the coming weeks, months, and years, you'll hardly remember anything about it, except maybe the colour of the blankets that Paul has been wrapped in. All the other details become insignificant. You will probably forget me too.'

She sat down, next to Olivia and took her hand without asking. 'You've been grieving since you recovered from the accident. I've been here before many times, believe me, in my opinion you've been suffering from survivor's guilt. Have you found yourself doing things lately you would never even consider doing in a million years?'

As the nurse looked her in the eyes, Olivia felt a compulsion to tell her the truth. Everything.

'Well, yes,' she stuttered. 'I've been drinking a lot lately, and then I've formed—'

'Shush now, woman. You don't have to tell me what you did.' There was a smile, filled with humour, even though it was only small. 'A lot of people want to tell me things like they think it's a form of confession or something. I don't have the power to forgive you, all I can do is maybe make you feel a little better about yourself. Let you know that you wouldn't be the first person to begin to steal things from shops or from work during this time in your life, or drinking, or even jumping into bed with people you don't know, or maybe people you do.'

She smiled a small but reassuring smile towards Olivia and gripped her hand a little tighter.

'It's OK, my love. Whatever you've done, you'll not be judged by Paul. In fact, to ease your conscience, he'll never know.'

Olivia smiled herself then. The woman really had made her feel better about herself and her stupid actions over the last seven months.

'You know that he's not going to make it back to you, don't you?' the nurse whispered kindly. 'I'm a specialist in this field. Some people in here call me the Butterfly of Death.' She laughed as she said this. 'It sounds harsh, but it's meant well. My mother called me Marie, because mariposa is the Spanish word for butterfly, so I kind of think that I was chosen for this,' she said, smiling and grasping Olivia's hand. 'I like to think that I have a way of easing the pain of the patient, and of their loved ones.'

'Well, I don't know about Paul, but you've made me feel a little better about myself.' Olivia smiled. *Is she here to give me my butterflies back? It seems such a coincidence,* she thought as she looked at the blue tint in her hair.

'I'll leave you now,' the Irish lilt came back stronger than ever. 'But if you need me at any time, just ask for Nurse Poser, and I'll come and see you... OK?'

Olivia began to cry again. 'OK,' she said as the small woman fluttered a little around Paul and then left, but not before giving Olivia's hand one more squeeze.

She was alone once again.

Alone with her thoughts, pondering on what Nurse Poser had said. She'd had plenty of time to prepare herself for this situation.

The truth was a hard pill to swallow, but somewhere, deep within her, she knew this eventuality was going to happen.

When she was waiting for him to wake up, she knew. When she cried herself to sleep, she knew. When she was dreaming about Richard, she must have known then too. Most of all, when she'd slept with him and the guilt the next day didn't, really, cripple her, she knew.

But she had been scared that what she knew made her a bad person! The truth of it all was that Nurse Poser was right, she had already grieved for Paul, and now it seemed that she may be over that grieving process already. Maybe Paul had sent Marie Poser to her, in a way *he* was giving her back her beautiful blue butterflies.

86.

WHEN ANTHONY ARRIVED at the hospital restaurant, he was a little flustered, as if he had rushed to be here by her side. Olivia was sitting on her own, holding a cup of coffee, and looking wistfully into space.

'Olivia, I'm sorry I took so long getting here, the traffic was horrendous. Are you OK?' he asked, slightly out of breath.

'Yeah, I'm fine,' she said, smiling as he sat opposite her.

He looked at her, there was confused light in his eyes. 'I was totally expecting you to be a gibbering mess about now.'

She gave him a look; it was a look of such clarity that it shocked him to see how together she was.

'Anthony, I'm tired... I've been living this day for the last seven months. I need to tell somebody something, and I need that somebody to tell me that I'm not a bad person for it.'

He looked a little unsure. 'Olivia, do you want to tell *me* this thing? I'm not sure if I would be the best person to tell. Remember I'm Paul's best friend, we've been as close as brothers since we were kids...'

Olivia just sat and looked at him. Her face was impassive, almost expressionless, but Anthony could see a strong determination in her eyes, and a deep, deep sorrow. He gave in. 'OK, I see. You need the somebody to be a somebody who cares as much about him as you do, don't you?'

Her eyes smiled more than her mouth did. 'Yes,' she whispered.

That was when he noticed there were tears in her eyes, they just hadn't fallen yet. 'Can't you tell Angela?' he asked.

She just shook her head. 'No, I can't. It's complicated, but I can't. It has to be you.'

He swallowed hard. He didn't like where this was going. He stared back at her, into her eyes, and steeled himself for what was coming. 'Go on then… tell me.'

Olivia sat and looked at him for about another minute. She was racking her brains for how to say it, and what to say. After all this time thinking about it, when it came down to the actually telling, it was something else entirely. 'Anthony,' she paused, taking in a deep mouthful of air. 'I have to tell you that I've moved on. I'm over my grieving period for Paul.' She stopped again and her dam broke. The tears swelled in her eyes and then burst down her cheeks. 'I'm over him and he's not even dead yet.'

She was sobbing now, deep, mournful sobs; dabbing at her eyes with a handkerchief. 'Anthony, please believe me, he was… is… the love of my life, but I'm just too tired to continue.'

He reached over to her and took her hand, she responded to his grip and squeezed back, and together they shared the moment.

'I've missed him every day for the last seven, nearly eight months. I've worked hard not to cry every night. Even when I've been occupied, it's been like only half of me was there, the other half has been lying here in this hospital. Can you understand what I'm saying?'

He nodded. He noticed that his eyes were tearing up too. 'Olivia, believe me, I understand. Since I got back, I've devoted a lot of my time to Paul. I've been here every day and studying every night. As much as I hate this situation, and as much as I hate to say it, Paul will be better off *not* pulling through this.' He paused for a moment to wipe the tears from his eyes and to collect himself before continuing. 'If he was to make it back, I mean before this swelling happened, it would have been years before he would have been back to the Paul we knew and loved before the accident; if *that* Paul ever came back at all.'

Olivia squeezed his hand again. The pair of them sat for just over an hour, neither saying a word. Both allowing their lover and their best friend to bring them together in memories.

87.

AS THE RESTAURANT was about to close for the night, they both ordered a large coffee to go.

'I need to go and sit with him for a while; I owe him that. I want to hold his hand; it isn't his fault that all of this has happened. I do still love him.'

'Olivia, you don't have to justify yourself to me. I want to sit with him too, if you'll let me, but I'll understand if you want to be alone.'

Olivia's eyes brightened, and she shook her head. 'No, I want you with me. You can tell me some stories about when you were boys.'

Anthony grinned; there was genuine, boyish humour in that smile, and Olivia liked it. 'Do you really want to hear these stories? I mean, are you ready for them?'

She smiled, it was a sad smile, but it was also full of hope. She needed cheering up on this blue day, and she'd decided Anthony was the one for the job.

88.

THEY TALKED FOR hours. The stories Anthony relayed were hilarious and sometimes, unbelievable. They laughed, they cried, they hugged. Olivia slept for a few hours; she was feeling jet lagged. While she slept, Anthony sought out Dr Hausen.

He knocked on the office door and walked in. 'Doctor Hausen, can I have a moment?'

Hausen looked up as Anthony entered the office. His eyes were pink, and his hair was askew. He regarded him for a moment, before the flicker of recognition animated him. 'Is something happening?'

'No, please relax. I just wanted an update on what's going on.'

The doctor shook his head slowly. 'I should come down to the room with you, Doctor. Is Paul's lovely lady wife down there too?'

'Yes, she's sleeping now, though.'

Dr Hausen pursed his lips. 'Best let her sleep for a while longer, she'll need all her strength for the day ahead. I fear it'll be a tough day, for her especially.' He sighed as he walked out of his office.

'And for me too,' Anthony muttered.

89.

BY THE TIME they had reached Paul's room, Olivia was awake. She was sitting up and holding her husband's hand, talking to him in hushed tones. The moment looked so special between them that Anthony was loath to disturb it. He held out his arm and stopped Dr Hausen from bustling in.

A little surprised at the obstacle, Hausen looked up and corrected his glasses. He then noticed the moment that was occurring in the room, pulled a small 'oops' face, and stood away from the door.

~~~~

She knew she looked tired, because she *was* tired, but there was no way she was going to be somewhere else for Paul's last day. Even though the doctors had told her he was past the point of no return, he was still here, with her, now, and that was good enough for her.

Sensing that there was someone behind her, she turned to see Anthony and Dr Hausen waiting outside the room. Carefully, she laid Paul's hand back onto the bed, and waved the two men in.

Butterflies

They both entered with sombre smiles.

'Anthony, I need you to do me an enormous favour. I need you to call Angela and let her know of this situation. There are reasons I can't call her myself that I'll tell you about, but not today.'

Anthony nodded. 'Do you want me to tell her to get home as quickly as they can?'

'Yes, please, she needs to be here too, if not for me, then for Paul. They loved each other dearly, didn't they?'

Anthony half laughed. 'Oh yes, devoted to each other, I'd say.' He turned and left the room, leaving her alone with Dr Hausen.

'So, Mrs Martelle, how are you keeping?' He looked at her with genuine concern.

Even through her soul searching, she was still feeling deeply emotional. 'Doctor, please tell me, how will it happen? How will he go?'

Dr Hausen removed his glasses and busied himself wiping them with a handkerchief. He was doing everything he could not to look at her. She could see how emotional he was, and this touched her. It touched her because of the empathy this man must have. He was a doctor, he must be around death all the time, and for him to show this much emotion regarding one of his patients showed his level of devotion.

It was a mark of the man, and Olivia respected him for it.

'It'll happen in the wink of an eye,' he said in his thick Germanic accent. 'He will simply be breathing one minute, and then not the next. I'm so sorry, Mrs Martelle, but I'm going to need you to sign some legal documents.' He turned and picked up a pad and clipboard resting on a small table.

Olivia looked a little confused. 'What documents, Doctor? What are they?'

Dr Hausen paused, almost embarrassed as he handed the papers to her. 'They are DNR forms, Mrs Martelle.'

She was still none the wiser. 'What are DNR forms?'

'It means Do Not Resuscitate. If... *when* we turn off the machines, he may go into arrest, we don't think he will, by the way, but there is a chance, and we will be bound by our Hippocratic oath to attempt resuscitation, even if it is not worth the effort. If this happens, in his state, we would want you to waiver us this action. Would you do that, Mrs Martelle?'

Tears began to flow down her cheeks. She couldn't really see the forms through her blurred eyes, but she could see the area that required her signature.

She signed her name as best she could and handed them back to him. She turned back towards the bed and broke down.

Anthony re-entered at that moment. He looked at Olivia crying with her head on the bed, and then he looked to Dr Hausen, himself looking distraught, holding the clipboard to his chest.

He understood the situation.

He was going to broach this scenario with her himself—maybe he would have done it a little smoother. He patted his colleague on the back and went to Olivia, putting his arms around her shoulders and easing her away from the bed. 'Come on now,' he soothed. 'You knew it was going to be tough, and you know *you'll* have to be tough too.'

She dried her eyes and wiped her nose on her sleeve. As she sniffed, she sobbed at the same time, causing her to laugh, just a little, at the noise.

Dr Hausen saw her laugh, and Anthony noted that he seemed to relax a little.

'I got hold of Angela,' he whispered. 'She's on the next flight home. They were due the day after tomorrow anyway. I told her straight because that's the way she works. I told her that it's odds on Paul won't see the day through.'

Olivia reached to her shoulder and grasped the hand resting there. 'Thank you, Anthony. I couldn't have done that, not today.'

'She did say that she'd want to come in and see him as soon as she lands. I said that wouldn't be a problem. Was that OK?'

Olivia nodded. 'Of course. She has every right to be here, more than me maybe…'

Anthony hugged her from behind and whispered, 'She doesn't. You're Paul's wife. You have more of a right than anyone.'

A very small beeping noise emanated from one of the machines. It alerted both Anthony and Dr Hausen at once.

'What is it?' Olivia asked, alarmed by their responses.

Dr Hausen was already by the bed, looking at the machines and taking notes on his clipboard.

Anthony gently, but firmly, guided her away from the bed and back towards the small settee against the wall. He looked at her, staring intently into her eyes.

'Olivia, I need you be strong right now,' he was nodding as his eyes stared into hers. 'It's starting.'

As he said this, as if on cue, three nurses entered.

She had time to notice that one of them was Nurse Poser.

90.

IN THE END, Paul's death was peaceful and dignified. As per Dr Hausen's explanation, he was simply there one minute and then not the next. All Olivia could do was stand and watch as the good doctor and three nurses fussed around the tubes and instruments surrounding his bed.

After about ten minutes, Dr Hausen hung the DNR form on the bottom of his bed. He looked at his watch with grim but professional determination. 'Time of death nineteen-thirty-two, second of December.'

One of the nurses made a note of this on Paul's clipboard at the bottom of the bed. Hausen turned towards Olivia and Anthony. Although there were no tears in his eyes, she could tell that this death had touched him deeply.

All the nurses filed out, each one making eye contact with Olivia and offering their condolences. Marie Poser stopped as she passed by and offered her arms out to her. She tore herself away from Anthony's embrace and gave the small Irish woman a big hug. The woman's strength surprised her, and the hug nearly crushed her ribs. After a few seconds that felt like minutes, they released each other.

Not one word passed between them, but they didn't need to. The sentiment was there for all to see.

Olivia looked up to Paul's bed. In her eyes, nothing had changed. Her husband was still lying on the bed with all the instruments hooked up to him. The only difference was the room was now silent.

She'd sometimes thought this room was one of the most peaceful places she could be, but now she knew every day she'd been in here there had been a veritable cacophony of noise. From the machines gently buzzing and bleeping, to the one that regulated his breathing. All these noises had gone, and although she shared the room with both Anthony and Dr Hausen, to her it was a moment of complete solitude.

She made her way over to the bed and once again took her husband's hand. It felt different somehow. Colder. It was strange to her that only moments ago she had been sitting, talking to him and holding his warm hand, and now he was already cold. Behind her she heard the door open and close. She assumed it was Anthony and Hausen leaving the room, as all her attention was on Paul.

'I'm so sorry,' she sobbed, finding the words difficult to form in her mouth. 'I love you, and I always will.' The tears came again. This time they were soft and beautiful instead of the harsh ones she had become used to. 'I'll cherish the time we had together and celebrate our wedding day for the rest of my life. We should have had, no, we deserved, a lot more time together. We should have grown old like that old couple in the lift. I love you, Paul, I always will. Goodnight, my sweet.'

She bent over and kissed his forehead before fixing his hair. She traced her hand along the smooth curve of his cheek and then his chin. She wiped her eyes and took in a shaky breath, before turning towards the door. Both Dr Hausen and Anthony were looking in on her. She nodded towards them, and Anthony walked in.

He went to her and hugged her, hard. She knew then that she'd have to get used to all the hugging all over again. Smiling through her tears, she said, 'I think I've only just got rid of all the hug bruises from Aunt Penny's death. I suppose I'm about to get new ones, aren't I?'

Anthony pulled away from the hug and held her at arm's length. He looked into her red, streaming eyes and smiled. 'I think you are, kid. But this time, you'll have someone to share them with.' Then he pulled her close again, and they embraced for a long time.

91.

PHONE CALLS HAD been made, and all the people who needed to be informed had been, with the exception of Angela and Richard. They must have been either at the airport in Philadelphia or in the air, Olivia couldn't remember the timings between when they were called and when Paul passed.

Anthony volunteered to take her home. Jan and Katie had offered to come and get her and make sure she was OK, but she couldn't see the point of that, not when Anthony was already there.

Dr Hausen was stood just outside the doorway to Paul's room. As Olivia walked out, he offered her a small smile. 'I really am sorry, Mrs Martelle. We did all we could.' His eyes dropped to the floor.

'I know you did, Doctor. I thank you from the bottom of my heart.' She gave him a hug and a kiss before walking away down the corridor towards the lifts. As he watched her being led away by Anthony, a small smile spread across his face.

~~~~

The drive home was a blur. She remembered crying a little as she got into the car, but not much else.

'Hey, Ollie, we're here.' Anthony was shaking her lightly, trying to rouse her from her sleep.

Slowly, her eyes flickered open, and she stared out at her driveway in amazement. 'Come on, sleepy head, you look like you need to get in a solid twelve-hour shift.'

She fumbled for the seatbelt as he got out of the car and made his way around to her door. He then opened it for her and helped her out. Somehow, he already had her keys in his hands. She didn't remember giving them to him but was glad he had them, as she didn't think she had the energy to even look for them.

He let them both in, and she turned off the alarm before wading through a pile of junk mail by the front door on their way upstairs. 'Are you going to be OK?' he asked as he supported her up the staircase.

'I think so. Do you want to stay over? The spare bedrooms are made up, you know.'

He looked like he appreciated the gesture. 'Yeah, I might just do that. I don't really fancy that drive back to my place, especially how I'm feeling right now. Thank you, Olivia.'

'It's no problem,' she said. 'Thanks for all your help today, and last night.' She walked up to him and gave him a light kiss on the cheek before turning around and letting herself into her bedroom.

He stood and watched as her door closed.

Butterflies

92.

SHE IS BACK in her hotel room on Lake Geneva. The room is dimly lit, and it's dark outside. Once again, the window overlooking the lake is reflective, like a great big mirror.

Olivia can see herself in the make-shift mirror. Standing in the centre of the room, she is studying her form.

Her bridal veil is pulled over her face, her long hair is hanging loose beneath it. She's wearing a white lace push up bra that accentuates her breasts and cleavage. Her tanned and slim stomach drags the eyes down towards her pleasing curves, which are highlighted by her white lace French knickers. The knickers in turn lead to her tanned, muscular thighs. Three quarters of the way up her legs are the rims to her white stockings, which fall gracefully down her long, shapely legs.

As she looks at herself in the window, she knows where she is, and remembers that this is the underwear she wore on the night of her wedding.

The sight of her in the flattering, dimmed light is spectacular, even if she does think so herself. She knows Paul is going to absolutely love the way she is dressed, or undressed, as the case maybe.

She waits for him to come. He's due any time now. She had something to tell him, but right now, she can't think what it is, but she knows it's important.

First and foremost, however, this is their wedding night. All she can think about is making love. The thought of him, all of him, excites her.

She walks over to the window and blocks the light from her eyes so she can see out. A large crowd has gathered below again. She was expecting them, as they'd been there every other time.

There is something different about them tonight; she can't quite put her finger on what it is, but it's there…

She sighs and moves away from the window. *Where can he be?* she thinks. *I've been here for ages.*

Butterflies

She turns back towards the window, and a slight movement in the reflection behind her catches her eye. It's the door, opening.

Her heart begins to flutter, like a butterfly in her chest. She smiles at that thought. She feels the familiar tug of her nipples hardening in anticipation of Paul and her night of unbridled bridal passion.

If only I can remember what I've got to tell him, she thinks.

She turns on her heel and sees him. His hair is immaculate, it's cut and styled, not a strand out of place. He's wearing his wedding suit, tailored to perfection. Its cut accentuates his firm frame—it fits where it touches.

He smiles at her, and she feels his eyes roaming all over her. She loves the sensation. 'I'm such a lucky man,' he whispers as his gaze continues to wander over her body.

She smiles. Her heart is his. She wants him, needs him, but there's something stopping her from going to him.

He has sensed it too.

His face changes to a confused frown. 'Ollie, what's going on? Why can't I get to you?'

There's no restraint that she can see, but she can feel it too. A force is blocking her from moving towards him. She gets an inkling of what she needs tell him, or is it the other way around? Was it something he had to tell her?

One of them must let go, but which one is it? She can't remember.

She sits down on the bed. Paul sits next to her, sighing in his own frustration. 'We're in a bit of a situation here, aren't we? I've got a feeling that this is our wedding night. You look amazing, I'm in the mood, and yet…'

He tries to reach out and touch her, but again, there is something, in the way.

'Paul!' Olivia remembers now what it is, she remembers that it's *her* who needs tell *him*. She needs to tell him that it's time for him to move on.

'Paul, I love you. I love you with all my heart and soul. That will never change. I don't think I ever loved anyone until the day I met you. I honestly don't know how I'm going to go on and love again.'

Paul looks a little shocked, 'Does this mean that I'm… dead?'

Butterflies

Olivia's eyes widen. 'I'm so sorry, I thought you kn—' She looks at him and sees he's smiling at her. Her face breaks into a big grin, and she begins to laugh. 'Oh, Paul! You really are a bastard.'

As she laughs, she falls forward a little, knocking his arm. Neither of them thinks anything of it, but then they both realise at the same time. They *can* touch each other.

Olivia holds out her hand towards him, and he takes it. They embrace. The fingers of their outstretched hands entwine. Olivia feels something she can only describe as magic coursing through her whole body. As she looks up at both their hands, she sees something, something that makes her smile— something she's missed.

As their fingers interlock, deep blue butterflies fly out from between the palms of their hands. They both sit and watch them fly. Olivia is moved to tears. 'Paul,' she sobs. 'Am I ever going to see you again?'

Already knowing the answer, she drops her head. Her tears fall onto her chest and disappear between her breasts.

Paul lifts her chin almost delicately. He looks deep into her eyes. 'I'll always be here, Ollie. In your dreams and in your thoughts.' He shakes his head slowly. 'You're my one true love. You're the love

I've taken to my grave. I want you to be happy, Olivia. I want you to be free, to release those butterflies you've kept locked up for so long.'

She opens her reddened eyes. The sight around her takes her breath away, and she's caught in an involuntary chuckle. The whole room is bursting with hundreds of thousands of the deepest blue butterflies she's ever seen.

'I have to go now.' He stands up, his wedding suite not even creased. 'Remember me, remember that you're still young, but most importantly, please remember…'

He stands and looks at her long and hard.

Something about him changes. He is lost, momentarily, in the fog of butterflies. He is still there, but she can only see his silhouette. Panicking, she stands and reaches out to him. Her fear abates as she feels his hand touch hers and she is able to pull him closer, out of the cloud of butterflies.

As she sees him, she bursts out laughing. She can't help it. His parting gift to her is so… Paul!

He is almost naked. The tight-fitting wedding suit has gone, to be replaced by a black thong. The front of the thong reads the word GROOM in white letters, below them there is a flashing red light.

Butterflies

He flashes her his dazzling grin. The one she fell in love with. Her heart pounds double time in her throat, in her ears, in her chest.

'...that you look fucking gorgeous.'

With that, he walks out of the room.

~~~

As the door closes behind him, she's forced into a half laugh and half sob. She gets up and walks to the window and puts her head to it to block out the light of the room. The people below are still there. Now she knows what is different about them: none of them are looking up towards the window.

She sees him then.

He is walking out of the hotel, towards the lake, towards where they took their wedding photographs. His wedding suit has returned, and his hands are in his pockets, and his head is dipped low. Suddenly, he turns towards her. She can feel him looking at her. He gestures for her to look behind her, then he waves.

She waves back before turning around. Most of the butterflies have gone now. Only a few remain, mostly on the bed.

Olivia turns back towards the window. She cocks her head to one side, as she isn't a hundred percent understanding what she's seeing. After a few moments, it opens up to her.

Written in the condensation of the window is a message:

YOU ARE FUCKING GORGEOUS. I WILL LOVE YOU FOREVER… PAUL xxx

She looks back out, down towards the dispersing crowd below. They've seen what they came here to see tonight. But Olivia hasn't finished looking. She wants to see him one last time.

He is stood at the edge of the lake. His hands are in his pockets, and he looks up towards her. There is a woman on his arm. She is tall, elegant, and beautiful. They both look up at her and wave before turning away and disappearing into the dissipating crowd.

Both Paul and Great Aunt Penny look at her one last time. They both smile and wave, and then… they are gone!

Butterflies

93.

OLIVIA WOKE WITH a start. She saw the early light of dawn just beginning to creep through her curtains. Considering it was early December, she estimated it must be about eight-thirty. From the corner of her eye, she swore she saw a blue butterfly fluttering from the bed and disappearing towards the window.

She picked up her mobile phone and was a little shocked to see that it was nearer ten. She had slept in. She flicked through the phone and opened the photo app and scrolled through several pics, mostly of her friends Katie and Jan, and Aunt Penny. She continued scrolling until she found the one she wanted.

She lay there for at least another ten minutes, looking at it, knowing that today was going to be a long, hard day, both physically and emotionally.

She had a lot to take in. First and foremost, she needed to make some sense out of that dream. Was it her messed up emotions that conjured the scenario, or had Paul really come back for her, to release her and let her know he'd always love her?

That would be one for her to ponder over for the next few days, or even years. Right now, she had to consider making funeral arrangements, letting people know what has happened, and possibly building some bridges with Angela.

She was going to be a problem again. Now, with Paul gone, she'd have complete control over his businesses—she didn't mind that bit, because she was a good businesswoman and Olivia wasn't. The problem was that Angela would now always be reporting directly to her, and with their history, especially recently, that might cause a problem.

But that was a problem for another time. Right now, her number-one concern was for her to get up, get showered, and make herself presentable for the rest of the world.

She looked at the photo of Paul on her phone, one last time. He was lying on the bed in the hotel in Geneva, naked except for the thong. She had taken the photo just as the red light flashed on, and the reflection from the Champagne bucket before him had caused the word GROOM to blur a little. But she didn't mind.

She knew it was there.

As she swung her legs out of bed, taking a moment to appreciate the scar on the top of her thigh, the little light at the top of the phone began to flash green, meaning she had a text. Clicking the button, a message flashed up that her text was from Anthony.

It read:

> Ollie just reminding you that I stayed in the spare room. Today is the start of a long journey, please know that I'll be here for you, come what may, every step. Ant xx

Butterflies

She lifted her head with her eyes closed and smiled. That was when she smelled the bacon cooking downstairs, and her stomach growled in response to it.

Anthony was in the kitchen. He still had the same clothes on as yesterday, but he looked showered and clean. He was standing by the cooker with two frying pans on the go, the grill, and a steaming kettle. 'I'm an early riser, so I thought I'd make you some breakfast.'

She beamed at him. At that precise moment, she realised that she hadn't eaten anything worth noting for... well she didn't even know how long.

Where did you get all this stuff from? I'm pretty sure I didn't have anything in when I left for America.'

He dangled her car keys in front of him and pulled an exaggerated, apologetic face. 'I sort of borrowed your car; I hope you don't mind.'

'Not if I'm getting a big cooked breakfast, I don't.'

'Well, I thought about the day we're going to have today, and I decided I wouldn't be a very good doctor if I let you go through it all on an empty stomach.'

She eased herself down onto a large kitchen stool on the breakfast nook and smiled as he fished the eggs and black pudding out of the frying pans, then removed the bacon from the grill.

'I took a leap on the black pudding.'

'I love black pudding.' She smiled as the plate was put in front of her along with a steaming cup of tea and two rounds of hot, buttered toast.

'This looks like it's exactly what I need,' she said, drowning everything in brown sauce before tucking in.

94.

WITH THE BREAKFAST finished and the dishes washed, they retired to the living room to finish off their mugs of tea.

'So, what's the deal with Angela, then?' he asked as they sat down in opposite chairs.

Olivia flushed. This was a question she was not expecting so soon, and it caught her off guard. 'I really can't tell you, not yet anyway,' she replied, taking a swig from her cup to avoid having to say anything more.

He sensed her reluctance to answer and gave up the line of inquiry. 'Well, I suppose that's between you two. She should be home this evening, her and Richard. Are they still living in the flat at the end of the garden?'

Olivia grimaced. She'd forgot all about that, so much had happened since their fight in America and her solo flight home.

Anthony laughed. 'Sorry, but the 'shut the fuck up' look on your face has just answered my question. I take it they *are* living there?'

'Look, something happened, and I don't want you to judge me because of it,' Olivia blurted. She couldn't believe that she was about to tell him the whole sordid mess, but apparently here she was, right in the middle of it. 'I've been through too much over the last year, and if I lost another friend and confidant, then I don't know what I'd do.'

He smiled a little, but Olivia could see he was forcing it. 'Jeez, Ollie, did you kill someone?' he laughed, although she sensed that it was only half a laugh.

'Only my own soul,' she replied.

'Your what?'

'There're some things you need to know regarding the background of this. I have to warn you that I just may burst out crying at any point during this conversation.'

Anthony reached into the back pocket of his jeans and produced a small pack of tissues. 'I used to be a cub scout. I'm always prepared.'

Olivia took one look at the tissues and began laughing, then she reached over and snatched them out of his hands.

'Well, I wasn't long out of hospital, and I was expecting Paul to wake up at any time, then Penny fell ill. She kept it from me for a while because she thought I was going through too much. She didn't want me to be worrying about her too.' Olivia opened the packet of tissues and removed one. She began to dab it in the corner of her eye before carrying on. 'You know all too well about the relationship between me and Angela, so I thought it best to give her the keys to the kingdom, as it were, to Paul's business. I'm not, by any stretch of the imagination, a businesswoman. She jumped at it without hesitation. I thought it would basically keep her out of my hair, and away from her meddling with Paul.'

'The part where she wanted power of attorney over him?'

'You heard about that?'

'Dr Hausen got me up to speed on a few points.'

'Anyway, she began going back and forth to America, doing a deal with a company over there and, in effect, widening our company's portfolio, or something like that.'

Anthony was nodding; he was taking it all in.

'Then Penny dropped her bombshell, she had terminal cancer, so I moved her in.' Olivia paused for a moment, dropping her head as she did. 'But she… she died and left me with no one in the whole world to talk to.'

'You had Jan and Katie, didn't you?'

Olivia pulled a little face, 'Yes, I do, you're right, but only to a degree. Their idea of talking things through is drinking a whole bottle of vodka, eating a whole pizza, then going out a having a shag with a complete stranger, which is quite ironic as it turns out.'

Anthony's eyes lit up at that last remark. 'Ironic?'

Olivia blushed. This was the part that she least wanted Anthony to know about—the part that could possibly push him away forever.

'Yeah, ironic,' she replied. 'I was lost, floating around. My butterflies were black, and I needed something to ground me. I was spending all my time in the hospital, then all my nights alone in here. We became close, just as friends mind…'

'Who?' Anthony asked looking genuinely interested.

'Well, you see, Penny died, we all got drunk, and I ended up in bed with—'

'Richard!' Anthony guessed.

Her face flushed bright red, and more tears began rolling down her cheeks. She nodded, then dabbed her eyes again. Her nose was turning red from her sniffing. She nodded, slowly, more than a little embarrassed. 'Yes, Richard. It was only because we were both drunk, and we were both vulnerable. Richard is a lovely guy. He's funny and witty and, as it happens, a real hero.'

Butterflies

Anthony stood up. Olivia's heart dipped as he did. She was expecting him to cross the room and head for the front door, but he didn't. He crossed the room and stood before her. He leaned in and gave her a massive hug.

Olivia felt guilty one more time, because right then, the very day after Paul died, she fell in love once again.

She was sobbing loud and hard, so hard that she could hardly breathe. 'D-d-don't you th-think I-I'm a b-b-bad p-p-person?'

He hugged her tighter. As he squeezed, she opened her eyes and saw all her tears soaking into the back of his shirt.

'No, I think you are a brave and resourceful person. Is this why you wouldn't speak to Angela the other day?'

'Yes, well there's a little more.'

Anthony stood back up and sat on the arm of the chair. He was still holding her hand.

She went on to tell him all about the night at the restaurant and the photographs. Then the fight just before she left America.

When she had spilled the whole thing, she sighed. 'Oh my God, how good does that feel getting it off my chest?' she said, more to herself than to Anthony.

He was looking at her, not saying anything.

She feared the silence between them; it seemed like a void, one that was getting a little wider as the seconds of silence ticked by.

'You really have moved on, haven't you? I mean, when you were talking last night, I thought it was just the grief talking, but it's not, it was actually you.'

She offered him a small but sincere smile, shrugging her shoulders slightly. 'Yes. I knew what I was saying. I hate myself for it, but I do feel like I've moved on.'

He hugged her again, tighter than last time. She let out a little laugh.

'What are you sniggering about?' he asked with an amused smile.

'If I tell you, please don't think I'm some sort of crazy bitch and run a million miles away, back to Thailand, or wherever, just to distance yourself from me. Promise?'

Anthony held up his hands 'I promise!' he exclaimed.

'I dreamt about Paul last night. He told me he loved me, I told him I loved him, then we shared butterflies again. Everything is all right between us.'

'Butterflies?' Anthony asked in confusion.

Olivia offered him a teary, lopsided grin. 'It's a long story...'

Butterflies

95.

OLIVIA FILLED HER next few days with chores. She needed to organise getting Paul from the hospital to the funeral directors. There were umpteen forms that required her signature. She needed to liaise with the church and the priest regarding the service. She needed to hire a hall and sort out a buffet and a disco. She needed to find her mother, who could have been anywhere in the world at that moment with God only knew who… but most of all, she needed to keep out of the way of Angela.

She had decided to book herself into a local hotel until after the funeral, that way she could control her dealings with Angela. She knew she was being a chicken, but if they could avoid any sort of confrontation until after the church, then there could be no scene made. Bitch or no bitch, angry or placid, Olivia knew Angela would not ruin her brother's funeral.

96.

OLIVIA AND ANTHONY had agreed to meet in the coffee shop annexed onto her hotel. They were enjoying the oasis of clarity amidst the madness of the funeral preparations. 'So, did you find your mother in the end?' he asked, taking a sip of his hot, frothy coffee.

Olivia harrumphed. 'Yeah, you'll never guess where she was.'

'Let me guess, a tent in Marrakesh, getting married to a Mugumbi warrior?'

'What's a Mugumbi warrior?' she asked, shaking her head and smiling. There had been very few smiles over the last few days, and doing it now felt good.

He shrugged. 'I don't know. I made it up!'

'No,' she continued. 'She was in Liverpool, working in a library. She met a man on the plane back to the Yemen, and they hit it off. She's in a nice semi-detached with a garden. Apparently, they're making plans to get married.'

Anthony shook his head and rolled his eyes. 'And she never even thought to let you know she was all right?'

Olivia laughed, which felt a million times better than simply smiling. 'My mother will always be all right. She knows she can phone me if she needs me. Anyway, are you going to give me some help on the eulogy for tomorrow? I want to do a fantastic speech to send him on his way.'

'Why don't you just write down what you told me the other day? Obviously leave out the bit about shagging Richard, that won't go down well in the church.' He held his hand to his chin. 'Hmmm, I wonder if that's true.'

She laughed again and hit him with the menu.

'That story will move people,' he laughed, attempting to dodge her attack. 'Seriously though, just let them know how Paul made you feel, you can't do any better than that.'

'You know what? You're right. I'll have a go at writing this down. Thanks once again, Ant, you've been a massive help.'

'That's what I'm here for.' He stood up and leaned into her to give her a kiss on the top of her head. At the same moment, she turned to face him. The embrace accidentally ended up as a full kiss on the lips for both of them.

They lingered slightly before breaking away, both looking a little embarrassed. 'Ollie, I'm so sorry, I was aiming for the top of your head,' he gushed, his face almost purple.

She laughed through her own deep crimson blush. 'If that's the case, don't take me shooting with you next time you go!'

They gave each other a brief, cheerful hug before parting, walking off in different directions, both smiling, both thinking about that kiss.

97.

THE MORNING OF the funeral, Olivia was alone in her room in the hotel. She was wearing the same dress she had worn for Aunt Penny's funeral as a sign of respect. It was her own way of saying she loved them both the same. There was a knock on the door, and Jan and Katie entered. They both looked stunning. They were a sight that her sore eyes needed right now, and she barely kept her tears at bay the moment they walked in. It was the first time they'd all been together since they had picked her up from the airport. For one reason or another, they'd all been busy.

Olivia was cheerful and bright, and it totally confused the girls.

'Ollie, are you OK? You look a little... too happy?' Jan asked, holding her out at arm's length.

Olivia looked at her two best friends in the world and smiled a big, genuine, beaming smile.

'Do you know what? I'm fine. Please don't think I've gone mad with grief and I'm bottling it all in. I assure you, I'm not. I feel good about myself. Don't get me wrong, I'm distraught about Paul, but I've had time to contemplate it. I'm going to live as Paul would have wanted me to. I'm going to bring the house down with my speech, then I'm going to, sorry, *we're* going to get drunk. I've booked the disco and paid for a late bar.' She wiped a rogue tear from her eye before continuing. 'It's how Paul would have wanted it.'

She looked around at her two best friends, noticing that neither of them was ready for a large drinking session. 'What wrong?' she asked, suddenly self-conscious.

Jan looked at her soberly. 'Oh, there's nothing wrong,' she said. 'Except, I'm not drinking today.'

Olivia was flabbergasted. 'What? What sort of celebration of my husband's life would be complete without the appearance of drunk Jan and Katie at the end of it?'

'Maybe… a celebration that involves Jan being pregnant?' Katie said, a smile twitching on her lips.

Olivia's eyes widened. Neither of the girls were expecting Olivia to be in this good a mood today. They hugged and cried together in the room, although for a completely different reason than the one they were all expecting.

'Jan?' Olivia asked. 'Do you even know who the father is?' Once the question was out, they all fell about laughing.

D E McCluskey

98.

IN AN APPROPRIATELY sombre mood at the church, Olivia watched as Paul's coffin was carried in. Richard and Anthony were at the front, and a few of his other friends were balancing the coffin on their shoulders.

Olivia had a handkerchief and was frantically dabbing at her eyes. The sadness at the loss of such a young life was made doubly tragic as the person also happened to be her husband, and the love of her life.

From the front of the church, she noticed Angela. As she saw her, her heart dropped into the pit of her stomach.

As she reached the front bench, Oliva stepped back to allow her in. Angela gave her the nicest smile Olivia had ever seen her produce. Even if it was tinged with sadness.

She smiled back. 'You look… good!' Olivia whispered.

'Well, all things considered, I am. Or should I say we are? And it's all thanks to you, really.'

'Me?'

'Yes, you. When you left, me and Richard talked. We really talked. We talked and talked and drank too. Richard explained to me your position, and his. By very unconventional means, you've managed to bring us back together. We realised that we do still love each other, and that life is too precious, we shouldn't give it up.'

Olivia was pleased, she was happy, and she was content, which was funny considering she was attending her husband's funeral.

'We're going to start trying for kids,' Angela continued. Olivia felt surprised as she felt her sister-in-law's hand grasp hers. 'Thank you, Olivia. You really have brought us back together.'

Olivia leaned in and kissed her on the cheek.

At that moment, she locked eyes with Anthony over the other side of the church. They held each other's gaze for a moment or two, far too long for it to be casual, then she looked away, smiling.

99.

OLIVIA GOT HOME just before ten-thirty p.m. She was tired, and she'd had a little too much to drink—Katie had seen to that. She removed her coat and hung it on the post of the staircase. Next, she removed her shoes, as they were killing her feet. 'I'm getting too old for this sort of thing,' she mumbled, losing her balance whilst swapping feet.

She made her way into the kitchen and poured herself a long glass of fresh orange juice, and then opened a small packet of tablets and put two in a glass before pouring water over them. The fizz began instantly. She picked up the glass and made her way upstairs.

As she reached the bedroom, she opened the door and put the light on. 'Ollie, turn that light off, will you?' came a mumble from underneath her covers.

'Oh, sorry,' she whispered, a little tipsy. She put her finger over her lips as if to 'shush' herself and turned the light off. She placed her drink on her nightstand and retired into the bathroom to remove her makeup.

She undid her dress at the back and lifted it off over her head. As she did, she mused over how much easier it was to take a dress off than to put one on. After she hung it on the bathroom floor, she looked into the full-length mirror on the wall.

Her hair was a little bit of a mess, but that could only be expected after the day she'd had. Her makeup was a little bit Addams Family, which is usually the case after a funeral. But as she looked down at the rest of herself, she was pleased with what she saw. There were bits that were beginning to wobble here and there, but after what she had been through recently, she wasn't surprised, or even that bothered.

She reached over to the cabinet next to the mirror and pulled out a few handfuls of moist tissues, then she began to work on her makeup, always the worst part of the regimen when she was a little bit drunk.

As she rubbed her eyes, she became aware of a presence in the doorway of the bathroom. 'Hey there, you,' she said with a smile.

'Hi, you woke me up,' he replied, rubbing his eyes, sleepily.

'I'm sorry. I didn't see you leave earlier.'

'Well, you looked like you were having fun, so I just sort of slipped out. You did get my text, though, didn't you?'

Olivia reached out for her phone, which she had put by the side of the sink, clicked it, and scrolled down to TEXT MESSAGES. There was one unread message from Anthony.

'Oops, looks like I did get it,' she giggled.

'Good. I'm going back to bed. Hurry up and join me, will you?' Anthony smiled at her as he moved back into the darkness of the room beyond the bathroom.

Her heart began to beat a little faster, and her excitement of his last statement caused her to abandon her makeup regimen until tomorrow morning. Making her way across the darkened bedroom, she was very pleased to find the semi-naked form of Anthony lying under the covers. She slipped in next to him in only her underwear and snuggled in.

'Shit, Ollie, you're freezing,' he laughed.

'I know. I need warming up,' she whispered.

Anthony didn't need any further encouragement. He leaned over and brushed her hair from her face before kissing her.

As their mouths touched, she felt a thrill slide through her whole body. The meeting of these innocuous, but powerful erogenous zones caused something to rouse and flutter around within her.

Anthony slipped his hand behind her and expertly unclipped her bra. As he discarded it onto the floor of the bedroom, the feel of the warm air on her exposed breasts was wonderful, but not half as wonderful as Anthony's mouth caressing them.

Slowly, he kissed from between her breasts, up her neck, and around to her ear. She squealed in delight as goose-bumps rose all over her exposed skin. His hands found purchase on her breasts, and his fingers danced expertly around her areola, causing her nipples to stiffen, instantly.

He moved back down towards her neck; small, light bites causing her to squirm beneath his embrace. Her leg brushed against his boxer shorts and she loved the feel of what was inside them. It seemed that all these kisses and bites were having the same effect on him as they were on her.

She traced his stomach and slipped her hand inside the waistline of his underwear. Antony's body stiffened as he breathed in a noisy gasp. She squeezed it again and got the same reaction. More than happy with herself, she allowed her hands to wander further down, and Anthony flopped onto his own side of the bed, laughing.

He reached over and grabbed her, pulling her to him. He put his hand around the back of her head and kissed her.

Butterflies

As they were kissing, she slipped him out of his boxers, enjoying the feel of his nakedness next to her.

'If I'm naked next to you,' he whispered. 'Then it's only fair that you are too.'

Giggling, Olivia slipped off her thong and waved it towards him. 'There, is that better for you?'

His face, in the dim light coming from the bathroom, was a picture. 'Absolutely,' he grinned.

Without warning, he was on top of her, flipping her underneath him. Then his mouth was on her. He leaned in and kissed her breasts, tantalising the nipples until they were almost bursting with tingles. She was longing for his teeth to be on them. She needed him to bite down on them, just a little, to relieve her pent-up tension. His hot breath and saliva were all over her flesh.

He began to move his kisses further, trailing them around her stomach and bellybutton. Then he moved down and lingered for a single, tantalising moment, before continuing even further down.

She wrapped her hands through the tight hair at the back of his head and pulled his face away from her. She wanted him, she needed him, her butterflies were screaming out for him to enter her.

With a wicked smile, he looked up at her.

'Fuck me,' she whispered, keeping eye contact with him.

He planted his feet onto the floor and twisted her body around on the bed, lifting her legs. Her butterflies swooped and swirled, battering her sensitive walls with their light blue wings. *It feels so good to have you back,* she said silently to all five hundred thousand of them.

The feel of him inside her was electric. There was something happening in her stomach, something that she'd missed and was so glad to feel again.

The butterflies fluttered; they were breaking free of their confinement, and she knew that very soon they would be amok, and she would fly with them.

Anthony was thrusting faster now, his erection caressing every part of her sensitivity, using his key to unlock the butterflies' cages. Her toes began to tingle, then her feet, before it spread up her legs to encompass her whole body.

Anthony was working harder. He had hit a rhythm, and she could read all the signs. She knew what was about to happen for both of them.

This was going to be glorious.

'Oh fuck!' she yelled as the butterflies finally broke free from their confinement. They fluttered everywhere around her body. Rushing their endorphins through every conduit, every nerve. She throbbed as they both reached the point of no return at the same time. She was about to yell again. The noise of it echoed through her head, but she wasn't one hundred percent sure it was her who screamed.

Then there was another scream.

As her orgasm tremors receded, she realised that the sound was coming from elsewhere in the house.

100.

THEY BOTH FELL back onto the bed, naked and concerned. The screaming was coming from the next bedroom. It had intensified, doubled.

They exchanged worried glances. 'I'll go,' Anthony said. As he got out of the bed, she could see the sweat of their exertions glistening on his back. He opened a drawer and took out a pair of pyjama bottoms and slipped them on. Olivia got up and danced naked into the en-suite.

She freshened herself up and walked back into the bedroom wearing only a silk night gown.

When she returned, the vision on the bed almost stopped her heart.

Anthony was sitting on the edge of the bed. In his arms were two babies wrapped in white blankets. 'Paul started it, then he woke Penny!' He shook his head. 'I don't think we're going to get much sleep tonight.'

'Oh, let me have them. I didn't get much of a chance to see them today, with all the too-ings and fro-ings going on.'

Olivia sat next to him on the bed as he passed the twins to her. They'd both stopped screaming almost instantaneously and were now cooing, obviously glad to see their mother.

'Hello, my little sweethearts. Did the big bad daddy scare you guys? Eh? Did he?'

'Erm, I think it was you who scared them, shouting *Oh fuck*,' Anthony laughed as he got up off the bed and stretched. 'Do you fancy a cup of tea before we feed them? You could probably do with one to counter all the alcohol in your system. I think we've got a long night ahead of us tonight.'

She wrinkled her nose, and he took that as his cue to go and make that cup of tea.

About ten minutes later, he returned with two steaming mugs and two half full bottles of milk. Olivia was relaxing back on the bed. There were two dirty nappy bags, tied and ready to be thrown away, lying on the floor. She shushed him as he approached, he could hear a very faint snore coming from one of the bundles. Anthony put the cups and bottles down on the night table and sat next to his family. He took one of the babies off her and sat back against the headboard nestling it in his arms.

'So, how was Katie today? I never really got a chance to see her, not with looking after these two and trying to keep Little Richard away from them all day. He means well for a two-year-old, but Angela and Richard need to start casting a little bit of discipline in him. I turned my head for one second, and the little bugger was head deep in the twins' bags. Everything was everywhere.'

Olivia let out a quiet chuckle.

'They seem to be getting along together nowadays,' he continued, 'I think that little bugger might have just saved them as a couple.'

Butterflies

Olivia smiled to herself. *Yeah, and me too*, she thought. 'Oh, Katie was fine. Her nanna had been sick for a while. In the end, I think she was more relieved that she's not in any more pain.'

He smiled at her and noticed the small tear in her eye, but he never mentioned it. 'And what about Jan, eh? Who would have ever thought that she'd end up getting married? If ever there was a lifelong spinster, she was the one,' he said, trying his best to get off the subject of funerals. 'Hey, Ollie. Are you OK?'

She looked at him, then her gaze fell upon their two small babies, one in her hands and the other in the safe hands of the man she loved most in the whole world. The tear that had been growing fell from her eye and trickled slowly down her cheek.

'Do you know what? I really think I am!' She smiled as she reached a hand over towards her husband.

He took it and squeezed it tight...

D E McCluskey

Butterflies

Author's notes and acknowledgements

Butterflies is a tale that I have had fluttering around my head for a while. Originally, I had the idea to make this into an erotic novel, where Olivia finds herself, again after the accident and the loss of her anchor, Aunt Penny, by sleeping her way through her list of friends.

When I read the original script back, it made the protagonist look like a horrible, unlikeable person; a million miles away from the flawed but strong woman that I wanted to portray. She came across as a slut, and a hard-faced one at that.

So, I cut the sleeping around out of the story, and suddenly I fell in love with Olivia again.

At this point, there was still a lot of sex in there, and some of it was rather hard-core too. I felt that this was detrimental to the story. It took away from the arc, from the journey Oliva needed to take. So, I removed the hard-core sex and made it kind of soft-core.

Also, as someone who is rather comfortable writing a graphic murder scene, or even an orgy of violence, I found myself rather uncomfortable writing sex… I know how crazy this sounds, as sex is a natural function, orgies of violence, not so much, but you have to write what you write!

So, this is the tale you have before you.

I need to thank a few people here at this point. I need to thank my sisters, Helen and Annmarie, for daring me to write a story like this (after reading a certain book with GREY in the title).

My proof-readers: Abigale Roylance, Stella Read, Bex Moore.

I must make a special announcement for one of my proof-readers as during the finishing of this book, Lauren Davies elevated herself from the position of proof-reader to fiancé. She had been chasing me for years!

I have to thank Naomi Gibson; she had a different name when I started this book. But without her help, this text would have been a pot-holed field of cliché and repetition, with a nasty protagonist.

I'd also like to thank Alan Jones for the fantastic wraparound cover, you can find more of his work at the following website: https://www.drawnbyalanjonesart.co.uk

Lisa Lee Tone has done an excellent job of editing this book for me. Both of us found ourselves out of our comfort zones on this one. She likes the horror books better, but like a real trouper, she took it on the chin and agreed to edit this romantic drama, with comedic bits...

I still have absolutely no idea of where to pitch this tale. All I know is that it's not horror!

Also, as always, I would like to, and need to, thank *you* for reading this book. I say it all the time, but I will say it again, and I mean it one hundred percent. Without you guys reading, there is no point in me writing...

Thank you, thank you, thank you!

Dave McCluskey
Liverpool
April 2018 (amendment July 2020)

Printed in Great Britain
by Amazon